John Churton Collins

Treasury of minor British poetry

Selected and arranged with notes

John Churton Collins

Treasury of minor British poetry
Selected and arranged with notes

ISBN/EAN: 9783337278755

Printed in Europe, USA, Canada, Australia, Japan

Cover: Foto ©Andreas Hilbeck / pixelio.de

More available books at **www.hansebooks.com**

A TREASURY

OF

MINOR BRITISH POETRY

SELECTED AND ARRANGED WITH NOTES

BY

J. CHURTON COLLINS, M.A.

μύρτα τε καὶ ἴα καὶ ἑλίχρυσος,
μᾶλά τε καὶ ῥόδα καὶ τέρεινα δάφνα

EDWARD ARNOLD

LONDON   NEW YORK
37 BEDFORD STREET   70 FIFTH AVENUE

1896

ERRATA

Page 22, line 12, *for* 'gailly' *read* 'gaylie' or 'gaily.'

,,   68, ,,   3, *for* 'statlie' *read* 'statelie.'

,,   98, at foot, *for* 'FLECKNO' *read* 'FLECKNOE.'

,, 102, line 12, *after* 'ty'd' *insert* (,).

,, ,, ,, 13, *after* 'them' and 'Waine' *insert* (,).

,, 132, line 4 from foot, *for* 'are' *read* 'aire.'

,, 134, at foot, *insert* 'ANON.'

PREFACE

A NEW Treasury of British poetry might almost seem an impertinence, so numerous, and in many cases so excellent, are collections of this kind. To go no farther than Mr. Francis Palgrave's *Golden Treasury*, Dean Trench's *Household Book of English Poetry*, Mr. Locker-Lampson's *Lyra Elegantiarum*, and Mr. Humphry Ward's *English Poets*, are not these, it may be asked, all that lovers of poetry could desire, and are not these in everybody's hands? I, for one, should certainly reply in the affirmative, and I should no more think of entering into competition with them than I should think of re-gathering and presenting again the flowers of their anthologies. If this collection has any relation to them it is that of the aftermath to the full harvest, of the gleaner to the binder of the sheaves. But I modestly claim for this little volume an independent place. It is an experiment, and it is, so far as I know, an experiment which has not been attempted before. The principle on which the poems have been selected, and the principle on which they have been arranged, I must ask permission to explain fully and precisely, and this is the more necessary as my book, unfortunately, labours under the disadvantage of being very imperfectly described by its title. It is commonly objected to anthologies that they copy each other, that they travel in a round, that the same poets, illustrated by the same poems, appear and reappear till they become trite by repetition, and that this applies not merely to poets who have long been classical and whose names are household words, but to the minor poets also. Thus, as surely as Ben Jonson, Herrick, and Waller are presented, so surely is the one the herald of *Drink to me only with thine eyes* and *Queen and Huntress*, the other of *Gather ye rosebuds* and *Faire Daffodils*, and the third of *Go, lovely rose*. A few original explorers of taste and judgment add from time to time to the treasury of gems, which soon passes into common property, till at last, as anthologies multiply, they become little more than compilations from compilations. As long as selections confine themselves to certain poets and to the very best things of their kind, to gems, so to speak, of the first water, it is difficult to see how this can be avoided; for poetry attaining a very high standard, though abundant, is soon exhausted, and repetition is inevitable. Without questioning the truth of the Greek proverb δὶς ἢ τρὶς τὰ καλὰ, that we cannot have too much of a good thing, I should yet not have ventured to add another volume to the volumes already dedicated to such good things. My chief object has been, if I may say so, to supplement those works and to introduce the general reader to poems which, though well worth his attention, are, as a rule, not to be found at all in popular anthologies, and in no case are among the stock-pieces in those collections, and with which presumably therefore he will not be familiar. I have for this reason excluded all those poets who may be regarded as classics, as well as those who are much in vogue. Thus Chaucer is passed over; thus in the Elizabethan Age, to say nothing of Spenser and Shakespeare, Marlowe and Ben Jonson have no place. In the eighteenth

century neither Pope nor Swift, neither Gray nor
Collins, neither Goldsmith nor Cowper is represented.
In the nineteenth century exclusion has even extended
to Moore and Southey. If I have included Waller,
Congreve, Prior, and Thomson, it is only because I have
sought to give prominence to one or two poems which
are not generally noticed. And what applies to them
applies to Crabbe.

But I have confined my area within stricter limits
still. Where a poet has only written two or three good
things, which have gone the round of the anthologies, I
have omitted him. Where a poet's work has been
abundant I have carefully avoided the "gems" with which
every one is familiar, and have chosen what seemed to
me best in the residue. I have thus had to deprive
my book of many diamonds, but I hope I have secured
in their place as many excellent pearls. I have not, it is
true, excluded all poems which are familiar even to the
general reader. I have inserted for instance Logan's
Braes of Yarrow and *Ode to the Cuckoo*, but I have
done my utmost to avoid what is trite.

But what has been restricted on one side has been
allowed latitude on another. I have not confined
myself to songs and lyrics, though songs and lyrics are
the staple of my collection. I have plucked a flower
wherever I could find it. I have occasionally detached
passages from voluminous narrative, philosophic, and
mock-heroic poems. From long lyrics I have chosen a
stanza or two, or even a few lines; I have not excluded
sonnets; I have not grudged a place to a good epigram.
Wherever in my rambles among tombs I have come
upon an epitaph which seemed worthy of preservation I
have inserted it, and I venture to think that I have thus
saved from perishing more than one of those compositions

which well deserve to be remembered. With all this variety every endeavour has been made to give a certain unity to the collection, and to prevent it from becoming, what it so easily might have become, a mere miscellany. It will be seen that each piece illustrates some phase it may be of thought, it may be of passion, it may be of sentiment in relation to life or to death, or in relation to supernaturalism or to nature—in other words, that the note throughout is lyrical. Within this limit the selections are in every possible tone between the intense expression of intense emotion, and the gayest and lightest abandon of the humorist and wit. Life itself, on its passive side, is little more than the record of what finds expression in these varied moods, and that its reflection may be the more faithfully returned in these poems, I have arranged them on a new principle. I have endeavoured to give them a sort of dramatic propriety by making them correspond, or at least roughly correspond, to the different stages of human experience. In each of the four books the poems pertaining to childhood and youth come first, and animal joy, passion, and pleasure are the themes. Next come poems of a more mingled yarn and in more diverse keys, expressive of the experiences of manhood. Then serious reflection begins to predominate, till

> About the rim
> Scull-things in order grim
> Grow out in graver mood, obey the sterner stress,

and the note is elegiac till death closes the scene on earth. Lastly come, as a fitting conclusion, poems in which hope and faith find expression. To this arrangement there is, however, one exception. It seemed desirable that, as the opening poems of the first book are in very obsolete language, they should not be distributed among the others, but be placed where they naturally would have been placed had the collection been arranged chronologically.

This Treasury has also another aim, a subordinate aim it is true, but one which has never been lost sight of, and that is to illustrate the history of our minor lyric poetry—not its form, that has been for obvious reasons impossible, but its essence and spirit. The period covered is from the first half of the thirteenth century to recent times, a period of some seven hundred years. The present collection extends to four books. The first book comprises selections from the minor poetry which appeared between the middle of the thirteenth century and the close of the Elizabethan Age; the selections in the second book range from 1625 to 1700; in the third book, from 1700 to 1798; in the fourth, from 1798 to recent times. Living poets have for obvious reasons been excluded.

Fletcher of Saltoun's famous saying about the ballads of a nation is susceptible of a much wider application than he gave to it. It is in the minor poetry of an age that contemporary life impresses itself most deeply, and finds perhaps its most faithful mirror. In the great masterpieces of poetry that life is presented in an ideal light, and in relation to ideal truth. What belongs to a time is subordinated to what belongs to all time, what is actual to what is typical, what is local to what is universal. There is, moreover, in genius of the higher order a dominant, a despotic individuality which tempers and assimilates the material on which it works to its own potent idiosyncrasy. It is not in the *Canterbury Tales* that the England of Edward III. becomes fully articulate, for where, even in a whisper, is heard the voice which pierces us to the soul in Langland? It is

not in the *Faerie Queen* or even in the Dramas of
Shakespeare that the England of Elizabeth and James
is presented to us on all its sides, for Spenser never
forgets that he is a didactic allegorist, and Shakespeare
that he is a dramatic artist.   Still less is the England
of the Revolution reflected in the masterpieces of Milton,
or the England of the latter part of the eighteenth and
the first part of the nineteenth century in the masterpieces of Byron, Scott, Wordsworth, and Shelley.   It is
otherwise with the minor poetry of any particular era.
Here for the eclecticism, if we may so express it, of the
great masters the age itself finds a tongue.   For the
voice which speaks in these poets is the voice of the
nation, of the courtier, of the statesman, and man of
affairs, of the scholar, and litterateur, of the churchman,
of the man of pleasure, of the busy citizen, of the recluse,
of the soldier and sailor, of the peasant, of the mechanic,
and of women of all classes and of all callings.   What
is moulding, what is colouring, what is in any way affecting the life of the time has its record here.   Is the pulse
of the nation quickened or depressed; are imagination
and passion, or fancy and sentiment, or reason and
reflection in the ascendant, is the prevailing tendency
in the direction of simplicity and nature, or towards
ingenuity and art, is the moral tone in society high or
low, is the period a period of progress, or of decadence,
or of transition, the answer to all this may be found,
and found in detail, in our collections of minor poetry.
Take, for instance, the poetry of the Sloane and Harleian
MSS. with the other poetry in Mr. Wright's Collections.
Here is the England of the thirteenth and fourteenth
centuries so fully, so faithfully depicted, that its social
and political history might be written from those anthologies.   Gushing from the heart as the song of a bird

ring out those primitive lyrics, with their gracious simplicity, their freshness, their abandon, their harmonious
responsiveness to the inspiring mood. Be the theme
what it may, sincerity, truth, and nature prevail. In the
love lyrics hope and despair, rapture and compliment
express themselves without conceits, and with charming
naïveté. No jarring chord of distrust or doubt is
audible in the religious poetry which is the simple
expression of thanksgiving, praise, and prayer. Let
us go forward to 1557 to Edward's *Paradise of Dainty
Devices* and to Tottel's *Miscellany*. Here all the characteristics of the period, stretching from the dawn of the
Reformation to the last two years of Mary's reign, have
full illustration, the influence exercised on our literature
by the Latin classics, by Italy, by Spain, the last notes
of mediævalism blending with the first notes of the new
world, the affectation of the forms and fashions of the
Renaissance, the large infusion of moral and religious
reflection, the gloom, depression, and anxiety which
darkened and vexed those sombre times. Let us pass
on to the beginning of the next century to *England's
Helicon* (1600), and to Davison's *Poetical Rhapsody*
(1602). Here we are at the acme of the great Elizabethan Age. The clouds have rolled away, all is
splendour, all is joy. The extraordinary complexity and
tropical luxuriance of that wonderful era which seems
to blend all that characterises the infancy, the maturity,
and the decadence of a literature in its entirety, are
fully displayed in those collections. But the predominating strain is rapture. It is the poetry of men
who are in different degrees, but in very truth inspired.
They may indulge in conceits, they may affect trivial
graces, their pedantry may sometimes jar on us, but the
unmistakable accent of enthusiasm is theirs. Let us go

forward eighty-two years to the next important *Treasury of Minor Poetry.* Between 1684 and 1716 appeared Tonson's *Miscellanies* in six parts. We turn over its pages; we are not only in another world but in a world which seems scarcely to retain any trace of the former. Imagination has disappeared, enthusiasm has disappeared, fervour, colour, richness all are gone; rhetoric has superseded passion; simplicity and naïveté have given place to ingenuity and wit, not the ingenuity and wit of the metaphysical school, but of a generation which has receded much farther from the sphere of poetry, and which seems indeed to have lost all touch with it. Pitched in as low a key as they well could be, both ethic and æsthetic have alike degenerated. High instincts, high aims, high actions are never the themes. Nothing is so rare as a touch of romance or transcendentalism. If the love poetry is not marked, as it frequently is, by cynicism and grossness, levity and libertinism are its characteristics, expressed, it is true, with so much grace and charm of style as not to be repulsive. It is the poetry of an age of reaction, and of reaction in a twofold sense, spiritually and morally against the ideals of Puritanism and of the religious party generally, artistically against the licence and extravagance of the Elizabethans and their immediate successors. But it is the poetry also of an age of revolution. As between the accession of Elizabeth and about 1616 everything contributed to subordinate the genius of science and criticism to the genius of romance and poetry, so at the time of the Restoration the tendency was exactly the reverse. A great scientific movement had passed over Europe and had become influential everywhere. The spirit of inquiry, of analysis, of reflection was at work in all directions. Men reasoned, where before they felt, and questioned, where before they accepted and enjoyed. To think clearly, to argue correctly, and to express the results in a precise and lucid style was the surest way of hitting the popular taste. The poets, under the dominion of the same influence, followed the prose-writers, and so far as essentials are concerned there is little to distinguish them. Both dealt with the same subjects and treated them in the same spirit. The charm of both lies partly in their moderation, knowledge of life, wit, and good sense, and partly in their power of expression. In both this reached a high degree of excellence. Nothing could be more finished than the style of some of these poets, than the style, for example, of Rochester, of Sedley, and of Congreve at its best. But the light of poetry burns very low in these the luminaries of Tonson's *Collection*, as it burnt very low in the sun of their system the great Dryden himself. Again let us go forward sixty-seven years and take the last edition of Dodsley's *Collection* with Pearch's Supplement published respectively in 1782 and 1783. We have here, illustrated from the writings of minor poets, a complete history of our poetry from the appearance of Pope to the dawn of the era of Wordsworth and Coleridge. And step by step we may trace its progress. First we mark the predominance of all that characterised the work of Pope and his school, those ethical commonplaces, that refined mock-heroic, that admirable satire, that point, that wit, that perfection of mechanical form. But side by side with this, *sotto voce* as it were, the pensive sentimentalism of Parnell, the genuine love of nature shown by Thomson and Dyer. As the century proceeds the note of Pope grows fainter, and the chords struck by Parnell, Thomson, and Dyer find more and more response. Soon all the signs of

reaction against the classical, or to speak more correctly,
the critical school of Dryden and Pope become conspicuous. The occasional substitution of Greek models
for Latin by Akenside, Gray, Mason, and Glover ; the revival of romanticism in such works as Percy's *Reliques*,—
and the Macpherson and Chatterton forgeries, some of the
Odes of Collins and of the Wartons, the enthusiasm for
nature, the cultivation of the ballad, the reappearance of
the sonnet, the increasing tendency to prefer incident to
reflection, the life of the country to the life of the town,
the affectation of simplicity, the large infusion of sentiment, the revival and accentuation of the spirit of liberty,
the awakening of the spirit of philanthropy,—of all this is
the poetry collected by Dodsley and Pearch the record.
In the work of many of these poets it is in some
respects but a step to the work of the great poets of the
next age. Nature had no more faithful votary or
painter in Wordsworth than she had in the authors of
Grongar Hill, of the *Ode to Evening*, of the *Ode to
Rural Elegance*, of *Flora's Fables*, of *The Enthusiast*, of
The Minstrel, of *Amwell*. The note which Scott struck
in *The Lay of the Last Minstrel* and *Marmion* had been
struck by Thomas Warton in his *Crusade* and *Grave of
King Arthur*. Crabbe is anticipated by Falconer and
Langhorne, Coleridge and Keats in some important
respects by Chatterton and others, and what has been
called the most original contribution ever made to poetry,
the *Lyrical Ballads* of Wordsworth and Coleridge, may be
resolved into elements, every one of which is to be traced
in our minor poetry between the accession of George
III. and 1790. As in social and political life, so also
in poetry, which is its expression, the great cataclysm
of the Revolution did but broaden and deepen into
torrents and rivers the rills which had their sources and

had defined their channels in the low tablelands of the England of Walpole and of Pulteney, of the Grenvilles and of Lord North. Twenty years later brings us to the *Poetical Register*, another twenty-two years to Alaric Watts' *Poetical Album*, another six decades or so to Mr. Alfred Miles' *Poets of the Century*. In these collections may be traced not merely the evolution of our lyrical poetry but its history from the end of the last century to the present time. We seem as we turn over the pages of the last two Anthologies—the *Poetical Register* is the asylum of mediocrity—to be once more amid the luxuriance and splendour, the rapture and glory of the Elizabethan Miscellanies. Passion and enthusiasm are again aglow and in a far intenser degree than in the lyrists of *England's Helicon* and the *Poetical Rhapsody*. A music as sweet, as liquid, as spontaneous as theirs, but infinitely richer, subtler, and more varied is in our ears. And it is heard on all sides, not in the strains of the master-singers only, but in those of the many who make up the chorus. The high level attained in the minor poetry of the first six decades of the present century has certainly no parallel in any preceding age. Between 1800 and 1860 there are at least a hundred poets, there are probably more, who have the note of distinction, whose note, that is to say, is not essentially commonplace or essentially imitative. Between 1860 and the present time talent has undoubtedly been more conspicuous than genius, but genius has not been rare, and the talent displayed, the standard reached in taste, in receptivity, in technique, and in expression are truly wonderful. It would be no exaggeration to say that many and very many of the minor poets of the last sixty years would, had they lived a century and a half ago, have become famous.

The distinguishing characteristic of the poetry of the present century, regarded comprehensively, is its extraordinary complexity. This has arisen partly from the faithfulness with which it has, in each generation, reflected the intense and manifold life of modern times, and partly from the natural tendency of an age of culture to eclecticism. We may trace in it the influence of every important movement which has from the beginning of the century affected politics and society. Now it has the note of the exaltation and excitement of the revolutionary era, now the note of the reactionary depression which succeeded it. Here it is the trumpet-voice of all that subsequently found vent in the cries for emancipation, relief, and reform, and in the demands and aspirations of the Chartists and Communists; here again it is the protest plaintive, indignant, or humorous of conservative opposition. Of every phase and mood in the conflict between Christianity and Agnosticism, between Transcendentalism and Science, between the creed of the optimist and the creed of the pessimist it is the faithful expression. The very Æolian harp of the Zeit-Geist, its chords have responded to every breath of the popular breeze. But if the poetry which has had its inspiration from the life of the age blends so many diverse notes, the poetry of culture has still more complexity. The tendency of culture is towards imitation, and imitation is naturally coextensive with what excites admiration and sympathy. Men are now universal students, and the note of the poetry of all ages and of all nations has been caught and returned by modern lyrists. One recalls the old Greek choruses, another the melic it may be of Sappho, or of Pindar, of Anacreon or of Simonides, another that of Catullus or of Horace. Here Hafiz or Omar is inspiration and model; here it is the accent of Dante

and his circle, or of Petrarch, or perhaps of Leopardi or
of Manzoni. Others recall the lyric of Spain, of Portugal,
or of France. One revives Villon, another Ronsard, or
the echo is the echo of Béranger, of De Musset, of
Victor Hugo. The old German ballads inspire some;
in many others the note is the note of Goethe, or of
Schiller, of Rückert, or of Heine. Of our own past and of
the past of Scotland and Ireland the poetry of every
century has its imitators. And the marvel is that so
large a portion of this essentially imitative poetry should
have so much intrinsic excellence. But excellence it
has and often of a high order. Longinus remarks that
if inspiration, in the proper sense of the term, is the gift
of Heaven, there is an inspiration not less genuine which
may be kindled by sympathy. This is the soul of
imitative poetry, the informing power which moulds a
copy into a counterpart and exalts servility into rivalry.
And in this lies the secret of the power and charm of so
much of modern poetry.

Such, in slight outline, has been the course of our
lyrical poetry, such its general characteristics, such the
influences which have at different periods affected it.
I have already said that in this selection I have been
obliged to subordinate historical illustration to other
considerations. I had originally inserted several poems
which were of interest because they were particularly
typical of the period to which they belonged, but on
second thoughts, for the reason which I have stated,
they were removed. Still the reader who cares to go
through these poems consecutively, in the order of the
books in which they are arranged, will discern broadly
the characteristics of our lyrical poetry at every important
stage in its progress, and so be able to trace, at least in
outline, the general course of its evolution.

No pains have been spared to secure a correct text in the selections; each poem has been carefully transcribed from the original editions, and where several editions with variants exist, they have been collated, and what seemed to be the best reading given. The old spelling has also been preserved, for, as Dr. Johnson remarked when he censured Lord Hailes for modernising the language of Hales of Eton, "an author's language is a characteristical part of his composition, and is also characteristical of the age in which he writes." In poetry the preservation of the old spelling, unsettled though it was, is more important, for its modernisation often, in my opinion, affects not only the rhythm but the tone and colour of a poem. The only alteration which I have ventured to make, and that because the old forms unnecessarily offend the eye, is to substitute "i" for "y" and "u" for "v." Except in the case of excerpts from long poems not lyrical, each piece has, as a rule, been printed in its entirety, but to this rule it has been found desirable to make exceptions. I have never scrupled to shorten poems when the choice lay between abbreviation or omission, as for example in Cowley's *Hymn to Light*, Akenside's *Hymn to Science*, and Smart's *Song to David*, or to excise a stanza here and there in the shorter pieces, where excision seemed a gain. I have never substituted plausible emendations for the authentic text; but where the text has been plainly wrong, as it has often been found to be, and the correction was obvious, it has been supplied.

To pass to another point. I should like to be allowed to add that if this compilation has been a task it has also been a pleasure. A glance at the names in the index will show that to remember the forgotten and to assist "buried merit," to assert or reassert itself has not been the least of my aims. There is no debt more sacred than that saddest of all debts, the expression of gratitude to those who are beyond the reach of it. To many, nay, to most perhaps of the poets who have a place in this volume, fame never came at all, or any adequate recognition, from any quarter, of their genius and work; some lived and died in obscurity, and are now, except to a small circle, little more than names. But if the world is indifferent the world is just, and it is pleasing to think that by contributing to bring these neglected or forgotten poets into notice I shall be contributing, if only imperfectly, to the reparation of the wrong which has inadvertently been done them. And this it is which induced me, somewhat inconsistently I fear, to include two poems by the Australian poet, poor Henry Kendall, to whose fine genius England has never done justice.

In the notes the source of each poem or extract has been indicated; notices have been given, where necessary, of the authors. When anything seemed to require explanation in the matter of the text, or in the text itself, it has been supplied. But I have carefully refrained from indulging in the sort of commentary which every reader can supply for himself, and which is commonly called æsthetic appreciation.

Where I have been indebted to other Collections due acknowledgment has been made in the notes, but I should like here to express my thanks for the use which Mr. Miles' *Poets of the Century* has been to me, not because I have drawn on the selections there given, but because that work directed my attention to two or three poets who were before unknown to me.

It remains for me to express my thanks to Mrs.

Calverley, Mrs. Locker-Lampson, the Earl of Crewe, Mr. Webster, Mr. John Murray, Messrs. Macmillan, Messrs. Ward and Lock, Messrs. Bell and Sons, Mr. George Allen of Ruskin House, and Messrs. Kegan Paul and Co., for permission to include poems which are still protected by copyright.

51 NORFOLK SQUARE, W.

BOOK I

CUCKOO-SONG

SuₘER is icumen in,
Lhude [1] sing cuccu !
Groweth sed, and bloweth med,
And springth the wude nu,
    Sing cuccu !

Awe bleteth after lomb
Lhouth after calvë cu ;
Bulluc sterteth,[2] bucke verteth,[3]
Murie sing cucu !

Cuccu, cuccu, well singes thu, cuccu,
Ne swike [4] thu naver nu ;
Sing, cuccu, nu, sing, cuccu
Sing cuccu, sing, cuccu, nu !

       ANON.

[1] Loud.   [2] Leaps about.
[3] Goes to harbour in the vert or fern.
    [4] Cease.

B

II

"BLOW NORTHERN WIND"

Ichot[1] a burde[2] in boure bryht,
That fully semly is on syht,
Menskful[3] maiden of myht
    Feir[4] ant fre to fonde;[5]
In al this wurhliche[6] won[7]
A burde of blod ant of bon;
Never yete y nuste[8] non
Lussomore[9] in londe.
      Blow northern wynd!
      Send thou me my suetyng![10]
      Blow, northern wynd! blou, blou, blou!

With lokkes lefliche[11] ant longe,
With frount ant face feir to fonge,[12]
With murthes monie mote[13] heo monge,[14]
    That brid[15] so breme[16] in boure
With lossom eye grete ant gode,
With browen blysfol underhode,
He that reste him on the rode,[17]
That leflych lyf honoure.
      Blou, northern wynd, etc.

---

[1] I know.   [2] Maiden.   [3] Graceful, noble.   [4] Fair.
[5] Meet with, or seek.   [6] Stately.   [7] Habitation.   [8] I never knew.
[9] Lovelier.   [10] Sweetheart.   [11] Lovely.   [12] Take hold of.
[13] Might.   [14] Mingle.   [15] Bird.   [16] Spirited.   [17] Cross.

Hire lure [18] lumes [19] liht [20]
Ase a launterne a nyht,
Hire bleo [21] blykyeth so bryht,
  So feyr heo is ant fyn.
A suetly [22] suyre heo hath to holde,
With armes shuldre ase mon wolde,
Ant fyngres feyre forte [23] folde,
God wolde hue [24] were myn !
  Blou northern wynd, etc.

Heo is coral of godnesse,
Heo is rubie of ryhtfulnesse,
Heo is cristal of clairnesse,
  Ant baner of bealtè.
Heo is lilie of largesse,
Heo is parvenke [25] of prouesse
Heo is solsecle [26] of suetnesse
  Ant lady of lealtè.

For hire love y carke ant care,
For hire love y droupne ant dare,
For hire love my blisse is bare
  Ant al ich waxe won,
For hire love in slep yslake,
For hire love al nyht ich wake,

[18] Complexion.
[19] Beams.
[20] Gay.
[21] Complexion.
[22] Sweetheart.
[23] For to, to.
[24] She.
[25] Flower.
[26] Sun-flower.

For hire love mournyng y make
  More then eny mon.
  Blou northern wynd!
  Send thou me my suetyng!
  Blou, northern wynd, blou, blou, blou!

ANON.

III

THE SONG OF THE ROSE

  Of a rose, a lovely rose,
  Of a rose is al myn song.
Lestenyt,[1] lordynges, bothe elde and zynge,[2]
How this rose began to sprynge;
Swych a rose to myn lykynge
  In al this world ne knowe I non.

The aungil cam fro hevene tour,
To grete Marye with gret honour,
And seyde sche xuld[3] bere the flour
  That xulde breke the fyndes bond.

The flour sprong in heye Bedlem,
That is bothe bryht[4] and schen :
The rose is Mary hevene qwyn,[5]
  Out of here bosum the blosme sprong.

The ferste braunche is ful of myht,
That sprang on Cyrstemesse nyht;
The sterre schon over Bedlem bryht
  That is bothe brod and long.

---

[1] Listen.   [2] Young.   [3] Should.   [4] Bright.   [5] Queen of heaven.

The secunde braunche sprong to helle,
The fendys power doun to felle :
Therein myht non sowle dwelle ;
    Blyssid be the time the rose sprong.

The thredde branche is good and swote,
It sprang to hevene crop and rote,
Therein to dwellyn and ben our bote ;
    Every day it schewit in prystes hond.

Prey we to here with gret honour,
Che that bar the blyssid flowr,
Che be our helpe and our socour
    And schyd us fro the fyndes bond.

                           ANON.

IV

THIS WORLD'S JOY

WYNTER wakeneth al my care,
    Nou this leues[1] waxeth bare ;
Ofte I sike ant mourne sare,
    When hit cometh in my thoht
Of this worldes joie, how hit goth al to noht.

Nou hit is, and nou hit nys,[2]
    Also hit ner nere[3] ywys ;
That moni mon seith, soth hit ys :
    Al goth bote[4] godes wille,[5]
Alle we shule deye,[6] thah[7] us like ylle.

---

[1] These leaves.   [2] Is not.   [3] As if it had never been.   [4] Except.
[5] Will.   [6] Die.   [7] Though evil pleases us.

Al that gren [8] me graueth grene,
　　Nou hit faleweth [9] albydene ; [10]
Jesu, help that hit be sene
　　Ant shild vs from helle,
For y not whider [11] y shal, ne hou longe her duelle. [12]

ANON.

V

A HYMN TO THE VIRGIN

OF on [1] that is so fayr and bright,
　　Velut maris stella,
Brighter than the day is light,
　　Parens et puella.
Ic crie to the, thou see to me
Levedy,[2] preye thi sone for me.
　　Tam pia,
That Ic mote come to the
　　Maria.

Al this world was for-lore
　　Eva peccatrice,
Tyl our Lord was y-bore
　　De te genetrice.
With ave it went away,
Thuster nyth and comz the day
　　Salutis ;
The welle springet hut of the
　　Virtutis.

Levedy, flour of alle thing,
Rosa sine spina,
Thu bere Jhesu hevene king
Gratia divina,
Of alle thu berst the pris,
Levedy, quenc of paradys,
Electa.
Mayde milde, moder es
Effecta.

ANON.

VI

A PLEA FOR PITY

Sweit rois [1] of vertew and of gentilness,
Delytsum [2] lyllie of everie lustynes,
Richest in bontie, and in bewtie cleir,
And every vertew that to hevin is deir,
Except onlie that ye ar mercyles.

Into your garthe [3] this day I did persew;
Thair saw I flouris that fresche wer of dew,
Baythe [4] quhyte [5] and reid most lusty wer to seyne,
And halsum [6] herbis upone stalkis grene;
Yet leif nor flour fynd could I nane of rew.

---

[1] Rose.   [2] Delightsome.   [3] Garden.   [4] Both.
[5] White.   [6] Wholesome.

I doute that Merche, with his cauld blastis keyne,[7]
Hes slane this gentil herbe, that I of mene;
Quhois [8] petewous [9] deithe dois to my hart sic pane,
That I would mak to plant his rute agane,
So confortand his levis unto me bene.

W. DUNBAR.

VII

BE MERRY, MAN

BE merrie, man, and tak nat sair in mind
The wavering of this wretchit warld of sorrow;
To God be humble, to thy friend be kind,
And with thy nichtbours gladly lend and borrow;
His chance to nicht, it may be thine to-morrow;
Be blythe in hearte for ony aventure,
For oft with wise men it has been said aforrow [1]
Without Gladness availes no Treasure.

Mak thee gude cheer of it that God thee sends,
For warld's wrak [2] but [3] weelfare nocht avails;
Nae gude is thine, save only that thou spends,
Remenant all thou bruikes [4] but with bailis; [5]
Seek to solace when sadness thee assailis;
In dolour lang thy life may not endure,
Wherefore of comfort set up all thy sailis :
Without Gladness availes no Treasure.

W. DUNBAR.

---

[7] Keen.   [8] Whose.   [9] Piteous.   [1] Before.
[2] Trash.   [3] Without health.   [4] Use, enjoy.   [5] Sorrow.

LIFE

WHAT is this life but a straight way to deid,
Which has a time to pass and none to dwell,
A sliding wheel us lent to seek remeid,
A free choice given to Paradise or Hell,
A prey to deid whom vain is to repell ;
A short torment for infinite gladness,
As short a joy for lasting heaviness.

W. DUNBAR.

IX

TO MAYSTRESS MARGARET HUSSEY

MIRRY Margaret,
As mydsomer flowre ;
Gentill as fawcoun
Or hawke of the towre :
With solace and gladness,

Moche mirthe and no madness,
All good and no badness,
So joyously,
So maydenly,
So womanly,
Her demenyng
In everythynge
Far, far passyng
That I can endyght,
Or suffyce to wryghte,
Of mirry Margarete,
As mydsomer flowre,
Gentyll as fawcoun
Or hawke of the towre,
As pacient and as styll,
And as full of good-wyll
   As faire Isaphill ;
    Colyaunder,
Swete pomaunder,
Goode Cassaunder ;
Stedfast of thought,
Wele made, wele wrought ;
Far may be sought,
Erst that ye can fynde
So corteise, so kynde,
As mirry Margaret,
This mydsomer floure,
Gentyll as faucoun
Or hawke of the towre.

             J. SKELTON.

AVE

WEEPE not my wanton, smile upon my knee,
When thou art olde, there's grief enough for thee.

Mother's wag, prettie boy,
Father's sorrow, father's joy;
When thy father first did see
Such a boy by him and me,
He was glad, I was woe;
Fortune changed made him so,
When he left his prettie boy,
Last his sorrow, first his joy.

Weepe not my wanton, smile upon my knee,
When thou art olde, there's grief enough for thee.

The wanton smil'd, father wept,
Mother cried, baby lept,
More he crow'd, more we cried,
Nature could not sorrow hide:
He must goe, he must kisse
Childe and mother, baby blisse,
For he left his prettie boy,
Father's sorrow, father's joy.

Weepe not my wanton, smile upon my knee,
When thou art olde, there's grief enough for thee.

R. GREENE.

XI

LULLABY

GOLDEN slumbers kisse your eyes,
Smiles awake you when you rise,
Sleepe, pretty wantons, doe not cry,
And I will sing a lullabie,
Rocke them, rocke them lullabie.

Care is heavie, therefore sleepe you,
You are care, and care must keep you ;
Sleepe pretty wantons, do not cry,
And I will sing a lullabie,
Rocke them, rocke them lullabie.

T. DEKKER (?)

XII

THE SIREN

Now I find thy lookes were fained,
Quickly lost and quicklie gained :

Soft thy skinne, like wool of wethers,
Hart unstable, light as feathers;
Tongue untrustie, subtil sighted,
Wanton will, with change delighted :
   Siren pleasant, foe to reason,
   Cupid plague thee for this treason.

Of thine eyes, I made my mirror,
From thy beautie came mine error,
All thy words I counted wittie,
All thy smyles I deemed pittie.
Thy false teares that me agrieved
First of all my trust deceived:
   Siren pleasant, foe to reason,
   Cupid plague thee for this treason.

Fain'd acceptance when I asked,
Lovely words with cunning masked,
Holie vowes, but hart unholie;
Wretched man ! my trust was follie :
Lillie white, and pretty winking,
Solemn vowes, but sorry thinking :
   Siren pleasant, foe to reason,
   Cupid plague thee for this treason.

Now I see (O seemely cruell !)
Others warme them at my fuell;
Wit shall guide me in this durance,
Since in Love is no assurance.

Change thy pasture, take thy pleasure,
Beautie is a fading treasure :
    Siren pleasant, foe to reason,
    Cupid plague thee for this treason.

T. LODGE.

XIII

TRUE LOVE

"Who is it that this darke night
Underneath my window playneth?"
It is one who from thy sight
Being, ah, exil'd, disdayneth
Every other vulgar light.

"Why, alas, and are you he?
Be not yet those fancies changèd?"
Deare, when you find change in me,
Though from me you be estrangèd,
Let my change to ruine be.

"Well, in absence this will dye;
Leave to see, and leave to wonder."
Absence sure will help, if I
Can learne how myselfe to sunder
From what in my hart doth lye.

"But time will these thoughts remove;
Time doth work what no man knoweth."
Time doth as the subject prove ;
With time still the affection groweth
In the faithful turtle-dove.

"What if we new beauties see,
Will not they stir new affection?"
I will thinke they pictures be
(Image-like, of saints' perfection),
Poorely counterfeiting thee.

"But your reason's purest light
Bids you leave such minds to nourish."
Deare, do reason no such spite ;
Never doth thy beauty flourish
More than in my reason's sight.

SIR P. SIDNEY.

XIV

SONG

AWAY delights, go seek some other dwelling,
For I must die :
Farewell, false love, thy tongue is ever telling
Lie after lie.

For ever let me rest now from thy smarts ;
   Alas, for pity go,
   And fire their hearts
That have been hard to thee, mine was not so.

Never again deluding Love shall know me,
   For I will die ;
And all those griefs that think to overgrow me,
   Shall be as I ;
For ever will I sleep, while poor maids cry
   " Alas, for pity stay,
   And let us die
With thee : men cannot mock us in the clay."

      BEAUMONT AND FLETCHER.

XV

SILENT MUSIC

ROSE-CHEEKED Laura, come ;
Sing thou smoothlie with beautie's
Silent music, either other
    Sweetly gracing.

Lovely forms doe flow
From concent divinely framed ;
Heav'n is music, and thy beautie's
    Birth is heavenlie.

These dull notes we sing
Discords need for helps to grace them,
Only beautie purely loving
    Knows no discord,

But still moves delight,
Like clear springs renewed by flowing,
Ever perfect, ever in them-
    selves eternal.

T. CAMPION.

XVI

A CRUEL BEAUTY

Thou art not faire, for all thy red and white,
For all those rosy ornaments in thee;
Thou art not sweete, though made of mere delight,
Nor faire, nor sweete, unless thou pity me.
I will not soothe thy fancies, thou shalt prove
That beautie is no beautie without love.

Yet love not me, nor seek thou to allure
My thoughts with beautie, were it more divine;
Thy smiles and kisses I cannot endure,
I'll not be wrapt up in those arms of thine:
Now show it, if thou be a woman right,—
Embrace and kisse and love me in despite!

T. CAMPION.

C

XVII

LOVE AND BEAUTY

GENTLE nymphs, be not refusing,
Love's neglect is time's abusing,
    They and beauty are but lent you ;
Take the one and keep the other :
Love keepes fresh what age doth smother,
    Beauty gone, you will repent you.

' Twill be said when ye have proved,
Never swaines more truely loved :
    O then fly all nice behaviour !
Pitty faine would (as her dutie)
Be attending still on Beautie,
    Let her not be out of favour.

                              W. BROWNE.

XVIII

LOVE'S CLAIM

LOVE for such a cherry lip
    Would be glad to pawn his arrows ;
Venus here to take a sip
    Would sell her doves and teams of sparrows.
        But they shall not so ;
        Hey nonny, nonny no !
    None but I this life must owe,
        Hey nonny, nonny, no !

Did Jove see this wanton eye,
  Ganymede must wait no longer ;
Phœbe here one night did lie,
  Would change her face and look much younger.

    But they shall not so ;
    Hey nonny, nonny no !
    None but I this life must owe ;
    Hey nonny, nonny no !

                              T. MIDDLETON.

XIX

SONG

Love, a childe, is ever crying;
Please him, and he straight is flying ;
Give him, he the more is craving,
Never satisfied with having.

His desires have no measure ;
Endless folly is his treasure ;
What he promiseth he breaketh,
Trust not one word that he speaketh.

He vows nothing but false matter ;
And to cozen you will flatter ;
Let him gaine the hand, he'll leave you,
And still glory to deceive you.

He will triumph in your wailing;
And yet cause be of your failing;
These his virtues are, and slighter
Are his gifts, his favours lighter.

Feathers are as firm in staying;
Wolves no fiercer in their preying :
As a childe, then, leave him crying;
Nor seeke him so given to flying.

LADY MARY WROATH.

XX

LOVE'S PLEA

FORGET not yet the tried intent
Of such a truth as I have meant;
My great travail so gladly spent,
                  Forget not yet!

Forget not yet when first began
The wearie life ye know, since whan
The suit, the service, none tell can,
                  Forget not yet!

Forget not yet the great assays,
The cruel wrong, the scornful ways,
The painful patience in delays,
                  Forget not yet!

Forget not ; oh ! forget not this,
How long ago hath been, and is
The mind that never meant amiss
                Forget not yet !

Forget not then thine own approved,
The which so long hath thee so loved,
Whose steadfast faith yet never moved :
                Forget not yet !

                          SIR T. WYATT.

XXI

THE SHEPHERD'S JOY

COME, sweet love, let sorrow cease,
Banish frownes, leave off dissension,
Love's warres make the sweetest peace,
Hearts uniting by contention.
Sunshine follows after raine,
After sorrow soone comes joy ;
Try me, prove me, trust me, love me,
        This will cure annoy ;
Sorrows ceasing, this is pleasing,
        All proves faire againe.

See these bright sunnes of thine eyes
        Clouded now with black disdaining ;
Shall such stormy tempests rise,
        To set love's faire dayes a raining ?

All are glad, the skies being cleare,
Lightly joying, sporting, toying,
　With their lovely cheare :
But as sad to see a shower,
Sadly drooping, lowring, powting,
　Turning sweet to sower.

Then, sweet love, dispearse this cloude
That obscures, this scornefull coying ;
When each creature sings aloude,
Filling hearts with over joying.
As every bird doth choose her mate,
Gailly billing, she is willing
　Her true love to take :
With such words let us contend,
Laughing, colling, kissing, playing,
　So our strife shall end.

ANON.

XXII

LOVE not me for comely grace,
For my pleasing eye or face,
Nor for any outward part,
No, nor for my constant heart:
　For these may faile, or turn to ill,
　So thou and I shall sever.

Keep therefore a true woman's eye,
And love me still, but know not why:
So hast thou the same reason still
　　To doat upon me ever.

ANON.

XXIII

LOVE

THE sea hath many thousand sands,
The sunne hath motes as many,
The skie is full of starres—and love
　　As full of woes as any;
Believe me that doe knowe the elfe,
And make no tryall by thyselfe.

It is in truth a prettie toye
　　For babes to play withall;
But O the honies of our youth
　　Are oft our age's gall;
Selfe-proofe in time will make thee know
　　He was a prophet told thee so.

A prophet that, Cassandra-like,
　　Tells truth without beliefe;
For headstrong youth will run his race,
　　Although his goal be griefe:

Love's martyr, when his heat is past,
Proves Care's Confessor at the last.

ANON.

XXIV

SONG

SOME say Love,
Foolish Love,
  Doth rule and govern all the gods :
I say Love,
Inconstant Love,
  Sets men's senses far at odds.
Some sweare Love,
Smooth-fac'd Love,
  Is sweetest sweete that men can have :
I say Love,
Sour Love,
  Makes virtue yield as beautie's slave,
A bitter sweete, a folly worst of all,
That forceth wisdom to be folly's thrall.

Love is sweete :
Wherein sweete ?
  In fading pleasures that do paine.
Beautie sweete :
Is that sweete
  That yieldeth sorrow for a gaine ?

If Love's sweetc,
Herein sweete,
   That minutes' joys are monthly woes :
'Tis not sweetc
That is sweete
   Nowhere, but where repentance growes ;
Then love who list, if beautie be so sour :
Labour for me, Love rest in prince's bower.

R. GREENE.

XXV

TO COLIN CLOUTE

BEAUTIE sat bathing by a spring,
   Where fairest shades did hide her,
The windes blew calme, the birds did sing,
   The coole streames ranne beside her.
My wanton thoughts entic'd mine eye
   To see what was forbidden :
But better memory said, fie,
   So, vaine desire was chidden.
      Hey nonnie, nonnie.

Into a slumber then I fell,
   When fond Imagination
Seemed to see, but could not tell,
   Her feature or her fashion.

But e'en as babes in dreames doe smile,
    And somctimes fall a weeping,
So I awakt, as wise this while,
    As when I fell a sleeping.
        Hey nonnie, nonnie.

ANON.

XXVI

PRESENCE IN ABSENCE

Absence, hear this my protestation
        Against thy strength,
        Distance, and length !
Do what thou canst for alteration,
        For hearts of truest mettle
Absence doth join, and Time doth settle.

Who loves a mistress of such quality,
        His mind hath found
        Affection's ground
Beyond time, place, and all mortality ;
        To hearts that cannot vary,
Absence is present, Time doth tarry.

My senses want their outward motion,
        Which now within
        Reason doth win,
Redoubled by her secret notion,

Like rich men that take pleasure
In hiding, more than handling treasure.

By absence this good means I gain,
    That I can catch her,
    Where none can watch her,
In some close corner of my brain.
    There I embrace her, and there kiss her,
    And so I both enjoy and miss her.

                  DONNE (?)

XXVII

WHAT IS LOVE?

Now what is Love? I praye thee, tell,
It is that fountaine and that well
Where pleasure and repentance dwell.
It is, perhaps, that sauncing bell,
That tolls all in to heaven or hell:
And this is Love, as I heare tell.

Yet what is Love? I praye thee saye,
It is a work on holie day;
It is December match'd with Maye:
When lustie blouds, in fresh araye,
Heare ten months after of their playe:
And this is Love, as I heare saye.

Yet what is Love? I prae thee saine,
It is a sunshine mix'd with raine;
It is a toothe-ache, or like paine;
It is a game where none doth gaine:
The lasse saith no, and would full faine:
And this is Love, as I heare saine.

Yet what is Love? I pray thee saie,
It is a yea, it is a nay,
A pretie kind of sporting fray,
It is a thing will soone away;
Then take the vantage while you may:
And this is Love, as I heare say.

Yet what is Love? I pray thee showe,
A thing that creepes, it cannot goe,
A prize that passeth to and fro,
A thing for one, a thing for mo;
And he that proves, must finde it so:
And this is Love, sweet friend, I troe.

SIR W. RALEIGH (?)

XXVIII

PHILLIDA AND CORYDON

In the merry month of May,
In a morne by breake of day,

Forth I walked by the wood-side,
When as May was in his pride :
There I spied all alone,
Phillida and Corydon.
Much ado there was, God wot,
He would love and she would not.
She said never man was true,
He said, none was false to you,
He said, he had lov'd her long,
She said, Love should have no wrong.
Corydon would kiss her then.
She said, maides must kiss no men,
Till they did for good and all :
Then she made the shepherd call
All the heavens to witnesse truth :
Never lov'd a truer youth.
Thus with many a pretty oath,
Yea and nay, and faith and troth,
Such as silly shepherds use
When they will not love abuse.
Love which had beene long deluded,
Was with kisses sweet concluded.
And Phillida with garlands gay,
Was made the lady of the May.

N. BRETON.

A SONG

Packe, cloudes, away, and welcome day,
With night we banish sorrow,
Sweete ayre, blow soft, mount, Larke, aloft,
To give my love good morrow.
Winges from the winde, to please her minde,
Notes from the Lark I'll borrow;
Bird, prune thy wing, nightingale, sing,
To give my love good morrow.
To give my love good morrow,
Notes from them all I'll borrow.

Wake from thy nest, robin red-brest,
Sing birds in every furrow,
And from each bill, let musicke shrill,
Give my faire love good morrow;
Blacke-bird and thrush, in every bush,
Stare, linnet, and cock-sparrow,
You pretty elves, amongst yourselves,
Sing my faire love good morrow.
To give my love good morrow,
Sing, birds, in every furrow.

T. HEYWOOD.

A SONG

Ye little birds that sit and sing
Amidst the shadie valleys,
And see how Phillis sweetly walkes
Within her garden alleyes ;
Goe pretty birds about her bowre,
Sing pretty birds she may not lowre,
Ah me, me thinkes I see her frowne,
   Ye pretty wantons warble.

Goe tune your voices harmonie,
And sing I am her lover ;
Straine loude and sweet, that every note,
With sweet content may move her :
And she that hath the sweetest voice,
Tell her I will not change my choice,
Yet still me thinkes I see her frowne,
   Ye pretty wantons warble.

O fly, make hast, see, see, she falles
Into a pretty slumber,
Sing round about her rosie bed
That waking she may wonder,

Say to her, 'tis her lover true,
That sendeth love to you, to you :
And when you heare her kinde reply,
Returne with pleasant warblings.

T. HEYWOOD.

XXXI

AN INVITATION

COME, shepherds, come !
        Come away
        Without delay,
Whilst the gentle time doth stay.
    Greene woods are dumb,
And will never tell to any
Those deare kisses, and those many
Sweete embraces that are given.
Dainty pleasures, that would even
Raise in coldest age a fire,
And give virgin blood desire.
        Then, if ever,
        Now or never,
    Come and have it ;
        Think not I
        Dare deny,
    If you crave it.

J. FLETCHER.

TO BACCHUS

God Lyæus, ever young,
Ever honour'd, ever sung;
Stain'd with blood of lusty grapes,
In a thousand lusty shapes;
Dance upon the mazer's brim,
In the crimson liquor swim;
From thy plenteous hand divine,
Let a river run with wine:
    God of youth, let this day here
    Enter neither care nor fear.

BEAUMONT AND FLETCHER.

LOVE AND TRUTH

Say that I should say, I love ye,
    Would you say, 'tis but a saying?
But if Love in prayers move ye,
    Will you not be mov'd with praying?

Thinke I thinke that love should know ye,
    Will you thinke 'tis but a thinking?
But if Love the thought doe show ye,
    Will ye loose your eyes with winking?

Write that I doe write you blessed,
   Will you write, 'tis but a writing?
But if Truth and Love confesse it,
   Will you doubt the true enditing?

No, I say, and thinke, and write it,
   Write, and thinke, and say your pleasure:
Love, and Truth, and I endite it,
   You arc blesséd out of measure.

                                   N. BRETON.

                    XXXIV

                    LOVE

FAIN would I change that note
To which fond love hath charm'd me
Long, long to sing by rote,
Fancying that that harm'd me:
Yet when this thought doth come,
   " Love is the perfect sum
   Of all delight,"
I have no other choice
Either for pen or voice
To sing or write.

O Love, they wrong thee much
That say thy sweet is bitter,

When thy rich fruit is such
As nothing can be sweeter.
Fair house of joy and bliss,
Where truest pleasure is,
 I do adore thee ;
I know thee what thou art,
I serve thee with my heart,
 And fall before thee.

ANON.

XXXV

STREPHON'S PALINODE

Sweet, I do not pardon crave,
 Till I have
By deserts this fault amended :
This, I only this desire,
 That your ire
May with penance be suspended.

Not my will, but Fate, did fetch
 Me, poor wretch,
Into this unhappy error ;
Which to plague, no tyrant's mind
 Pain can find
Like my heart's self-guilty terror.

Then, O then, let that suffice!
Your dear eyes
Need not, need not more afflict me;
Nor your sweet tongue, dipped in gall,
Need at all
From your presence interdict me.

Unto him that Hell sustains,
No new pains
Need be sought for his tormenting.
Oh! my pains Hell's pains surpass;
Yet, alas!
You are still new pains inventing.

By my love, long, firm, and true,
Borne to you;
By these tears my grief expressing;
By this pipe, which nights and days
Sounds your praise;
Pity me, my fault confessing.

Or, if I may not desire,
That your ire
May with penance be suspended;
Yet let me full pardon crave,
When I have
With soon death my fault amended.

F. DAVISON.

TO HIS LOVE

COME away, come sweet Love,
The golden morning breakes :
All the earth, all the ayre
Of love and pleasure speakes.
Teach thine armes then to embrace,
And sweet rosie lips to kisse :
And mix our soules in mutual blisse.
Eyes were made for beautie's grace,
Viewing, ruing love's long paine :
Procur'd by beautie's rude disdaine.

Come away, come sweet Love,
The golden morning wasts :
While the sunne from his sphere
His fierie arrowes casts,
Making all the shadowes flie,
Playing, staying in the grove,
To entertaine the stealth of love.
Thither, sweet love, let us hie
Flying, dying, in desire,
Wing'd with sweet hopes and heavenly fire.

Come away, come sweet Love,
Doe not in vaine adiorne
Beautie's grace that should rise,
Like to the naked morne.

Lillies on the river's side,
And faire Cyprian flowers newe blowne
Desire no beauties but their owne.
Ornament is nurse of pride,
Pleasure, measure, Love's delight:
Haste then, sweet Love, our wished flight.

ANON.

XXXVII

A WARNING FOR WOOERS

SOME love for wealth and some for hue,
And none of both these loves are true;
For when the mill hath lost her sailes,
Then must the miller lose his vailes:
                    Of grass comes hay,
And flowers faire will soon decay:
                    Of ripe comes rotten,
In age all beautie is forgotten.

Some love too high and some too lowe,
And of them both great griefs do growe;
And some do love the common sort,
And common folk use common sport.
                    Look not too high,
Lest that a chip fall in thine eye:
                    But high or lowe,
Ye may be sure she is a shrewe.

But, sirs, I use to tell no tales,
Each fish that swims doth not bear scales ;
In every hedge I find not thornes,
Nor every beast doth carry hornes :
    I say not soe,
That every woman causeth woe.
     That were too broad :
Who loves not venom must shun the toad.

Who useth still the truth to tell,
May blamed be, though he say well ;
Say crow is white, and snow is black,
Lay not the fault on woman's back :
    Thousands were good,
But few scap'd drowning in Noe's flood :
     Most are well bent,
I must say so, lest I be spent.

         ANON.

XXXVIII

A MARRIAGE BLESSING

VERTUE, if not a God, yet God's chiefe part,
Be thou the knot of this their open vow,
That still he be her head, she be his heart ;
He leane to her, she unto him doe bow,
   Each other still allow ;

Like oak and misletoe,
Her strength from him, his praise from her doe growe ;
In which most lovely traine,
O Hymen, long their coupled joyes maintaine !

SIR P. SIDNEY.

XXXIX

A BRIDAL SONG

ROSES, their sharpe spines being gone,
   Not royal in their smells alone,
    But in their hue ;
Maiden-pinkes, of odour faint,
Daisies smel-lesse, yet most quaint,
    And sweet thyme true ;

Primrose, first-born child of Ver,
Merry spring-time's harbinger,
    With her bells dimme ;
Oxlips, in their cradles growing,
Marigolds, on death-beds blowing,
    Lark-heeles trimme.

All dear Nature's children swecte,
Lie 'fore bride and bridegroome's feet,
    Blessing their sensc.

Not an angel of the aire,
Bird melodious, or bird faire,
    Is absent hence.

The crow, the slanderous cuckoo, nor
The boding raven, nor chough hoar,
    Nor chattring pie,
May on our bride-house perch or sing,
Or with them any discord bring,
    But from it fly.

J. FLETCHER.

XL

ROSALIND'S MADRIGAL

Love in my bosome, like a bee,
    Doth sucke his sweete :
Now with his wings he playes with me,
    Now with his feete :
Within mine eyes he makes his nest,
His bed amidst my tender breast,
My kisses are his daily feast,
And yet he robs me of my rest.
    Ah, wanton, will ye ?

And if I sleepe, then percheth he
    With pretty flight :
And makes his pillow of my knee
    The live-long night.

Strike I my lute, he tunes the string,
He music playes if so I sing,
He lends me every lovely thing,
Yet cruel he my heart doth sting :
 Ah, wanton, will ye ?

Else I with roses every day
 Will whip ye hence,
And bind you, when you long to play,
 For your offence ;
I'll shut mine eyes to keep you in,
I'll make you fast it for your sinne,
I'll count your power not worth a pinne,
Alas ! what hereby shall I winne,
 If he gain-say me ?

What if I beate the wanton boy
 With many a rod ?
He will repay me with annoy,
 Because a God.
Then sit thou safely on my knee,
And let thy bowre my bosome be ;
Lurk in mine eyes, I like of thee,
O, Cupid, so thou pity me !
 Spare not, but play thee.

                    T. LODGE.

XLI

DAMELUS SONG TO HIS DIAPHENIA

DIAPHENIA, like the daffa-down-dilly,
White as the sunne, faire as the lilly,
  Heigh ho, how I doe love thee !
I doe love thee as my lambs
Are beloved of their dams,
  How blest were I if thou would'st prove me !

Diaphenia, like the spreading roses,
That in thy sweetes all sweetes encloses,
  Faire sweet how I doe love thee !
I doe love thee as each flower
Loves the sunne's life-giving power,
  For dead, thy breath to life might move me.

Diaphenia, like to all things blessed,
When all thy praises are expressed,
  Deare joy, how I do love thee !
As the birds doe love the Spring,
Or the bees their careful king,
  Then in requite, sweet virgin love me.

                                   H. CONSTABLE.

TO HIS COY LOVE

I PRAY thee, leave ; love me no more,
    Call home the heart you gave me ;
I but in vaine that saint adore
    That can, but will not save me.
These poore halfe kisses kill me quite ;
    Was ever man thus served ?
Amidst an ocean of delight,
    For pleasure to be sterved.

Show me no more those snowie breasts,
    With azure riverets branched,
Where, whilst mine eye with plentie feasts,
    Yet is my thirst not stanched.
O Tantalus ! thy paines ne'er tell ;
    By me thou art prevented :
'Tis nothing to be plagu'd in hell,
    But thus in heaven tormented.

Clip me no more in those deare armes,
    Nor thy life's comfort call me ;
O ! these are but too powerful charmes,
    And doe but more enthral me.

But see how patient I am growne,
In all this coile about thee ;
Come, nice thing, let thy heart alone,
I cannot live without thee.

M. DRAYTON.

XLIII

WHAT IS LOVE?

TELL me, dearest, what is love?
'Tis a lightning from above,
'Tis an arrow, 'tis a fire,
'Tis a boy they call Desire.
    'Tis a grave,
    Gapes to have
Those poor fools that long to prove.

Tell me more, are women true?
Yes, some are, and some as you.
Some are willing, some are strange,
Since you men first taught to change.
    And till troth
    Be in both,
All shall love, to love anew.

Tell me more yet, can they grieve?
Yes, and sicken sore, but live,
And be wise, and delay,
When you men are as wise as they.

Then I see,
Faith will be,
Never till they both believe.

BEAUMONT AND FLETCHER.

XLIV

LIFE'S PAGEANT

WHETHER men do laugh or weepe,
Whether they do wake or sleepe,
Whether they die young or olde,
Whether they feel heat or colde,
There is underneath the sunne
Nothing in true earnest done.

All our pride is but a jeste,
None are worst and none are beste ;
Grief and joye and hope and feare,
Play their pageants everywhere ;
Vaine opinion all doth sway,
And the worlde is but a play.

Powers above in cloudes do sit,
Mocking our poor apish wit,
That so lamely, with such state
Their high glory imitate :
No ill can be felt but paine,
And that happy men disdaine.

T. CAMPION.

TO SPRING AND DEATH

SWEET spring, thou turn'st with all thy goodly traine,
Thy head with flames, thy mantle bright with flowers,
The zephyres curl the green locks of the plaine,
The clouds for joy in pearls weep down their showers.

Turn thou, sweet youth ; but ah ! my pleasant hours
And happy days with thee come not againe,
The sad memorials only of my paine
Do with thee turn, which turn my sweets to sours.

Thou art the same which still thou wert before,
Delicious, lusty, amiable, fair ;
But she whose breath embalm'd thy wholesome air
Is gone ; nor gold, nor gems can her restore.

Neglected Virtue ! seasons go and come,
While thine, forgot, lie closed in a tomb.

W. DRUMMOND.

SURSUM COR

LEAVE me, O Love, which reachest but to dust ;
And thou, my mind, aspire to higher things ;
Grow rich in that which never taketh rust ;
Whatever fades, but fading pleasure brings.

Draw in thy beames, and humble all thy might
To that sweet yoke where lasting freedomes be ;
Which breakes the cloudes, and opens forth the light,
That doth both shine, and give us sight to see.

O take fast hold; let that light be thy guide
In this small course which birth draws out of death,
And thinke how ill becometh him to slide
Who seeketh heav'n and comes of heavenly breath.

Then farewell, world ; thy uttermost I see :
Eternal Love, maintaine thy life in me.

SIR P. SIDNEY.

XLVII

CONTENT

ART thou poore, yet hast thou golden slumbers :
      O sweet content !
Art thou rich, yet is thy minde perplexed :
      O punishment !
Dost thou laugh to see how fooles are vexed
To add to golden numbers, golden numbers :
      O sweet content !
   Worke apace, apace, apace, apace ;
   Honest labour beares a lovely face ;
   Then hey noney, noney, hey noney, noney.

Canst drinke the waters of the crisped spring :
    O sweet content !
Swim'st thou in wealth, yet sink'st in thine owne
    teares,
    O punishment !
Then he that patiently want's burden beares,
No burden beares, but is a king, a king,
    O sweet content !
      Work apace, apace, etc.

T. DEKKER (?)

XLVIII

THE HAPPY LIFE

MARTIAL, the things that do attain
    The happy life, be these, I finde.
The richesse left, not got with pain ;
    The fruitful ground, the quiet minde ;

The equal friend, no grudge, no strife ;
    No charge of rule, nor governance ;
Without disease, the healthful life ;
    The household of continuance ;

The meane diet, no delicate fare ;
    True wisdom join'd with simplenesse ;
The night discharged of all care,
    Where wine the wit may not oppresse.

E

The faithful wife, without debate;
  Such sleepes as may beguile the night;
Contented with thine owne estate,
  Ne wish for death, ne feare his might.

EARL OF SURREY.

XLIX

THE CHARACTER OF A HAPPY LIFE

How happy is he born and taught,
  That serveth not another's will;
Whose armour is his honest thought,
  And simple truth his utmost skill;

Whose Passions not his masters are;
  Whose Soul is still prepar'd for Death,
Unti'd unto the world by care
  Of publick Fame or private Breath;

Who envies none that chance doth raise,
  Nor Vice; who never understood
How deepest wounds are given by praise;
  Nor Rules of State, but Rules of good.

Who hath his life from Rumours freed;
  Whose conscience is his strong retreat;
Whose State can neither Flatterers feed,
  Nor Ruin make oppressors great;

Who God doth late and early pray
More of His grace than gifts to lend ;
And entertains the harmless day
With a Religious Book or Friend.

This man is freed from servile bands
Of hope to rise or fear to fall :—
Lord of himself, though not of Lands,
And, having nothing, yet hath all.

SIR H. WOTTON.

L

PARVUM SUFFICIT

HOMELY hearts doe harbour quiet,
　　Little feare, and mickle solace :
States suspect their bed and diet,
　　Feare and craft do haunt the palace.
Little would I, little want I,
　　Where the minde and store agreeth,
Smallest comfort is not scantie,
　　Least he longs that little seeth.
Time hath beene that I have longed,
　　Foolish I, to like of folly,
To converse where honour thronged,
　　To my pleasures linked wholly.

Now I see, and seeing sorrow,
    That the day consum'd returns not:
Who dare trust upon to-morrow,
    When nor time, nor life sojourns not.

T. LODGE.

LI

FORTUNE AND VIRTUE

DAZZLED thus with height of place,
Whilst our Hopes our Wits beguile,
No man marks the narrow space
'Twixt a Prison and a Smile.

Then, since Fortune's favours fade,
You, that in her arms do sleep,
Learn to swim, and not to wade;
For the Hearts of Kings are deep.

But if Greatness be so blind
As to trust in Towers of Air,
Let it be with Goodness lin'd,
That at least the Fall be fair.

Then, though dark'ned, you shall say,
When Friends fail, and Princes frown,
Vertue is the roughest way,
But proves at Night a Bed of Down.

SIR H. WOTTON.

LII

LOSS IN DELAY

SHUN delayes, they breede remorse ;
     Take thy time while time is lent thee ;
Creeping snailes have weakest force,
     Fly their fault lest thou repent thee.
Good is best when soonest wrought,
Linger'd labours come to nought.

Hoist up sail while gale doth last,
     Tide and winde stay no man's pleasure ;
Seeke not time when time is past,
     Sober speede is wisdom's leisure.
After-wits are dearly bought,
Let thy fore-wit guide thy thought.

Seek thy salve while sore is green,
     Fester'd woundes ask deeper lancing ;
After cures are seldome seen,
     Often sought scarce ever chancing.
Time and place give best advice,
Out of season, out of price.

Tender twigs are bent with ease,
  Aged trees do breake with bending;
Young desires make little prease,
  Growth doth make them past amending.
Happy man, that soone doth knock
Babel's babes against the rock !

R. SOUTHWELL.

LIII

A PORTRAIT

A SWEET attractive kinde of grace,
A full assurance giv'n by lookes,
Continual comfort in a face,
The lineaments of Gospell bookes.
I trowe that countenance cannot lie
Whose thoughts are legible in the eye.

Was never eye did see that face,
Was never eare did heare that tong,
Was never minde did minde his grace,
That ever thought the travell long;
But eyes, and eares, and ev'ry thought
Were with his sweete perfections caught.

M. ROYDON.

A CONTENTED MIND

I weigh not Fortune's frowne or smile,
I joy not much in earthly joyes,
I seeke not state, I seeke not stile,
I am not fond of fancie's toyes.
 I rest so pleas'd with what I have,
 I wish no more, no more I crave.
I quake not at the thunder's crack,
I tremble not at noise of warre,
I swound not at the newes of wrack,
I shrink not at a blazing-starre ;
 I fear not losse, I hope not gaine,
 I envie none, I none disdaine.
I see Ambition never pleas'd,
I see some Tantals starv'd in store,
I see gold's dropsie seldome eas'd,
I see even Midas gape for more ;
 I neither want, nor yet abound,
 Enough's a feast, content is crown'd.
I faine not friendship where I hate,
I fawne not on the great (in show),
I prize, I praise a meane estate,
Neither too lofty nor too low ;
 This, this is all my choice, my cheere,
 A minde content, a conscience cleere.

J. SYLVESTER.

LV

THE STURDY ROCK

The sturdy rock, for all his strength,
  By raging seas is rent in twaine;
The marble stone is pearst at length,
  With little drops of drizzling rain:
The ox doth yeeld unto the yoke,
The steele obeyeth the hammer stroke.

The stately stagge, that seems so stout,
  By yalping hounds at bay is set;
The swiftest bird that flies about,
  Is caught at length in fowler's net:
The greatest fish, in deepest brooke,
Is soon deceived by subtill hooke.

Yea, man himself, unto whose will
  All thinges are bounden to obey;
For all his wit and worthie skill,
  Doth fade at length and fall away.
There is nothing but time doth waste;
The heavens, the earth, consume at last.

But vertue sits triumphing still,
  Upon the throne of glorious fame;
Though spiteful death man's body kill,
  Yet hurts he not his vertuous name.

By life or death what so betides,
The state of vertue never slides.

ANON.

LVI

THE LIE

Go, Soul, the body's guest,
　Upon a thankless arrant :
Fear not to touch the best ;
　The truth shall be thy warrant :
　　Go, since I needs must die,
　　And give the world the lie.

Say to the Court, it glows
　And shines like rotten wood ;
Say to the Church, it shows
　What's good, and doth no good :
　　If Church and Court reply,
　　Then give them both the lie.

Tell Potentates, they live
　Acting by others' action ;
Not loved unless they give,
　Not strong but by a faction :
　　If Potentates reply,
　　Give Potentates the lie.

Tell men of high condition.
That manage the estate,
Their purpose is ambition,
Their practice only hate :
And if they once reply,
Then give them all the lie.

Tell them that brave it most,
They beg for more by spending,
Who, in their greatest cost,
Seek nothing but commending :
And if they make reply,
Then give them all the lie.

Tell zeal it wants devotion ;
Tell love it is but lust ;
Tell time it metes but motion ;
Tell flesh it is but dust :
And wish them not reply,
For thou must give the lie.

Tell age it daily wasteth ;
Tell honour how it alters ;
Tell beauty how she blasteth ;
Tell favour how it falters :
And as they shall reply,
Give every one the lie.

Tell wit how much it wrangles
   In tickle points of niceness ;
Tell wisdom she entangles
   Herself in over-wiseness :
     And when they do reply,
     Straight give them both the lie.

Tell physic of her boldness ;
   Tell skill it is pretension ;
Tell charity of coldness ;
   Tell law it is contention :
     And as they do reply,
     So give them still the lie.

Tell fortune of her blindness ;
   Tell nature of decay ;
Tell friendship of unkindness ;
   Tell justice of delay :
     And if they will reply,
     Then give them all the lie.

Tell arts they have no soundness,
   But vary by esteeming ;
Tell schools they want profoundness,
   And stand too much on seeming :
     If arts and schools reply,
     Give arts and schools the lie.

Tell faith it's fled the city;
　Tell how the country erreth;
Tell, manhood shakes off pity,
　Tell, virtue least preferreth:
　　And if they do reply,
　　Spare not to give the lie.

So when thou hast, as I
　Commanded thee, done blabbing,—
Although to give the lie
　Deserves no less than stabbing,—
　　Stab at thee he that will,
　　No stab the soul can kill!

SIR W. RALEIGH.

LVII

THE LULLABY OF A LOVER

SING lullaby, as women doe,
　Wherewith they bring their babes to rest;
And lullaby can I sing too,
　As womanly as can the best.
With lullaby they still the childe,
And if I be not much beguil'd,
Full many wanton babes have I,
Which must be still'd with lullaby.

First lullaby, my youthful yeares !
  It is nowe time to go to bed,
For crooked age and hoary hairs
  Have won the haven within my head :
With lullaby then, youth, be still,
With lullaby content thy will ;
Since courage quayles, and comes behind,
Go sleepe, and so beguile thy minde.

Next lullaby, my gazing eyes,
  Which wonted were to glance apace ;
For every glasse may nowe suffice
  To shewe the furrowes in my face.
With lullaby then winke awhile,
With lullaby your lookes beguile :
Let no faire face, nor beautie brighte
Entice you eft with vaine delighte.

And lullaby, my wanton will !
  Let reason's rule nowe reigne thy thought,
Since all too late I finde by skill
  Howe deare I have thy fancies bought :
With lullaby nowe take thine ease,
With lullaby thy doubtes appease ;
For, trust to this, if thou be still,
My body shall obey thy will.

G. GASCOIGN.

LVIII

ON TIME

TIME ! I ever must complaine
 Of thy craft and cruell cunning;
Seeming fix'd here to remaine,
 When thy feete are ever running;
  And thy plumes
  Still resumes
Courses new, repose most shunning.

Like calme winds thou passest by us;
 Lin'd with feathers are thy feete;
Thy downie wings with silence flie us,
 Like the shadowes of the night:
  Or the streame,
  That no beame
Of sharpest eye discernes to fleet.

Therefore mortals all deluded
 By thy grave and wrinkled face,
In their judgements have concluded,
 That thy slow and snaile-like pace
  Still doth bend
  To no end,
But to an eternal race.

Budding youth's vaine blooming wit
Thinks the spring shall ever last,
And the gaudie flowers that sit
    On Flora's brow shall never taste
        Winter's scorne,
        Nor forlorne,
    Bend their heads with chilling blast.

Riper age expects to have
    Harvests of his proper toile,
Times to give, and to receive
    Seedes and fruits from fertile soile ;
        But at length,
        Doth his strength,
    Youth and beauty all recoile.

Cold December hope retaines,
    That the spring, each thing reviving,
Shall throughout his aged veines
    Pour fresh youth, past joys repriving ;
        But thy sithe
        Ends his strife,
    And to Lethe sends him driving.

J. HAGTHORPE.

WHAT IS THE WORLD?

SWIFTLY water sweepeth by:
Swifter winged arrowes fly,
Swiftest yet, the winde that passes
When the nether clouds it chases.
But the joyes of earthly mindes,
Worldly pleasures, vain delights,
Far out-swift far sudden flights,
Waters, arrowes, and the windes.
What is the world? tell, Worldling (if thou know it),
If it be good, why do all ills o'erflow it?
If it be bad, why dost thou like it so?
If it be sweet, how comes it bitter then?
If it be bitter, what bewitcheth men?
If it be Friend, why kills it, as a Foe,
Vain-minded men that over-love and lust it?
If it be Foe, Fondling, how dar'st thou trust it?

J. SYLVESTER.

As Noah's pigeon, which return'd no more,
　　Did show she footing found, for all the flood;
So when good soules, departed through Death's doore,
　　Come not againe, it shewes their dwelling good.

SIR J. DAVIES.

LXI

THE WORLD A GAME

THIS world a hunting is,
The prey, poor man, the Nimrod fierce is death;
His speedy greyhounds are
Lust, sickness, envy, care,
Strife that ne'er falls amiss,
With all those ills which haunt us while we breathe.
Now if by chance we fly
Of these the eager chase,
Old age with stealing pace
Casts up his nets, and there we panting die.

W. DRUMMOND.

LXII

EPITAPH

I WAS, I am not; smil'd, that since did weepe;
Labour'd, that rest; I wak'd, that now must sleepe;
I play'd, I play not; sung, that now am still;
Saw, that am blind; I would, that have no will;
I fed that, which feeds worms; I stood, I fell:
I bad God save you, that now bid farewell;
I felt, I feel not; followed, was pursued;
I warr'd, have peace; I conquer'd, am subdued;

F

I mov'd, want motion; I was stiffe, that bow
Below the earth; then something, nothing now.
I catch'd, am caught; I travel'd, here I lie;
Liv'd in the world, that to the world now die.

T. HEYWOOD.

LXIII

LAY a garland on my hearse
    Of the dismal yew;
Maidens, willow-branches bear
    Say I died true.
My love was false, but I was firm
    From my hour of birth.
Upon my buried body lie
    Lightly, gentle earth.

BEAUMONT AND FLETCHER.

LXIV

NATURE'S LESSONS

WHEN the leaves in Autumn wither,
    With a tawny, tanned face;
Warpt and wrinkled-up together,
    Th' year's late beauty to disgrace:

There thy life's glass mayst thou finde thee,
Green now, gray now, gone anon ;
Leaving, Worldling, of thine own
Neither fruit nor leaf behind thee.

When chill Winter's cheer wee see
Shrinking, shaking, shivering, cold ;
See ourselves, for such are wee
After youth, if ever old.
After Winter, Spring (in order)
Comes again ; but earthly thing
Rotting here, not rooting further,
Can thy Winter hope a Spring?

J. SYLVESTER.

LXV

ILLUSION

If Fortune's dark eclipse cloud glorie's light,
Then what availes that pomp which pride doth claim ?
A meere illusion made to mock the sight,
Whose best was but the shadow of a dreame.

Let greatnesse of her glassie scepters vaunt,
Not scepters, no, but reeds, soone bruis'd, soone
broken ;
And let this worldlie pompe our wits enchant,
All fades and scarcelie leaves behinde a token.

Those golden palaces, those gorgeous halls,
  With furniture superfluously faire ;
Those statlie courts, those sky-encount'ring walls
  Evanish all—like vapours in the aire.

Our painted pleasures but apparell paine ;
  We spend our dayes in dread, our lives in dangers,
Balls to the starres, and thralls to Fortune's reigne,
  Knowne unto all, yet to ourselves but strangers.

ALEXANDER, EARL OF STIRLING.

LXVI

ON THE TOMBS IN WESTMINSTER ABBEY

Mortality, behold, and fear,
What a change of flesh is here !
Think how many royal bones
Sleep within this heap of stones.
Here they lie, had realms and lands,
Who now want strength to stir their hands ;
Where, from their pulpits seal'd with dust,
They preach, " In greatness is no trust."
Here's an acre sown indeed
With the richest, royal'st seed,
That the earth did e'er suck in
Since the first man died for sin :
Here the bones of birth have cried
" Though gods they were, as men they died."

Here are sands, ignoble things
Dropt from the ruin'd sides of kings;
Here's a world of pomp and state
Buried in dust, once dead by fate.

F. BEAUMONT.

LXVII

TO DEATH

DEATH, be not proud, though some have called thee
Mighty and dreadful, for thou art not so;
For those, whom thou think'st thou dost overthrow,
Die not, poor Death, nor yet canst thou kill me.

From rest and sleep which but thy picture be,
Much pleasure, then, from thee much more must flow;
And soonest our best men with thee do go,
Rest of their bones, and soul's delivery.

Thou'rt slave to Fate, chance, kings, and desperate men,
And dost with poison, war, and sickness dwell,
And poppy or charms can make us sleep as well,
And better than thy stroke. Why swell'st thou then?

One short sleep past, we wake eternally,
And Death shall be no more; Death, thou shalt die.

DR. DONNE.

A PRAYER

VIEW me, Lord, a work of Thine :
Shall I then lie drowned in night ?
Might Thy grace in me but shine,
I should seeme made all of light.

But my soul still surfeits so
On the poisoned baits of sinne,
That I strange and ugly grow,
All is dark and foul withinne.

Cleanse me, Lord, that I may kneele
At thine altar, pure and white :
They that once Thy mercies feele,
Gaze no more on earth's delight.

Worldly joys, like shadows, fade
When the heavenly light appears;
But the covenants Thou hast made,
Endless, knowe nor dayes nor yeares.

In Thy Word, Lord, is my trust,
To Thy mercies past I flye ;
Though I am but clay and dust,
Yet Thy grace can lift me highe.

T. CAMPION.

LXIX

THE BURNING BABE

As I in hoary winter's night stood shiveringe in the snowe,
Surpris'd I was with sudden heat, which made my heart
    to glowe ;
And lifting up a fearful eye to view what fire was neare,
A prettie babe all burning bright, did in the air appeare,
Who, scorchèd with exceeding heate, such floodes of teares
    did shed,
As though His floodes should quench His flames which
    with His teares were fed;
Alas ! quoth He, but newly borne, in fiery heates I fry,
Yet none approach to warme their heartes or feele my fire
    but I !
My faultless breast the furnace is, the fuel woundinge
    thornes,
Love is the fire, and sighes the smoke, the ashes shame
    and scornes;
The fuel Justice layeth on, and Mercy blowes the coales;
The metal in this furnace wrought are men's defiled
    soules,
For which, as nowe a fire I am, to worke them to their
    good,
So will I melt into a bath, to washe them in my bloode :

With this He vanish'd out of sight, and swiftly shrunk
    awaye,
And straight I called unto mind that it was Christmas-
daye.

R. SOUTHWELL.

LXX

A HYMN TO GOD THE FATHER

WILT Thou forgive that sin where I begun,
    Which was my sin, though it were done before?
Wilt thou forgive that sin through which I run
    And do run still, though still I do deplore?
When Thou hast done, Thou hast not done,
                For I have more.

Wilt Thou forgive that sin which I have won
    Others to sin, and made my sins their door?
Wilt Thou forgive that sin which I did shun
    A year or two, but wallow'd in a score?
When Thou hast done Thou hast not done,
                For I have more.

I have a sin of fear, that when I've spun
    My last thread, I shall perish on the shore;
But swear by Thyself, that at my death Thy Son
    Shall shine, as He shines now and heretofore;
And having done that, Thou hast done,
                I fear no more.

DR. DONNE.

TIME AND HOPE

EVEN such is time, that takes in trust
Our youth, our joyes, our all we have,
And pays us but with Earth and Dust ;
Who, in the dark and silent Grave,
(When we have wandred all our ways),
Shuts up the story of our days ;
But from this Earth, this Grave, this Dust,
    My God shall raise me up, I trust !

SIR W. RALEIGH.

EVEN-SONG

O MORTALL folke, you may beholde and see
Howe I lye here, sometime a mighty knight ;
The end of joye and all prosperitee
Is death at last, thorough his course and mighte,
After the daye there cometh the darke night,
For though the daye be never so long,
At last the belle ringeth to even-song.

S. HAWES.

BOOK II

A FATHER'S BLESSING

WHAT I shall leave thee none can tell,
But all shall say I wish thee well ;
I wish thee, Vin, before all wealth,
Both bodily and ghostly health :
Nor too much wealth, nor wit, come to thee,
So much of either may undoe thee.
I wish thee learning, not for show,
Enough for to instruct, and know ;
Not such as gentlemen require,
To prate at table, or at fire.
I wish thee all thy mother's graces,
Thy father's fortunes, and his places.
I wish thee friends, and one at court,
Not to build on, but support ;
To keep thee, not in doing many
Oppressions, but from suffering any.
I wish thee peace in all thy ways,
Nor lazy nor contentious dayes ;
And when thy soul and body part,
As innocent as now thou art.

R. CORBET.

LXXIV

THE RETREAT

Happy those early dayes, when I
Shin'd in my angel infancy!
Before I understood this place
Appointed for my second race.
Or taught my soul to fancy ought
But a white, celestial thought;
When yet I had not walkt above
A mile or two from my first love,
And looking back, at that short space,
Could see a glimpse of his bright face;
When on some gilded Cloud or Flowre
My gazing soul would dwell an houre,
And in those weaker glories spy
Some shadows of eternity;
Before I taught my tongue to wound
My conscience with a sinful sound,
Or had the black art to dispense
A sev'rall sin to ev'ry sense;
But felt through all this fleshly dresse
Bright shootes of everlastingnesse.
O how I long to travel back,
And tread again that ancient track!
That I might once more reach that plaine
Where first I left my glorious traine;

From whence th' enlightened spirit sees
That shady city of palme trees.
But ah ! my soul with too much stay
Is drunk, and staggers in the way !
Some men a forward motion love,
But I by backward steps would move ;
And, when this dust falls to the urn,
In that state I came, return.

H. VAUGHAN.

LXXV

THE ALCHEMY OF LOVE

WHAT pearls, what rubies can
Seem so lovely fair to man,
As her lips whom he doth love,
When in sweet discourse they move,
Or her lovelier teeth, the while
She doth bless him with a smile ?
Stars indeed fair creatures bee :
Yet amongst us where is hee
Joys not more the whilst he lies
Sunning in his mistress' eyes,
Than in all the glimmering light
Of a starrie winter's night ?
Note the beautie of an eye—
And if aught you praise it bye

Leave such passion in your mind,
Let my reason's eye be blind.
Mark if ever red or white
Anywhere gave such delight,
As when they have taken place
In a worthie woman's face.

G. WITHER.

LXXVI

LOVE

ALL love, at first, like gen'rous wine,
Ferments and frets, until 'tis fine ;
But when 'tis settled on the lee,
And from th' impurer matter free,
Becomes the richer still, the older,
And proves the pleasanter, the colder.
Love is too great a happiness
For wretched mortals to possess :
For, could it hold inviolate
Against those cruelties of Fate,
Which all felicities below
By rigid laws are subject to,
It would become a bliss too high
For perishing mortality,
Translate to earth the joys above ;
For nothing goes to Heaven but love.

S. BUTLER.

THE PRIMROSE

ASKE me why I send you here
This sweet Infanta of the yeare?
Aske me why I send to you
This primrose, thus bepearl'd with dew?
I will whisper to your eares
The sweets of love are mixt with tears.

Ask me why this flower does show
So yellow-green, and sickly too?
Ask me why the stalk is weak
And bending, yet it doth not break?
I will answer, These discover
What fainting hopes are in a lover.

R. HERRICK.

AGAINST THEM WHO LAY UNCHASTITY TO THE SEX OF WOMEN

THEY meet but with unwholesome springs,
And summers which infectious are;

G

They heare but when the mermaid sings,
    And onely see the falling starre,
        Who ever dare,
Affirme no woman chaste and faire.

Goe cure your fevers ; and you'll say
    The dog-dayes scorch not all the yeare ;
In copper mines no longer stay,
    But travell to the West, and there
        The right ones see,
And grant all gold's not alchemie.

What madman, 'cause the glow-worme's flame
    Is cold, sweares there's no warmth in fire ?
'Cause some make forfeit of their name,
    And slave themselves to man's desire,
        Shall the sex, free
From guilt, damn'd to the bondage be ?

Nor grieve, Castara, though 'twere fraile ;
    Thy vertue then would brighter shine,
When thy example should prevaile,
    And every woman's faith be thine :
        And were there none,
'Tis majesty to rule alone.

W. HABINGTON.

LXXIX

CASTARA

LIKE the violet which alone
    Prospers in some happy shade ;
My Castara lives unknown,
    To no looser eye betray'd.
        For she's to herself untrue,
        Who delights i' the public view.

Such is her beauty, as no arts
    Have enriched with borrowed grace ;
Her high birth no pride imparts,
    For she blushes in her place.
        Folly boasts a glorious blood,
        She is noblest, being good.

She her throne makes reason climbe,
    While wild passions captive lie,
And each article of time
    Her pure thoughts to heaven fly :
        All her vowes religious be,
        And her love she vowes to me.

W. HABINGTON.

LXXX

THE NIGHT-PIECE TO JULIA

HER eyes the glow-worme lend thee,
The shooting starres attend thee ;
    And the elves also,
    Whose little eyes glow,
Like the sparks of fire, befriend thee.

No Will-o'-th'-Wispe mislight thee ;
Nor snake, or slow-worme bite thee :
    But on, on thy way,
    Not making a stay,
Since ghost there's none t' affright thee.

Let not the darke thee cumber ;
What though the moon does slumber ?
    The starres of the night
    Will lend thee their light
Like tapers cleare without number.

Then Julia let me woo thee,
Thus, thus to come unto me ;
    And when I shall meet
    Thy silv'ry feet,
My soul I'll poure into thee.

R. HERRICK.

THE POWER OF LOVE

THERE are two births, the one when light
First strikes the new awaken'd sense ;
The other when two souls unite,
And we must count our life from thence :
When you lov'd me and I lov'd you,
Then both of us were born anew.

Love then to us did new souls give,
And in those souls did plant new powers ;
Since when another life we live,
The breath we breathe is his not ours :
Love makes those young, whom age doth chill,
And whom he finds young, keeps young still.

W. CARTWRIGHT.

TO HIS COY MISTRESS

HAD we but world enough, and time,
This coyness, lady, were no crime,
We would sit down, and think which way
To walk, and pass one long, love's day.

Thou by the Indian Ganges' side
Should'st rubies find; I by the tide
Of Humber would complain. I would
Love you ten years before the flood,
And you should, if you please, refuse
Till the conversion of the Jews;
My vegetable love should grow
Vaster than empires and more slow;
An hundred years should go to praise
Thine eyes, and on thy forehead gaze;
Two hundred to adore each breast,
But thirty thousand to the rest;
An age at least to every part,
And the last age should show your heart.
For, lady, you deserve this state,
Nor would I love at lower rate.

But at my back I always hear
Time's winged chariot hurrying near;
And yonder all before us lie
Deserts of vast eternity.
Thy beauty shall no more be found,
Nor, in thy marble vault, shall sound
My echoing song: then worms shall try
That long preserv'd virginity;
And your quaint honour turn to dust,
And into ashes all my lust:
The grave's a fine and private place,
But none, I think, do there embrace.

Now therefore, while the youthful hue
Sits on thy skin like morning dew,
And while thy willing soul transpires
At every pore with instant fires,
Now let us sport us while we may,
And now, like am'rous birds of prey,
Rather at once our time devour,
Than languish in his slow-chapt pow'r.
Let us roll all our strength and all
Our sweetness up into one ball ;
And tear our pleasures with rough strife,
Thorough the iron gates of life ;
Thus, though we cannot make our sun
Stand still, yet we will make him run.

A. MARVELL.

LXXXIII

SONG

PHILLIS is my only joy,
      Faithless as the winds or seas ;
Sometimes coming, sometimes coy,
      Yet she never fails to please ;
            If with a frown
            I am cast down,
            Phillis smiling
            And beguiling,
Makes me happier than before.

Though, alas ! too late I find
Nothing can her fancy fix,
Yet the moment she is kind,
I forgive her all her tricks ;
    Which though I see,
    I can't get free ;
    She deceiving,
    I believing ;
What need lovers wish for more ?

SIR C. SEDLEY.

LXXXIV

AMORET

FAIR Amoret is gone astray,
    Pursue and seek her, ev'ry lover ;
I'll tell the signs by which you may
    The wand'ring shepherdess discover.

Coquette and coy at once her air,
Both studied, tho' both seem neglected ;
Careless she is, with artful care,
Affecting to seem unaffected.

With skill her eyes dart ev'ry glance,
Yet change so soon you'd ne'er suspect them,
For she'd persuade they wound by chance,
Tho' certain aim and art direct them.

She likes herself, yet others hates
For that which in herself she prizes;
And, while she laughs at them, forgets
She is the thing that she despises.

LXXXV

SEMELE TO JUPITER

With my frailty don't upbraid me,
I am woman as you made me;
Causeless doubting or despairing,
Rashly trusting, idly fearing.
    If obtaining,
    Still complaining;
    If consenting,
    Still repenting;
    Most complying,
    When denying,
And to be follow'd only flying.

With my frailty don't upbraid me,
I am woman as you made me.

W. CONGREVE.

CHANSON A BOIRE

COME, let's mind our drinking,
Away with this thinking ;
   It ne'er, that I heard of, did any one good ;
Prevents not disaster,
But brings it on faster,
   Mischance is by mirth and by courage withstood.

He ne'er can recover
The day that is over,
   The present is with us, and does threaten no ill ;
He's a fool that will sorrow
For the thing call'd to-morrow,
   But the hour we've in hand we may wield as we
   will.

There's nothing but Bacchus
Right merry can make us,
   That virtue particular is to the vine ;
It fires ev'ry creature
With wit and good-nature,
   Whose thoughts can be dark when their noses do
   shine ?

A night of good drinking
Is worth a year's thinking,
    There's nothing that kills us so surely as sorrow ;
Then to drown our cares, boys,
Let's drink up the stars, boys,
    Each face of the gang will a sun be to-morrow.

C. COTTON.

LXXXVII

LOVE ARMED

Love in fantastic triumph sat,
    Whilst bleeding hearts around him flow'd ;
For whom fresh pains he did create,
    And strange tyrannic power he show'd.
From thy bright eyes he took his fire,
    Which round about in sport he hurl'd ;
But 'twas from mine he took desire,
    Enough t' inflame the amorous world.

From me he took his sighs and tears,
    From thee his pride and cruelty;
From me his languishments and fears,
    And every killing dart from thee.
Thus thou and I the god have arm'd,
    And set him up a deity ;
But my poor heart alone is harm'd,
    Whilst thine the victor is, and free.

APHRA BEHN.

LXXXVIII

LOVE AND MARRIAGE

In vain does Hymen, with religious vows
   Oblige his slaves to wear his chains with ease ;
A privilege alone that Love allows,
   'Tis Love alone can make our fetters please.

The angry tyrant lays his yoke on all,
   Yet in his fiercest rage is charming still ;
Officious Hymen comes whene'er we call,
   But haughty Love comes only when he will.

APHRA BEHN.

LXXXIX

THE SIEGE

'Tis now, since I sat down before
   That foolish fort, a heart,
(Time strangely spent !) a year and more,
   And still I did my part :

Made my approaches, from her hand
   Unto her lip did rise ;
And did already understand
   The language of her eyes :

Proceeded on with no less art,
(My tongue was engineer;)
I thought to undermine the heart
By whispering in the ear.

When this did nothing, I brought down
Great cannon-oaths, and shot
A thousand thousand to the town,
And still it yielded not.

I then resolv'd to starve the place,
By cutting off all kisses,
Praising and gazing on her face,
And all such little blisses.

To draw her out and from her strength,
I drew all batteries in ;
And brought myself to lie, at length,
As if no siege had been.

When I had done what man could do,
And thought the place mine own,
The enemy lay quiet too,
And smil'd at all was done.

I sent to know from whence, and where
These hopes and this relief?
A spy inform'd, Honour was there,
And did command in chief.

"March, march," quoth I; "the word straight give,
Let's lose no time, but leave her;
That giant upon air will live,
And hold it out for ever."

SIR J. SUCKLING.

XC

THE OLD MAN'S WISH

IF I live to grow old, for I find I go down,
Let this be my fate : in a country town,
May I have a warm house, with a stone at the gate,
And a cleanly young girl to rub my bald pate.
  May I govern my passion with an absolute sway,
  And grow wiser and better as my strength wears
    away,
  Without gout or stone, by a gentle decay.

Near a shady grove, and a murmuring brook,
With the ocean at distance, whereon I may look,
With a spacious plain without hedge or stile,
And an easy pad-nag to ride out a mile.
  May I govern, etc.

With Plutarch and Horace, and one or two more
Of the best wits that lived in the ages before;
With a dish of roast mutton, not ven'son or teal,
And clean, though coarse linen, at every meal.
    May I govern, etc.

With a pudding on Sunday, with stout humming liquor,
And remnants of Latin to puzzle the Vicar;
With a hidden reserve of Burgundy wine,
To drink the king's health as oft as I dine.
    May I govern, etc.

I hope I shall have no occasion to send
For priests or physicians, till I'm so near my end,
That I have eat all my bread and drank my last glass,
Let them come then and set their seals to my pass.
    May I govern, etc.

With courage undaunted may I face my last day,
And when I am dead may the better sort say,—
In the morning when sober, in the evening when mellow,
He's gone, and has left not behind him his fellow;
    For he governed his passion with an absolute sway,
    And grew wiser and better as his strength wore
      away,
    Without gout or stone, by a gentle decay.

                        DR. W. POPE.

XCI

THE BAG OF THE BEE

About the sweet bag of a bee,
  Two Cupids fell at odds ;
And whose the pretty prize should be
  They vow'd to ask the gods.

Which Venus hearing, thither came,
  And for their boldness stript them ;
And taking thence from each his flame,
  With rods of myrtle whipt them.

Which done, to still their wanton cries,
  When quiet grown she had seen them,
She kiss'd and wip'd their dove-like eyes,
  And gave the bag between them.

R. HERRICK.

XCII

AGAINST PLEASURE

There's no such thing as pleasure here,
  'Tis all a perfect cheat,
Which does but shine and disappear,
  Whose charm is but deceit ;

The empty bribe of yielding souls,
Which first betrays, and then controls.

'Tis true, it looks at distance fair;
    But if we do approach,
The fruit of Sodom will impair,
    And perish at a touch :
It being then in fancy less,
And we expect more than possess.

For by our pleasures we are cloy'd,
    And so desire is done ;
Or else, like rivers, they make wide
    The channel where they run ;
And either way true bliss destroys,
Making us narrow, or our joys.

We covet pleasure easily,
    But ne'er true bliss possess ;
For many things must make it be,
    But one may make it less ;
Nay, were our state as we could choose it,
'Twould be consum'd by fear to lose it.

What art thou, then, thou winged air,
    More weak and swift than fame,
Whose next successor is Despair,
    And its attendant Shame ?
Th' experienced prince then reason had,
Who said of pleasure—" It is mad."

KATHERINE PHILIPS.

XCIII

LOVE AND DEATH

Love and Death o' th' way once meeting,
Having past a friendly greeting,
Sleep their weary eyelids closing,
Lay them downe themselves reposing.
Love, whom divers cares molested,
Could not sleep, but whilst Death rested,
All in haste away he posts him,
But his haste full dearly costs him ;
For it chanc'd that going to sleeping,
Both had giv'n their darts in keeping
Unto Night, who, Error's mother,
Blindly knowing not one from t'other,
Gave Love Death's, and ne'er perceiv'd it,
While as blindly Love received it.
Since which time their darts confounding,
Love now kills instead of wounding ;
Death our hearts with sweetness filling,
Gently wounds, instead of killing.

R. FLECKNO.

FAIR HELEN OF KIRCONNEL

'I wish I were where Helen lies,
Nicht and day on me she cries ;
Oh, that I were where Helen lies,
    On fair Kirconnel lee !
Oh, Helen fair, beyond compare,
I'll mak' a garland o' thy hair,
Shall bind my heart for ever mair,
    Until the day I dee.

Oh, think na ye my heart was sair,
When my love dropt down and spak nae mair !
She sank, and swoon'd wi' mickle care,
    On fair Kirconnel lee.
Curst be the heart that thocht the thocht,
And curst the hand that shot the shot,
When in my arms burd Helen dropt,
    And died to succour me.

As I went down the water-side,
None but my foe to be my guide,
None but my foe to be my guide,
    On fair Kirconnel lee.

I lichtit doun, my sword did draw,
I hackit him in pieces sma',
I hackit him in pieces sma',
 For her sake that died for me.

Oh, that I were where Helen lies !
Nicht and day on me she cries,
Out of my bed she bids me rise—
 Oh, come, my love, to me !
Oh, Helen fair ! Oh, Helen chaste !
If I were with thee I were blest,
Where thou lies low and takes thy rest,
 On fair Kirconnel lee.

I wish my grave were growin' green,
A windin' sheet drawn ower my een,
And I in Helen's arms lying,
 On fair Kirconnel lee.
I wish I were where Helen lies,
Nicht and day on me she cries ;
And I am weary of the skies,
 For her sake that died for me.

ANON.

XCV

BEAUTY'S BEAUTY

CAN you paint a thought ? or number
 Every fancy in a slumber ?
Can you count soft minutes roving
From a dial's point by moving ?

Can you grasp a sigh? or, lastly,
Rob a virgin's honour chastely?
No, oh no! yet you may
Sooner do both that and this,
This and that, and never miss,
Than by any praise display
 Beauty's beauty; such a glory,
 As beyond all fate, all story,
  All arms, all arts,
  All loves, all hearts,
 Greater than those, or they,
 Do, shall, and must obey.

J. FORD.

XCVI

WHAT IS LOVE?

'Tis a child of phansie's getting,
 Brought up between hope and fear,
Fed with smiles, grown by uniting
 Strong, and so kept by desire;

'Tis a perpetual vestal fire
 Never dying,
Whose smoak like incense doth aspire
 Upwards flying.

'Tis a soft magnetique stone
 Attracting hearts by sympathie,

Binding up close two souls in one,
Both discoursing secretlie :

'Tis the true Gordian knot that tyes
Yet ne'er unbinds,
Fixing thus two lovers eyes
As wel as mindes.

'Tis the sphere's heavenly harmonie
Where two skilful hearts do strike,
And everie sound expressively
Marries sweetly with the like.

'Tis the world's everlasting chain
That all things ty'd
And bid them like the fixed Waine
Unmov'd to bide.

R. HEATH.

XCVII

THE DIRGE

WHAT is th' existence of man's life,
But open war, or slumber'd strife ;
Where sickness to his sense presents
The combat of the elements ;
And never feels a perfect peace
Till Death's cold hand signs his release ?

It is a storme, where the hot blood
Outvies in rage the boiling flood;
And each loose passion of the minde
Is like a furious gust of winde,
Which beats his bark with many a wave,
Till he casts anchor in the grave.

It is a flowre, which buds and grows,
And withers as the leaves disclose;
Whose spring and fall faint seasons keep,
Like fits of waking before sleep;
Then shrinks into that fatal mould
Where its first being was enroll'd.

It is a dreame, whose seeming truth
Is moralis'd in age and youth;
Where all the comforts he can share
As wandering as his fancies are;
Till, in a mist of dark decay,
The dreamer vanish quite away.

It is a dial, which points out
The sunset, as it moves about;
And shadows out in lines of night
The subtle stages of time's flight;
Till all-obscuring earth hath laid
The body in perpetual shade.

It is a wearie interlude,
Which doth short joys, long woes include ;
The world the stage, the prologue tears,
The acts vain hope and varied fears ;
The scene shuts up with loss of breath,
And leaves no epilogue but death.

H. KING.

XCVIII

RESPICE FINEM

My soul, sit thou a patient looker on ;
Judge not the play before the play is done :
Her plot has many changes : every day
Speaks a new scene ; the last act crowns the play.

F. QUARLES.

XCIX

THE WORLD'S PROMISES

False world, thou ly'st ; thou canst not lend
⠀⠀⠀⠀⠀The least delight :
Thy favours cannot gain a friend,
⠀⠀⠀⠀⠀They are so slight :
Thy morning pleasures make an end
⠀⠀⠀⠀⠀To please at night :

Poor are the wants that thou supply'st,
And yet thou vaunt'st, and yet thou vy'st
With heaven : fond earth, thou boast'st ; false world,
    thou ly'st.

Thy babbling tongue tells golden tales
        Of endless treasure :
Thy bounty offers easy sales
        Of lasting pleasure :
Thou ask'st the conscience what she ails,
        And swear'st to ease her :
There's none can want where thou supply'st,
There's none can give where thou deny'st ;
Alas ! fond world, thou boast'st ; false world, thou ly'st.

What well-advised ear regards
        What earth can say ?
Thy words are gold, but thy rewards
        Are painted clay :
Thy cunning can but pack the cards,
        Thou can'st not play :
Thy game at weakest, still thou vy'st,
If seen, and then revy'd, deny'st ;
Thou art not what thou seem'st : false world, thou ly'st.

Thy tinsel bosom seems a mint
        Of new-coin'd treasure ;
A paradise that has no stint,
        No change, no measure :

A painted cask, but nothing in't
        Nor wealth, nor pleasure:
Vain earth! that falsly thus comply'st
With man; vain man! that thou rely'st
On earth; vain man, thou doat'st; vain earth, thou ly'st.

What mean dull souls, in this high measure,
        To haberdash
In earth's base wares, whose greatest treasure
        Is dross and trash;
The height of whose enchanting pleasure
        Is but a flash?
Are these the goods that thou supply'st
Us mortals with?   Are these the high'st?
Can these bring cordial peace?   False world, thou
    ly'st.

                                F. QUARLES.

C

A REQUIEM

SLEEPE on, my Love, in thy cold bed
Never to be disquieted!
My last good-night! thou wilt not wake
Till I thy fate shall overtake:
Till age, or grief, or sickness must
Marry my body to that dust

It so much loves; and fill the room
My heart keeps empty in thy tomb.
Stay for me there; I will not faile
To meet thee in that hollow vale.
And think not much of my delay:
I am already on the way,
And follow thee with all the speed
Desire can make, or sorrows breed.
Each minute is a short degree,
And ev'ry houre a step towards thee.

DR. H. KING.

CI

HYMN TO LIGHT

Thou tide of glory which no rest dost know,
    But ever ebb and ever flow!
    Thou golden shower of a true Jove!
Who does in thee descend, and Heav'n to earth make
    love.

Say from what golden quivers of the sky,
    Do all thy winged arrows fly?
    Swiftness and power by birth are thine:
From thy great sire they came, thy sire the word Divine.

Thou in the moon's bright chariot proud and gay,
    Dost thy bright wood of stars survey;
    And all the year dost with thee bring
Of thousand flowry lights thine own nocturnal spring.

Thou Scythian-like dost round thy lands above
    The Sun's gilt tent for ever move,
    And still as thou in pomp do'st go,
The shining pageants of the world attend thy show.

When, goddess, thou lift'st up thy wak'ned head,
    Out of the morning's purple bed,
    Thy quire of birds about thee play,
And all the joyful world salutes the rising day.

All the world's brav'ry that delights our eyes
    Is but thy sev'ral liveries,
    Thou the rich dye on them bestow'st;
Thy nimble pencil paints this landscape as thou go'st.

A crimson garment in the rose thou wear'st;
    A crown of studded gold thou bear'st;
    The virgin lillies in their white,
Are clad but with the lawn of almost naked light.

With flame condens'd thou do'st thy jewels fix,
    And solid colours in it mix:
    Flora herself envies to see
Flowers fairer than her own, and durable as she.

Through the soft wayes of Heav'n, and air, and sea,
    Which open all their pores to Thee,
    Like a clear river thou do'st glide,
And with thy living stream through the close channels
    slide.

But the vast ocean of unbounded day
    In th' empyræan Heaven does stay.
    Thy rivers, lakes, and springs below,
From thence took first their rise, thither at last must
    flow.

A. COWLEY.

CII

FAITH AND REASON

Some blind themselves, 'cause possibly they may
    Be led by others a right way ;
They build on sands, which if unmov'd they find,
    'Tis but because there was no wind.
Less hard 'tis, not to erre ourselves, than know
    If our forefathers err'd or no.
When we trust men concerning God, we then
    Trust not God concerning men.

The Holy Book, like the eighth sphere, does shine
With thousand lights of truth divine.
So numberless the stars, that to the eye,
    It makes but all one galaxie.
Yet Reason must assist too, for in seas
    So vast and dangerous as these,
Our course by stars above we cannot know,
    Without the compass too below.

Though Reason cannot through Faith's mysteries see,
    It sees that there and such they be ;
Leads to Heaven's door, and there does humbly keep,
    And there through chinks and key-holes peep.
Though it, like Moses, by a sad command,
    Must not come in to th' Holy Land,
Yet thither it infallibly does guide ;
    And from afar 'tis all descry'd.

A. COWLEY.

CIII

THE GARDEN

WHAT wond'rous life is this I lead !
Ripe apples drop about my head ;
The luscious clusters of the vine
Upon my mouth do crush their wine ;

The nectarine, and curious peach,
Into my hands themselves do reach ;
Stumbling on melons, as I pass,
Insnared with flowers, I fall on grass.

Meanwhile the mind, from pleasure less,
Withdraws into its happiness ;
The mind, that ocean where each kind
Does straight its own resemblance find ;
Yet it creates, transcending these,
Far other worlds, and other seas,
Annihilating all that's made,
To a green thought in a green shade.

Here at the fountain's sliding foot,
Or at some fruit-tree's mossy root,
Casting the body's vest aside,
My soul into the boughs does glide :
There, like a bird, it sits and sings,
Then whets and claps its silver wings,
And, till prepared for longer flight,
Waves in its plumes the various light.

Such was that happy garden state,
While man there walked without a mate :
After a place so pure and sweet,
What other help could yet be meet !
But 'twas beyond a mortal's share
To wander solitary there :
Two paradises are in one,
To live in Paradise alone.

How well the skilful gardener drew
Of flow'rs, and herbs, this dial new,
Where, from above, the milder sun
Does through a fragrant zodiac run,
And, as it works, the industrious bee
Computes its time as well as we!
How could such sweet and wholesome hours
Be reckon'd but with herbs and flowers?

A. MARVELL.

CIV

PHOSPHORE REDDE DIEM

Will't ne'er be morning?   Will that promis'd light
    Ne'er break, and clear those clouds of night?
Sweet Phosphor, bring the day,
    Whose conqu'ring ray
May chase these fogs; sweet Phosphor, bring the day.

How long!   How long shall these benighted eyes
    Languish in shades, like feeble flies
Expecting spring?   How long shall darkness soil
    The face of earth, and thus beguile
The souls of sprightful action?   When, when will day
    Begin to dawn, whose new-born ray

May gild the weather-cocks of our devotion,
And give our unsoul'd souls new motion?
　　Sweet Phosphor, bring the day,
　　　　Thy light will fray
These horrid mists; sweet Phosphor, bring the day.

Alas! my light in vain expecting eyes
　　Can find no objects, but what rise
From this poore mortal blaze, a dying spark
　　Of Vulcan's forge, whose flames are dark,
A dang'rous, a dull blue-burning light,
　　As melancholy as the night:
Here's all the sunnes that glister in the sphere
　　Of earth: ah me! what comfort's here?
　　　　Sweet Phosphor, bring the day;
　　　　　　Haste, haste away,
Heav'n's loit'ring lamp; sweet Phosphor, bring the day.

F. QUARLES.

CV

PRESENT AND FUTURE

How we dally out our days!
How we seek a thousand ways
To find death! the which, if none
We sought out, would show us one.

I

Never was there morning yet,
Sweet as is the violet,
Which man's follie did not soon
Wish to be expir'd in noon :
As though such an haste did tend
To our bliss, and not our end.

Nay, the young ones in the nest
Sucke this folly from the breast;
And no stammering ape but can
Spoil a prayer to be a man.

Sooner shall the wandering star
Learn what rest and quiet are ;
Sooner shall the slippery rill
Leave his motion and stand still.

Be it joy, or be it sorrow,
We refer all to the morrow ;
That, we think, will ease our paine ;
That, we do suppose again,
Will increase our joy ; and soe
Events, the which we cannot know,
We magnify, and are (in sum)
Enamour'd of the time to come.

Well, the next day comes, and then
Another next, and soe to ten,
To twenty we arrive, and find
No more before us than behind

Of solid joy; and yet haste on
To our consummation;
Till the forehead often have
The remembrance of a grave;
And, at last, of life bereav'd,
Die unhappy and deceiv'd.

R. GOMERSALL.

CVI

DEPARTED FRIENDS

THEY are all gone into the world of light!
    And I alone sit ling'ring here!
Their very memory is faire and bright,
    And my sad thoughts doth clear.

It glows and glitters in my cloudy breast
    Like stars upon some gloomy grove,
Or those faint beams in which this hill is drest
    After the Sun's remove.

I see them walking in an air of glorie,
    Whose light doth trample on my days;
My days, which are at best but dull and hoarie,
    Mere glimmering and decays.

O holy Hope ! and high Humility !
   High as the Heavens above ;
These are your walks, and you have shew'd them me
   To kindle my cold love.

Dear, beauteous death ; the Jewel of the Just !
   Shining no where but in the dark ;
What mysteries do lie beyond thy dust,
   Could man outlook that mark !

He that hath found some fledg'd bird's nest may know
   At first sight if the bird be flown ;
But what fair dell or grove he sings in now,
   That is to him unknown.

And yet, as Angels in some brighter dreams
   Call to the soul when man doth sleepe,
So some strange thoughts transcend our wonted themes,
   And into glory peepe.

If a star were confin'd into a tombe,
   Her captive flames must needs burn there ;
But when the hand that lockt her up gives roome
   She'll shine through all the spheare.

O Father of eternal life, and all
   Created glories under thee !
Resume thy spirit from this world of thrall
   Into true libertie !

Either disperse these mists, which blot and fill
My perspective still as they passe :
Or else remove me hence unto that hill,
Where I shall need no glasse.

H. VAUGHAN.

CVII

AN EPITAPH

In this marble buri'd lyes
Beauty may inrich the skyes
And add light to Phœbus' eyes.

Sweeter than Aurora's aire,
When she paints the lillies faire,
And gilds cowslips with her haire.

Chaster than the virgin Spring,
Ere her blossomes she doth bring,
Or cause Philomel to sing.

If such goodnesse live 'mongst men
Bring me it ! I shall know then
She is come from heaven agen.

But if not, ye standers by,
Cherish me, and say that I
Am the next designed to dye.

R. HERRICK (?)

CVIII

INVOCATION TO SILENCE

STILL-BORN Silence ! thou that art
Flood-gate of the deeper heart !
Offspring of a heavenly kinde,
Frost o' th' mouth, and thaw o' th' minde.
Secrecy's confident, and he
Who makes religion mystery !
Admiration's speaking'st tongue !
Leave, thy desart shades among,
Reverend hermit's hallow'd cells,
Where retir'dst Devotion dwells !
With thy enthusiasms come,
Seize our tongues, and strike us dumbe.

R. FLECKNO.

CIX

THE ASPIRATION

How long great God, how long must I
Immur'd in this dark prison lye !
Where at the grates and avenues of sense
My Soul must watch to have intelligence ;

Where but faint gleams of thee salute my sight,
Like doubtful moonshine in a cloudy night.
    When shall I leave this magic Sphere,
    And be all mind, all eye, all ear!

How cold this clime! and yet my sense
Perceives even here thy influence.
Even here thy strong magnetic charms I feel,
And pant and tremble like the amorous steel.
To lower good, and beauties less divine,
Sometimes my erroneous needle does decline;
    But yet, so strong the sympathy,
    It turns, and points again to thee.

I long to see this excellence
Which at such distance strikes my sense.
My impatient Soul struggles to disengage
Her wings from the confinement of her cage.
Would'st thou great Love this prisoner once set free,
How would she hasten to be link'd with thee!
    She'd for no Angel's conduct stay,
    But fly, and love on all the way.

                              J. NORRIS OF BEMERTON.

PRAISE AND PRAYER

PRAISE is devotion, fit for mighty mindes,
The diff'ring world's agreeing sacrifice;
Where Heav'n divided faiths united findes:
But prayer, in various discord, upward flies.

For prayer the ocean is, where diversely
Men steer their course, each to a sev'ral coast;
Where all our interests so discordant be,
That half beg windes by which the rest are lost.

By penitence, when we ourselves forsake,
'Tis but in wise design on piteous Heaven;
In praise we nobly give what God may take,
And are without a beggar's blush forgiven.

SIR W. DAVENANT.

SAINT TERESA

O THOU undaunted daughter of desires !
By all thy dower of lights and fires,
By all the eagle in thee, all the dove,
By all thy lives and deaths of love,

By thy large draughts of intellectual day,
And by thy thirsts of love more large than they ;
By all thy brim-fill'd bowls of fierce desire,
By thy last morning's draught of liquid fire,
By the full kingdom of that final kiss
That seiz'd thy parting soul, and seal'd thee his ;
By all the heavens thou hast in him
Fair sister of the seraphim !
By all of him we have in thee,
Leaving nothing of myself in me :
Let me so read thy life that I
Unto all life of mine may die.

R. CRASHAW.

CXII

A TRANQUIL SOUL

THY soul within such silent pomp did keep,
As if humanity were lulled asleep ;
So gentle was thy pilgrimage beneath,
    Time's unheard feet scarce make less noise,
Or the soft journey which a planet goes :
    Life seemed all calm as its last breath.
A still tranquillity so husht thy breast,
    As if some Halcyon were its guest,
        And there had built her nest ;
    It hardly now enjoys a greater rest.

As that smooth sea which wears the name of Peace,
　Still with one even face appears,
And feels no tides to change it from its place,
　No waves to alter the fair form it bears ;
So thy unvary'd mind was always one,
And with such clear serenity still shone,
As caused thy little world to seem all temperate zone.

　　　　　　　　　　　　J. OLDHAM.

CXIII

THE MAGNET

LIKE to the arctic needle, that doth guide
　The wand'ring shade by his magnetic power,
And leaves his silken gnomon to decide
　The question of the controverted hour ;
First frantics up and down, from side to side,
　And restless beats his crystal'd iv'ry case
With vain impatience ; jets from place to place,
And seeks the bosome of his frozen bride ;
　At length he slacks his motion and doth rest
His trembling point at his bright pole's beloved breast.

Ev'n so my soul, being hurried here and there,
　By ev'ry object that presents delight,
Fain would be settled, but she knows not where ;
　She likes at morning what she loaths at night.

She bowes to honour; then she lends an eare
    To that sweet swan-like voice of dying pleasure,
    Then tumbles in the scatter'd heaps of treasure:
Now flatter'd with false hope; now foil'd with fear:
    Thus finding all the world's delights to be
But empty toyes, good God, she points alone to Thee.

F. QUARLES.

CXIV

PRAYER

LORD, when the sense of Thy sweet grace
Sends up my soul to seek Thy face,
Thy blessed eyes breed such desire,
I die in love's delicious fire.
    O Love, I am thy sacrifice,
    Be still triumphant, blessed eyes;
    Still shine on me, fair suns! that I
    Still may behold though still I die.

R. CRASHAW.

CXV

AN ELEGY

MY sweet companion, and my gentle peer,
Why hast thou left me thus unkindly here,
Thy end for ever, and my life to moan;
    Oh, thou hast left me all alone!

Thy soul and body when Death's agony
    Besieg'd around thy noble heart,
    Did not with more reluctance part
Than I, my dearest Friend, do part from thee.

My dearest Friend, would I had died for thee !
Life and this world henceforth will tedious be.
Nor shall I know hereafter what to do
    If once my griefs prove tedious too.
Silent and sad I walk about all day,
    As sullen ghosts stalk speechless by,
    Where their hid treasures lie ;
Alas, my Treasure's gone, why do I stay ?

Say, for you saw us, ye immortal lights,
How oft unweari'd have we spent the nights ?
Till the Ledaean stars so fam'd for love,
    Wonder'd at us from above.
We spent them not in toys, in lusts, or wine ;
    But search of deep philosophy,
    Wit, Eloquence, and Poetry,
Arts which I lov'd, for they, my Friend, were thine.

Ye fields of Cambridge, our dear Cambridge, say,
Have ye not seen us walking every day ?
Was there a tree about which did not know
    The love betwixt us two ?

Henceforth, ye gentle trees, for ever fade ;
　　Or your sad branches thicker join,
　　And into darksome shades combine,
Dark as the grave wherein my Friend is laid.

Large was his Soul ; as large a Soul as ere
Submitted to inform a body here,
High as the place 'twas shortly in Heaven to have,
　　But low, and humble as his grave.
So high that all the Virtues there did come
　　　As to their chiefest seat
　　　Conspicuous, and great ;
So low that for me too it made a room.

So strong a wit did Nature to him frame,
As all things but his judgment overcame ;
His judgment like the heav'nly moon did show,
　　Temp'ring that mighty sea below.
Oh had he lived in learning's world, what bound
　　　Would have been able to control
　　　His over-powering Soul ?
We have lost in him arts that not yet are found.

But happy Thou, ta'en from this frantic age,
Where ignorance and hypocrisy does rage !
A fitter time for Heav'n no soul ere chose,
　　The place now only free from those.

There 'mong the blest thou dost for ever shine,
   And wheresoe'er thou casts thy view
   Upon that white and radiant crew,
See'st not a soul cloth'd with more light than Thine.

A. COWLEY.

CXVI

EPITAPH

SHE on this clayen pillow layed her head,
As brides do use the first to go to bed.
He missed her soon and yet ten months he trys
To live apart and lykes it not and dyes.

ANON.

CXVII

AN EPITAPH UPON HUSBAND AND WIFE WHO DIED AND WERE BURIED TOGETHER

To these, whom Death again did wed,
This grave's the second marriage bed.
For though the hand of Fate could force
'Twixt soul and body a divorce,
It could not sever man and wife
Because they both liv'd but one life.

Peace, good reader, do not weep !
Peace ! the lovers are asleep.
They, sweet turtles, folded lie
In the last knot that Love could tie.
Let them sleep, let them sleep on,
Till the stormy night be gone,
And th' eternal morrow dawn ;
Then the curtains will be drawn,
And they waken with that light
Whose day shall never sleep in night.

R. CRASHAW.

CXVIII

DEATH

To die is landing on some silent shore,
Where billows never break, nor tempests roar ;
Ere well we feel the friendly stroke, 'tis o'er.
The wise through thought th' insults of death defy ;
The fools through blest insensibility.
'Tis what the guilty fear, the pious crave ;
Sought by the wretch, and vanquish'd by the brave :
It eases lovers, sets the captive free,
And, though a tyrant, offers liberty.

SIR S. GARTH.

CXIX

OLD AGE

THE seas are quiet when the winds give o'er ;
So calm are we when passions are no more,
For then we know how vain it was to boast
Of fleeting things, so certain to be lost.

Clouds of affection from our younger eyes
Conceal that emptiness which age descries ;
The soul's dark cottage, batter'd and decay'd,
Lets in new light through chinks which time has made :

Stronger by weakness, wiser men become,
As they draw near to their eternal home.
Leaving the old, both worlds at once they view,
That stand upon the threshold of the new.

                                        E. WALLER.

CXX

Like to the falling of a Starre,
Or as the flights of eagles are,
Or like the fresh spring's gaudy hue,
Or silver drops of morning dew ;

Or like a wind that chafes the flood,
Or bubbles which on water stood ;
Even such is man, whose borrow'd light
Is straight call'd in, and paid to-night.
  The Wind blowes out, the bubble dies,
  The Spring entomb'd in Autumn lies ;
  The Dew's dried up, the Starre is shot,
  The Flight is past, and man forgot

DR. H. KING (?)

CXXI

THE PULLEY

WHEN God at first made man,
Having a glass of blessings standing by ;
Let us, said He, pour on him all we can,
Let the world's riches, which dispersed lie,
    Contract into a spanne.

So strength first made a way ;
Then beautie flow'd, then wisdom, honoure, pleasure :
When almost all was out, God made a staye,
Perceiving that alone of all his treasure
    Rest at the bottom laye.

K

For if I should, said he,
Bestowe this jewel also on my creature,
He would adore my gifts instead of me
And rest in Nature, not the God of nature,
So both should losers be.

Yet let him keepe the rest,
But keepe them with repining restlessness,
Let him be rich and wearie, that at least
If goodness lead him not, yet weariness
May toss him to my breast.

G. HERBERT.

CXXII

A FAREWELL TO THE WORLD

THE night is come, like to the day;
Depart not Thou, great God, away.
Let not my sins, black as the night,
Eclipse the lustre of Thy light.
Keep still in my horizon: for to me
The sun makes not the day, but Thee.

Thou whose nature cannot sleep
On my temples sentry keep;
Guard me 'gainst those watchful foes,
Whose eyes are open while mine close.
Let no dreams my head infest,
But such as Jacob's temples blest;
While I do rest, my soul advance,
Make my sleep a holy trance;
That I may, my rest being wrought,
Awake into some holy thought,
And with as active vigour run
My course as doth the nimble sun.
Sleep is a death;—O make me try,
By sleeping, what it is to die!
And as gently lay my head
On my grave, as now my bed.
Howe'er I rest, great God, let me
Awake again at last with Thee.
And thus assur'd, behold I lie
Securely, or to wake or die.
These are my drowsy days; in vain
I do now wake to sleep again:
O come that hour, when I shall never
Sleep again, but wake for ever!

SIR T. BROWNE.

SOUL AND BODY

GREAT Nature cloaths the Soul, which is but thin,
With fleshly garments, which the Fates do spin ;
And when these garments are grown old and bare,
With sickness torn, Death takes them off with care,
Doth fold them up in peace and quiet rest,
And lays them safe within an earthly chest ;
Then scours them well, and makes them sweet and clean,
Fit for the soul to wear those cloaths again.

MARGARET, DUCHESS OF NEWCASTLE

PURIFICATION

My God ! If 'tis Thy great decree
That this must the last moment be
Wherein I breathe this are ;
My heart obeys, joy'd to retreate
From the false favours of the great
And treachery of the faire.

When Thou shalt please this soule t' enthrone
Above impure corruption,
 What should I grieve or feare
To think this breathlesse body must
Become a loathsome heape of dust
 And ne'er againe appeare?

For in the fire when ore is tryed,
And by that torment purified,
 Doe we deplore the losse?
And when Thou shalt my soule refine,
That it thereby may purer shine,
 Shall I grieve for the drosse?

W. HABINGTON.

CXXV

IN BLISS

BRAVE spirits, whose advent'rous feet
 Have to the mountain's top aspir'd,
Where fair desert and honour meet:
 Here, from the toiling press retir'd,
Secure from all disturbing evil,
For ever in my temple revel.
With wreaths of stars circled about,
 Gild all the spacious firmament,

And smiling on the panting rout
That labour in the steep ascent,
With your resistless influence guide
Of human change th' uncertain tide.

T. CAREW.

CXXVI

WELCOME, welcome, happy paire,
To these abodes, where spicy aire
Breathes perfumes, and every sense
Doth find his object's excellence :
Where's no heate, nor cold extreme,
No winter's ice, nor summer's scorching beame,
Where's no sun, yet never night,
Day always springing from eternal light ;
    All mortal sufferings laid aside,
    Here in endless blisse abide.

T. NABBES.

CXXVII

AN EPITAPH

A VIRGIN blossom in her May
Of youth and virtues turn'd to clay ;
Rich earth accomplish'd with those graces
That adorn Saints in heavenly places.
Let not Death boast his conquering power,
She'll rise a Star, that fell a Flower.

BOOK III

LIFE'S PROGRESS

How gaily is at first begun
Our Life's uncertain race !
Whilst yet that sprightly morning sun,
With which we just set out to run,
Enlightens all the place.

How soft the first ideas prove,
Which wander through our minds !
How full the joys, how free the love,
Which does that early season move,
As flow'rs the western winds !

Our sighs are then but vernal air,
But April-drops our tears,
Which swiftly passing, all grows fair,
Whilst beauty compensates our care,
And youth each vapour clears.

But oh ! too soon, alas, we climb,
    Scarce feeling we ascend,
The gently rising hill of Time,
From whence with grief we see that prime,
    And all its sweetness end.

The die now cast, our station known,
    Fond expectation past ;
The thorns, which former days had sown,
To crops of late repentance grown,
    Thro' which we toil at last.

Whilst ev'ry care's a driving harm,
    That helps to bear us down ;
Which faded smiles no more can charm,
But ev'ry tear's a winter storm,
    And ev'ry look's a frown.

Till with succeeding ills opprest,
    For joys we hop'd to find ;
By age too, rumpl'd and undrest,
We, gladly sinking down to rest,
    Leave following crowds behind.

                          ANNE, COUNTESS OF WINCHILSEA.

A SIMILE

By this flow'ry meadow walking,
To this prattling echo talking,
As along the stream I pass,
Gazing on my floating face ;
Lo ! the ruffling winds arise,
To snatch the prospect from my eyes ;
The mimic form their fury braves,
And proudly triumphs o'er the waves ;
Yet, tho' with ev'ry wave 'tis tost,
The reflection is not lost.
Virtue wages such a strife,
In this turbulent stream of life ;
Rack'd with passions, tost with fears,
Vex'd with jealousies and cares :
But a good unspotted soul,
Tho' subject, yet knows no control
Whilst it turns on Virtue's pole.
But lo ! the clouds obscure the sun,
Swift shadows o'er the waters run !
Trembling too, my shadow flies,
And by its very likeness dies.

W. PATTISON.

LIVE TO-DAY

SHALL man from Nature's sanction stray,
With blind Opinion for his guide,
And, rebel to her rightful sway,
Leave all her bounties unenjoy'd?
Fool! Time no change of motion knows;
With equal speed the torrent flows
To sweep fame, power, and wealth away:
The past is all by death possest;
And frugal Fate that guards the rest,
By giving, bids him live to-day.

E. FENTON.

CXXXI

THE TOPER

CONTENTED I am, and contented I'll be,
For what can this world more afford,
Than a lass who will sociably sit on my knee,
And a cellar as sociably stored,
My brave boys?

My vault door is open, descend and improve :
  That cask,—ay, that we will try ;
'Tis as rich to the taste as the lips of your love,
  And as bright as her cheeks to the eye,
    My brave boys.

In a piece of slit hoop, see my candle is stuck,
  'Twill light us each bottle to hand ;
The foot of my glass for the purpose I broke,
  As I hate that a bumper should stand,
    My brave boys.

Astride on a butt, as a butt should be strod,
  I gallop the brusher along ;
Like grape-blessing Bacchus, the good fellow's god,
  And a sentiment give, or a song,
    My brave boys.

We are dry where we sit, though the oozing drops seem
  With pearls the moist walls to emboss ;
From the arch mouldy cobwebs in gothic taste stream,
  Like stucco-work cut out of moss,
    My brave boys.

When the lamp is brimful, how the taper flame shines,
  Which, when moisture is wanting, decays ;
Replenish the lamp of my life with rich wines,
  Or else there's an end of my blaze,
    My brave boys.

Sound those pipes,—they're in tune, and those bins are
    well fill'd,
View that heap of old Hock in your rear;
Yon bottles are Burgundy! mark how they're piled,
    Like artillery, tier over tier,
            My brave boys.

My cellar's my camp, and my soldiers my flasks,
    All gloriously ranged in review;
When I cast my eyes round, I consider my casks
    As kingdoms I've yet to subdue,
            My brave boys.

Like Macedon's madman, my glass I'll enjoy,
    Defying hyp, gravel, or gout;
He cried when he had no more worlds to destroy,
    I'll weep when my liquor is out,
            My brave boys.

On their stumps some have fought, and as stoutly will I,
    When reeling, I roll on the floor;
Then my legs must be lost, so I'll drink as I lie,
    And dare the best buck to do more,
            My brave boys.

'Tis my will when I die, not a tear shall be shed,
    No *Hic jacet* be cut on my stone;
But pour on my coffin a bottle of red,
    And say that his drinking is done,
            My brave boys.

                                        G. A. STEVENS.

APOLLO MAKING LOVE

I AM,—cry'd Apollo, when Daphne he woo'd,
And panting for breath, the coy virgin pursued,
When his wisdom, in manner most ample, express'd
The long list of the graces his godship possess'd,

I'm—the god of sweet song, and inspirer of lays;
Nor for lays, nor sweet song, the fair fugitive stays;
I'm the god of the harp—stop, my fairest—in vain;
Nor the harp, nor the harper, could fetch her again.

Every plant, every flower, and their virtues I know,
God of light I'm above, and of physic below;
At the dreadful word physic, the nymph fled more fast;
At the fatal word physic she doubled her haste.

Thou fond god of wisdom, then, alter thy phrase,
Bid her view thy young bloom, and thy ravishing rays,
Tell her less of thy knowledge, and more of thy charms,
And, my life for't, the damsel will fly to thy arms.

T. TICKELL.

CXXXIII

CHLOE'S TRIUMPH

I SAID to my heart, between sleeping and waking,
"Thou wild thing, that always art leaping or aching,
What black, brown, or fair, in what clime, in what nation,
By turns has not taught thee a pit-a-patation?"

Thus accused, the wild thing gave this sober reply :—
"See, the heart without motion, though Celia pass by!
Not the beauty she has, not the wit that she borrows,
Give the eye any joys, or the heart any sorrows.

"When our Sappho appears, she, whose wit so refined
I am forced to applaud with the rest of mankind—
Whatever she says is with spirit and fire;
Ev'ry word I attend, but I only admire.

"Prudentia as vainly would put in her claim,
Ever gazing on heaven, though man is her aim :
'Tis love, not devotion, that turns up her eyes—
Those stars of this world are too good for the skies.

"But Chloe so lively, so easy, so fair,
Her wit so genteel, without art, without care :
When she comes in my way—the motion, the pain,
The leapings, the achings, return all again."

O wonderful creature ! a woman of reason !
Never grave out of pride, never gay out of season ;
When so easy to guess who this angel should be,
Would one think Mrs. Howard ne'er dreamt it was she ?

C. MORDAUNT, EARL OF PETERBOROUGH.

CXXXIV

THE PLAYTHING

KITTY's charming voice and face,
    Syren-like, first caught my fancy ;
Wit and humour next take place,
    And now I doat on sprightly Nancy.

Kitty tunes her pipe in vain,
    With airs most languishing and dying ;
Calls me false, ungrateful swain,
    And tries in vain to shoot me flying.

Nancy with resistless art,
    Always humorous, gay, and witty,
Has talk'd herself into my heart,
    And quite excluded tuneful Kitty.

Ah, Kitty ! Love, a wanton boy,
    Now pleas'd with song, and now with prattle,
Still longing for the newest toy,
    Has chang'd his whistle for a rattle.

ANON.

L

CXXXV

I LOVED thee beautiful and kind,
   And plighted an eternal vow;
So alter'd are thy face and mind,
   'Twere perjury to love thee now.

LORD NUGENT.

CXXXVI

ADVICE

CEASE, fond shepherd—cease desiring
   What you never must enjoy;
She derides your vain aspiring,
   She to all your sex is coy.

Cunning Damon once pursu'd her,
   Yet she never would incline;
Strephon too as vainly woo'd her
   Tho' his flocks are more than thine.

At Diana's shrine aloud,
   By the zone around her waist,
Thrice she bow'd, and thrice she vow'd
   Like the goddess to be chaste.

ANSWER

Tho' I never get possession,
    'Tis a pleasure to adore ;
Hope, the wretch's only blessing,
    May in time procure me more.

Constant courtship may obtain her,
    Where both wealth and merit fail,
And the lucky minute gain her,—
    Fate and fancy must prevail.

At Diana's shrine aloud,
    By the bow and by the quiver,
Thrice she bow'd, and thrice she vow'd
    Once to love—and that for ever.

LADY MARY WORTLEY MONTAGU.

CXXXVII

SONG

Oh ! forbear to bid me slight her,
    Soul and senses take her part ;
Could my death itself delight her,
    Life should leap to leave my heart.
Strong, though soft, a lover's chain,
Charm'd with woe, and pleas'd with pain.

Though the tender flame were dying,
　　Love would light it at her eyes ;
Or, her tuneful voice applying,
　　Through my ear my soul surprise.
Deaf, I see the fate I shun ;
Blind, I hear I am undone.

　　　　　　　　　　　A. HILL.

CXXXVIII

MIRA'S SONG

SEE those cheeks of beauteous dye,
Lovely as the dawning sky,
Innocence that ne'er beguiles,
Lips that wear eternal smiles :
Beauties to the rest unknown,
Shine in her and her alone.

Now the rivers smoother flow,
Now the op'ning roses glow,
The woodbine twines her odorous charms
Round the oak's supporting arms :
Lilies paint the dewy ground
And ambrosia breathes around.

Come, ye gales that fan the spring,
Zephyr, with thy downy wing,
Gently waft to Mira's breast
Health, Content, and balmy Rest.
Far, O far from hence remain
Sorrow, Care, and sickly Pain.

Thus sung Mira to her lyre,
Till the idle numbers tire :
"Ah ! Sappho sweeter sings," I cry,
And the spiteful rocks reply,
(Responsive to the jarring strings)
" Sweeter—Sappho sweeter sings."

MARY LEAPOR.

CXXXIX

A SONG

When thy beauty appears
In its graces and airs,
All bright as an angel new dropt from the sky ;
At distance I gaze, and am awed by my fears,
So strangely you dazzle my eye !

But when, without art,
Your kind thought you impart,
When your love runs in blushes through every vein ;
When it darts from your eyes, when it pants in your
heart,
Then I know you're a woman again.

" There's a passion and pride
In our sex," she replied,
" And thus, (might I gratify both,) I would do :
Still an angel appear to each lover beside,
But still be a woman to you."

T. PARNELL.

CXL

THE INDIFFERENT

IF from the lustre of the sun,
To catch your fleeting shade you run,
    In vain is all your haste, Sir ;
But if your feet reverse the race,
The fugitive will urge the chace,
    And follow you as fast, Sir.

Thus, if at any time, as now,
Some scornful Chloe you pursue,
    In hopes to overtake her ;
Be sure you ne'er too eager be,
But look upon't as cold as she,
    And seemingly forsake her.

So I and Laura, t'other day,
Were coursing round a cock of hay,
  While I could ne'er o'er get her ;
But, when I found I ran in vain,
Quite tir'd I turn'd me back again,
  And, flying from her, met her.

W. PATTISON.

CXLI

TO A LADY MAKING LOVE

GOOD madam, when ladies are willing,
  A man must needs look like a fool ;
For me, I would not give a shilling
  For one who would love out of rule.

You should leave us to guess by your blushing,
  And not speak the matter so plain ;
'Tis our's to write and be pushing,
  'Tis your's to affect a disdain.

That you're in a terrible taking,
  By all these sweet oglings I see ;
But the fruit that can fall without shaking,
  Indeed is too mellow for me.

LADY MARY WORTLEY MONTAGU.

AE HAPPY HOUR

THE dark grey o' gloamin',
 The lone leafy shaw,
The coo o' the cushat,
 The scent o' the haw;
The brae o' the burnie
 A' bloomin in flower,
An' twa faithfu' lovers,
 Make ae happy hour.

A kind winsome wifie,
 A clean cantie hame,
An' smilin' sweet babies,
 To lisp the dear name;
Wi' plenty o' labour,
 An' health to endure,
Make time to row round aye
 The ae happy hour.

Ye, lost to affection,
 Whom avarice can move
To woo an' to marry
 For a' thing but love;

Awa' wi' your sorrows,
Awa' wi' your store,
Ye ken na the pleasure
O' ae happy hour !

A. LAING.

CXLIII

THE SECOND MARRIAGE

"THEE, Mary, with this ring I wed,"
So, fourteen years ago, I said—
Behold another ring !—"For what ?"
"To wed thee o'er again—why not ?"

With that first ring I married Youth,
Grace, Beauty, Innocence, and Truth ;
Taste long admir'd, sense long rever'd,
And all my Molly then appear'd.
If she, by merit since disclos'd,
Prove twice the woman I suppos'd,
I plead that double merit now,
To justify a double vow.

Here then, to-day, (with faith as sure,
With ardour as intense and pure,
As when, amidst the rites divine,
I took thy troth, and plighted mine),

To thee, sweet girl, my second ring
A token and a pledge I bring:
With this I wed, till death us part,
Thy riper virtues to my heart;
These virtues, which, before untry'd,
The wife has added to the bride;
Those virtues, whose progressive claim,
Endearing wedlock's very name,
My soul enjoys, my song approves,
For Conscience' sake, as well as Love's.

For why?—They show me every hour,
Honour's high thought, affection's power,
Discretion's deed, sound Judgment's sentence,
And teach me all things—but Repentance.

S. BISHOP.

CXLIV

EUPHELIA AND CLOE

THE merchant, to secure his treasure,
   Conveys it in a borrowed name:
Euphelia serves to grace my measure;
   But Cloe is my real flame.

My softest verse, my darling lyre,
  Upon Euphelia's toilet lay ;
When Cloe noted her desire,
  That I should sing, that I should play.

My lyre I tune, my voice I raise,
  But with my numbers mix my sighs ;
And whilst I sing Euphelia's praise,
  I fix my soul on Cloe's eyes.

Fair Cloe blushed : Euphelia frowned :
  I sung and gazed : I played and trembled ;
And Venus to the Loves around
  Remark'd, how ill we all dissembled.

                                    M. PRIOR.

CXLV

THE HAPPY SWAIN

HAVE ye seen the morning sky,
When the dawn prevails on high,
When, anon, some purple ray
Gives a sample of the day,
When, anon, the lark, on wing,
Strives to soar, and strains to sing ?

Have ye seen th' ethereal blue
Gently shedding silvery dew,
Spangling o'er the silent green,
While the nightingale, unseen,
To the moon and stars full bright,
Lonesome chants the hymn of night?

Have ye seen the broider'd May
All her scented bloom display,
Breezes opening, every hour,
This, and that, expecting flower,
While the mingling birds prolong,
From each bush, the vernal song?

Have ye seen the damask-rose
Her unsully'd blush disclose,
Or the lily's dewy bell,
In her glossy white, excell,
Or a garden vary'd o'er
With a thousand glories more?

By the beauties these display,
Morning, evening, night, or day;
By the pleasures these excite,
Endless sources of delight!
Judge, by them, the joys I find,
Since my Rosalind was kind,
Since she did herself resign
To my vows, for ever mine.

A. PHILIPS.

SILVIA AND THE BEE

As Silvia in her garden stray'd,
  Where each officious rose,
To welcome the approaching maid
  With fairer beauty glows.

Transported from their dewy beds,
  The new-blown lilies rise ;
Gay tulips wave their shining heads,
  To please her brighter eyes.

A bee that sought the sweetest flow'r,
  To this fair quarter came :
Soft humming round the fatal bow'r
  That held the smiling dame.

He searched the op'ning buds with care
  And flew from tree to tree :
But, Silvia, finding none so fair,
  Unwisely fixed on thee.

Her hand obedient to her thought,
  The rover did destroy ;
And the slain insect dearly bought
  Its momentary joy.

O, Silvia, cease your anger now
    To this your guiltless foe ;
And smooth again that gentle brow,
    Where lasting lilies blow.

Soft Cynthio vows when you depart,
    The sun withdraws its ray,
That nature trembles like his heart,
    And storms eclipse the day.

Amintor swears a morning sun's
    Less brilliant than your eyes ;
And tho' his tongue at random runs,
    You seldom think he lies.

They tell you, those soft lips may vie
    With pinks at op'ning day ;
And yet you slew a simple fly
    For proving what they say.

Believe me, not a bud like thee
    In this fair garden blows ;
Then blame no more the erring bee,
    That took you for the rose.

                              MARY LEAPOR.

SLIGHTED LOVE

The tears I shed must ever fall,
 I mourn not for an absent swain;
For thoughts may past delights recall,
 And parted lovers meet again.
I weep not for the silent dead,
 Their toils are past, their sorrows o'er;
And those they loved their steps shall tread,
 And death shall join to part no more.

Though boundless oceans roll'd between,
 If certain that his heart is near,
A conscious transport glads each scene,
 Soft is the sigh, and sweet the tear.
E'en when by death's cold hand remov'd,
 We mourn the tenant of the tomb,
To think that e'en in death he lov'd,
 Can gild the horrors of the gloom.

But bitter, bitter are the tears
 Of her who slighted love bewails;
No hope her dreary prospect cheers,
 No pleasing melancholy hails.
Hers are the pangs of wounded pride,
 Of blasted hope, of wither'd joy;
The flattering veil is rent aside;
 The flame of love burns to destroy.

In vain does memory renew
    The hours once tinged in transport's dye ;
The sad reverse soon starts to view,
    And turns the past to agony.
E'en time itself despairs to cure
    Those pangs to ev'ry feeling due ;
Ungenerous youth ! thy boast how poor,
    To win a heart—and break it too.

MRS. DUGALD STEWART.

CXLVIII

LOVE'S TRIUMPH

OH, how could I venture to love one like thee,
And you not despise a poor conquest like me,
On lords, thy admirers, could look wi' disdain,
And knew I was naething, yet pitied my pain ?
You said, while they teased you with nonsense and
    dress,
When real the passion, the vanity's less ;
You saw through that silence which others despise,
And, while beaux were a-talking, read love in my eyes.

Oh, how shall I fauld thee, and kiss a' thy charms,
Till, fainting wi' pleasure, I die in your arms ;
Through all the wild transports of ecstasy tost,
Till, sinking together, together we're lost !

Oh, where is the maid that like thee ne'er can cloy,
Whose wit can enliven each dull pause of joy;
And when the short raptures are all at an end,
From beautiful mistress turn sensible friend?

In vain do I praise thee, or strive to reveal,
(Too nice for expression), what only we feel:
In a' that ye do, in each look and each mien,
The graces in waiting adorn you unseen.
When I see you I love you, when hearing adore;
I wonder and think you a woman no more:
Till, mad wi' admiring, I canna contain,
And, kissing your lips, you turn woman again.

With thee in my bosom, how can I despair?
I'll gaze on thy beauties, and look awa care;
I'll ask thy advice, when with troubles opprest,
Which never displeases, but always is best.
In all that I write I'll thy judgment require:
Thy wit shall correct what thy charms did inspire.
I'll kiss thee and press thee till youth is all o'er,
And then live in friendship, when passion's no more.

A. WEBSTER.

CXLIX

O TELL ME HOW TO WOO THEE

If doughty deeds my ladye please,
  Right soon I'll mount my steed ;
And strong his arm, and fast his seat,
  That bears frae me the meed.
I'll wear thy colours in my cap,
  Thy picture in my heart ;
And he, that bends not to thine eye,
  Shall rue it to his smart.
        Then tell me how to woo thee, love ;
          O tell me how to woo thee !
        For thy dear sake, nae care I'll take,
          Tho' ne'er another trow me.

If gay attire delight thine eye,
  I'll dight me in array ;
I'll tend thy chamber door all night,
  And squire thee all the day.
If sweetest sounds can win thy ear,
  These sounds I'll strive to catch ;
Thy voice I'll steal to woo thysell,
  That voice that nane can match,
        Then tell me how to woo thee, love ;
          O tell me how to woo thee !
        For thy dear sake, nae care I'll take,
          Tho' ne'er another trow me.

But if fond love thy heart can gain,
 I never broke a vow ;
Nae maiden lays her skaith to me,
 I never loved but you.
For you alone I ride the ring,
 For you I wear the blue ;
For you alone I strive to sing
 O tell me how to woo !
  O tell me how to woo thee, love ;
   O tell me how to woo thee !
  For thy dear sake, nae care I'll take,
   Tho' ne'er another trow me.

                          GRAHAM OF GARTMORE.

                    CI.

            WILLIE AND HELEN

" WHAREFORE sou'd ye tauk o' love,
   Unless it be to pain us ?
 Wharefore sou'd ye tauk o' love
   When ye say the sea maun twain us ? "

 " It's no because my love is light,
   Nor for your angry deddy ;
  It's a' to buy ye pearlins bright
   And busk ye like a leddy."

"O Willy, I can caird an' spin,
    Sac ne'er can want for cleedin ;
    An gin I ha'e my Willy's heart
    I ha'e a' the pearls I'm heedin.

"Will it be time to praise this cheek
    Whan years an' tears ha'e blench't it ?
    Will it be time to tauk o' love
    When cauld an' care ha'e quencht it ? "

H. AINSLIE.

CLI

THE WORLD'S TREASURES

STRUCTURES, rais'd by morning dreams,
Sands, that trip the flitting streams,
Down, that anchors on the air,
Clouds, that paint their changes there.

Seas, that smoothly dimpling lie,
While the storm impends from high,
Showing, in an obvious glass,
Joys, that in possession pass.

Transient, fickle, light and gay,
Flatt'ring only to betray ;
What, alas, can life contain !
Life, like all it circles—vain !

Will the stork, intending rest,
On the billow build her nest?
Will the bee demand her store
From the bleak and bladeless shore?

Man alone, intent to stray,
Ever turns from wisdom's way;
Lays up wealth in foreign land,
Sows the sea, and ploughs the sand.

E. MOORE.

CLII

DISILLUSION

Ah me, my friend! it will not, will not last!
This fairy scene, that cheats our youthful eyes!
The charm dissolves; th' aerial music's past,
The banquet ceases, and the vision flies.

Where are the splendid forms, the rich perfumes,
Where the gay tapers, where the spacious dome?
Vanish'd the costly pearls, the crimson plumes,
And we, delightless, left to wander home!

And now, 'tis o'er, the dear delusion's o'er!
A stagnant breezeless air becalms my soul;
A fond aspiring candidate no more,
I scorn the palm, before I reach the goal.

O life! how soon of every bliss forlorn!
   We start false joys, and urge the devious race;
A tender prey, that cheers our youthful morn,
   Then sinks untimely, and defrauds the chace.

W. SHENSTONE.

CLIII

THE DEFILED SANCTUARY

I saw a chapel all of gold
   That none did dare to enter in,
And many weeping stood without,
   Weeping, mourning, worshipping.

I saw a serpent rise between
   The white pillars of the door,
And he forced and forced and forced,
   Till he the golden hinges tore:

And along the pavement sweet,
   Set with pearls and rubies bright,
All his shining length he drew,—
   Till upon the altar white

He vomited his poison out
   On the bread and on the wine.
So I turned into a sty,
   And laid me down among the swine.

W. BLAKE.

WINIFREDA

Away; let nought to love displeasing,
　My Winifreda, move your care;
Let nought delay the heavenly blessing,
　Nor squeamish pride, nor gloomy fear.

What tho' no grants of royal donors,
　With pompous titles grace our blood;
We'll shine in more substantial honors,
　And, to be noble, we'll be good.

Our name, while virtue thus we tender,
　Will sweetly sound where-e'er 'tis spoke:
And all the great ones, they shall wonder
　How they respect such little folk.

What though, from fortune's lavish bounty,
　No mighty treasures we possess;
We'll find, within our pittance, plenty,
　And be content without excess.

Still shall each returning season
　Sufficient for our wishes give;
For we will live a life of reason,
　And that's the only life to live.

Through youth and age, in love excelling,
    We'll hand in hand together tread ;
Sweet-smiling peace shall crown our dwelling,
    And babes, sweet-smiling babes, our bed.

How should I love the pretty creatures,
    While round my knees they fondly clung;
To see them look their mother's features,
    To hear them lisp their mother's tongue.

And when with envy, Time transported,
    Shall think to rob us of our joys,
You'll in your girls again be courted,
    And I'll go wooing in my boys.

ANON.

CLV

THE TOUCH STONE

A FOOL and knave with different views
    For Julia's hand apply ;
The knave to mend his fortune sues,
    The fool to please his eye.

Ask you how Julia will behave,
    Depend on't for a rule,
If she's a fool she'll wed the knave—
    If she's a knave, the fool.

S. BISHOP.

BEN BLOCK

BEN BLOCK was a veteran of naval renown,
  And renown was his only reward;
For the Board still neglected his merit to crown,
  As no interest he held with "my lord."

Yet brave as old Benbow was sturdy old Ben,
  And he'd laugh at the cannon's loud roar,
When the death-dealing broadside made worm's-meat of
      men,
  And the scuppers were streaming with gore.

Nor could a Lieutenant's poor stipend provoke
  The staunch Tar to despise scanty prog:
But his biscuit he'd crunch, turn his quid, crack his joke,
  And drown care in a jorum of grog.

Thus year after year in a subaltern state,
  Poor Ben for his King fought and bled;
Till time had unroof'd all the thatch from his pate,
  And the hair from his temples had fled.

When on humbly saluting, with sinciput bare,
  The first Lord of the Admiralty once,
Quoth his Lordship, "Lieutenant, you've lost all your hair
  Since I last had a peep at your sconce!"

"Why, my Lord," replied Ben—"it with truth may be
　　said,
While a bald pate I long have stood under;
There are so many Captains walk'd over my head,
　　That to see me quite scalp'd were no wonder!"

J. COLLINS.

CLVII

FOR MY OWN MONUMENT

As doctors give physic by way of prevention,
　　Mat, alive and in health, of his tombstone took care;
For delays are unsafe, and his pious intention
　　May haply be never fulfilled by his heir.

Then take Mat's word for it, the sculptor is paid;
　　That the figure is fine, pray believe your own eye:
Yet credit but lightly what more may be said,
　　For we flatter ourselves, and teach marble to lie.

Yet, counting as far as to fifty his years,
　　His virtues and vices were as other men's are;
High hopes he conceived, and he smothered great fears,
　　In a life party-coloured, half pleasure, half care.

Nor to business a drudge, nor to faction a slave,
　He strove to make interest and freedom agree ;
In public employments industrious and grave,
　And alone with his friends, lord, how merry was he !

Now in equipage stately, now humbly on foot,
　Both fortunes he tried, but to neither would trust ;
And whirl'd in the round, as the wheel turn'd about,
　He found riches had wings, and knew man was but
　　dust.

This verse little polish'd, though mighty sincere,
　Sets neither his titles nor merit to view ;
It says that his relics collected lie here,
　And no mortal yet knows too if this may be true.

Fierce robbers there are that infest the highway,
　So Mat may be kill'd, and his bones never found ;
False witness at court, and fierce tempests at sea,
　So Mat may yet chance to be hang'd, or be drown'd.

If his bones lie on earth, roll in sea, fly in air,
　To fate we must yield, and the thing is the same ;
And if passing thou giv'st him a smile, or a tear,
　He cares not—yet pr'ythee be kind to his fame.

M. PRIOR.

CLVIII

A REASONABLE AFFLICTION

On his death-bed poor Lubin lies,
  His spouse is in despair :
With frequent sobs, and mutual cries,
  They both express their care.

A different cause, says parson Sly,
  The same effect may give ;
Poor Lubin fears that he shall die ;
  His wife, that he may live.

M. PRIOR.

CLIX

THE POWER OF MUSIC

When Orpheus went down to the regions below,
  Which men are forbidden to see,
He tun'd up his lyre, as old histories show,
  To set his Eurydice free.

All hell was astonish'd a person so wise,
Should rashly endanger his life,
And venture so far—but how vast their surprise !
When they heard that he came for his wife.

To find out a punishment due to his fault
Old Pluto had puzzl'd his brain ;
But hell had no torments sufficient, he thought,
—So he gave him his wife back again.

But pity succeeding found place in his heart,
And, pleas'd with his playing so well,
He took her again in reward of his art ;
Such merit had music in hell.

DR. T. LISLE.

CLX

A NIGHT PIECE

How deep yon azure dyes the sky !
Where orbs of gold unnumber'd lie,
While through their ranks in silver pride
The nether crescent seems to glide.
The slumbering breeze forgets to breathe,
The lake is smooth and clear beneath,
Where once again the spangled show
Descends to meet our eyes below.

The grounds, which on the right aspire,
In dimness from the view retire ;
The left presents a place of graves,
Whose wall the silent water laves ;
That steeple guides thy doubtful sight
Among the livid gleams of night.
There pass, with melancholy state,
By all the solemn heaps of fate,
And think, as softly-sad you tread
Above the venerable dead,
" Time was, like thee, they life possest,
And time shall be, that thou shalt rest."

Those graves, with bending osier bound,
That nameless heave the crumbled ground,
Quick to the glancing thought disclose,
Where toil and poverty repose.

The flat smooth stones that bear a name,
The chisel's slender help to fame,
(Which ere our set of friends decay
Their frequent steps may wear away),
A middle race of mortals own,
Men, half ambitious, all unknown.

The marble tombs that rise on high,
Whose dead in vaulted arches lie,
Whose pillars swell with sculptur'd stones
Arms, angels, epitaphs, and bones,

These, all the poor remains of state,
Adorn the rich, or praise the great ;
Who, while on earth in fame they live,
Are senseless of the fame they give.

T. PARNELL.

CLXI

ORIGIN OF EVIL

EVIL, if rightly understood,
Is but the Skeleton of good,
Divested of its Flesh and Blood.

While it remains, without Divorce,
Within its hidden, secret Source,
It is the Good's own Strength and Force.

As Bone has the supporting Share,
In human Form divinely fair,
Altho' an Evil when laid bare ;

As Light and Air are fed by Fire,
A shining Good, while all conspire,
But (separate) dark, raging Ire ;

As Hope and Love arise from Faith,
Which then admits no Ill, nor hath ;
But, if alone, it would be Wrath ;

Or any Instance thought upon,
In which the Evil can be none,
Till Unity of Good is gone.

So, by abuse of Thought and Skill,
The greatest Good, to wit, Free-Will,
Becomes the Origin of Ill.

Thus when rebellious Angels fell,
The very Heav'n, where good ones dwell,
Became th' apostate Spirits' Hell.

Seeking, against eternal Right,
A Force without a Love and Light,
They found, and felt its evil might.

Thus Adam, biting at their Bait,
Of Good and Evil when he ate,
Died to his first thrice happy State.

Fell to the Evils of this Ball,
Which, in harmonious Union all,
Were Paradise before his Fall.

And, when the Life of Christ in Men
Revives its faded Image, then,
Will all be Paradise again.

J. BYROM.

CLXII

CONTEMPLATION

THE world can't hear the small still voice,
    Such is its bustle and its noise;
Reason the proclamation reads,
But not one riot passion heeds.
Wealth, honour, power, the graces are,
Which here below our homage share:
They, if one votary they find
To mistress more divine inclin'd,
In truth's pursuit, to cause delay,
Throw golden apples in his way.
Place me, O Heaven, in some retreat;
There let the serious death-watch beat,
There let me self in silence shun,
To feel thy will, which should be done.
    Then comes the Spirit to our hut,
When fast the senses' doors are shut;
For so divine and pure a guest,
The emptiest rooms are furnish'd best.
    O Contemplation! air serene!
From damps of sense, and fogs of spleen!
Pure mount of thought! thrice holy ground,
Where grace, when waited for, is found.
    Here 'tis the soul feels sudden youth,
And meets, exulting, virgin Truth;

N

Here, like a breeze of gentlest kind,
Impulses rustle through the mind ;
Here shines that light with glowing face,
The fuse divine, that kindles grace ;
Which, if we trim our lamps, will last,
Till darkness be by dying past,
And then goes out, at end of night,
Extinguish'd by superior light.

M. GREEN.

CLXIII

FALLENTIS SEMITA VITÆ

THRICE happy you, whoe'er you are,
From life's low cares secluded far,
   In this sequester'd vale !—
Ye rocks on precipices pil'd !
Ye ragged deserts, waste and wild !
   Delightful horrors hail !

What joy within these sunless groves,
Where lonely Contemplation roves,
   To rest in fearless ease !
Save weeping rills, to see no tear,
Save dying gales, no sigh to hear,
   No murmur but the breeze.

Say, would you change that peaceful cell
Where sanctity and silence dwell,
    For splendor's dazzling blaze?
For all those gilded toys that glare
Round high-born power's imperial chair,
    Inviting fools to gaze?

Ah friend!   Ambition's prospects close,
And, studious of your own repose,
    Be thankful here to live:
For, trust me, one protecting shed
And nightly peace, and daily bread
    Is all that life can give.

DR. J. LANGHORNE.

CLXIV

ILLUSION

HOWE'ER, 'tis well, that while mankind
    Through Fate's perverse meander errs,
He can imagined pleasures find,
    To combat against real cares.

Fancies and notions he pursues,
    Which ne'er had being but in thought;
Each, like the Grecian artist, woos
    The image he himself has wrought.

Against experience he believes;
   He argues against demonstration;
Pleas'd, when his reason he deceives;
   And sets his judgment by his passion.

The hoary fool, who many days
   Has struggled with continued sorrow,
Renews his hope, and blindly lays
   The desperate bet upon to-morrow.

To-morrow comes; 'tis noon, 'tis night;
   This day like all the former flies:
Yet on he runs, to seek delight
   To-morrow, till to-night he dies.

Our hopes, like towering falcons, aim
   At objects in an airy height;
The little pleasure of the game
   Is from afar to view the flight.

Our anxious pains we, all the day,
   In search of what we like, employ;
Scorning at night the worthless prey,
   We find the labour gave the joy.

At distance through an artful glass
   To the mind's eye things well appear;
They lose their forms, and make a mass
   Confus'd and black, if brought too near.

If we see right, we see our woes;
Then what avails it to have eyes?
From ignorance our comfort flows,
The only wretched are the wise.

M. PRIOR.

CLXV

PRAYER FOR INDIFFERENCE

I ASK no kind return of love,
No tempting charm to please;
Far from the heart those gifts remove,
That sighs for peace and ease.

Nor peace, nor ease, the heart can know,
Which, like the needle true,
Turns at the touch of joy or woe,
But, turning, trembles too.

Far as distress the soul can wound,
'Tis pain in each degree:
'Tis bliss but to a certain bound—
Beyond—is agony.

Take then this treacherous sense of mine,
Which dooms me still to smart;
Which pleasure can to pain refine,
To pain new pangs impart.

O ! haste to shed the sacred balm !
    My shatter'd nerves new-string ;
And for my guest, serenely calm,
    The nymph, Indifference, bring.

At her approach, see Hope, see Fear,
    See Expectation fly ;
And Disappointment in the rear,
    That blasts the promis'd joy.

The tear, which Pity taught to flow,
    My eye shall then disown ;
The heart that melts for others' woe,
    Shall then scarce feel its own.

The wounds which now each moment bleed,
    Each moment then shall close,
And tranquil days shall still succeed
    To nights of sweet repose.

O fairy elf ! but grant me this,
    This one kind comfort send ;
And so may never-fading bliss
    Thy flow'ry paths attend !

So may the glow-worm's glimm'ring light
    Thy tiny footsteps lead,
To some new region of delight,
    Unknown to mortal tread.

And be thy acorn goblet fill'd
With heaven's ambrosial dew,
From sweetest, freshest flowers distill'd,
That shed fresh sweets for you.

And what of life remains for me,
I'll pass in sober ease;
Half-pleas'd, contented will I be,
Content—but half to please.

MRS. GREVILLE.

CLXVI

THE MODERN ARISTIPPUS

PRITHEE tease me no longer, dear troublesome friend,
On a subject which wants not advice;
You may make me unhappy, but never can mend
Those ills I have learnt to despise.

You say I'm dependent; what then?—if I make
That dependence quite easy to me,
Say why should you envy my lucky mistake,
Or why should I wish to be free.

Many men of less worth, you partially cry,
To splendor and opulence soar;
Suppose I allow it, yet. pray sir, am I
Less happy because they are more?

But why said I happy? I aim not at that,
    Mere ease is my humble request;
I would neither repine at a niggardly fate,
    Nor stretch my wings far from my nest.

Nor e'er may my pride or my folly reflect
    On the fav'rites whom Fortune has made,
Regardless of thousands, who pine with neglect
    In pensive Obscurity's shade;

With whom, when comparing the merit I boast,
    Tho' rais'd by indulgence to fame,
I sink in confusion, bewilder'd and lost,
    And wonder I am what I am!

And what are these wonders, these blessings refin'd,
    Which splendour and opulence shower?
The health of the body, and peace of the mind,
    Are things which are out of their power.

To contentment's calm sunshine, the lot of the few,
    Can insolent greatness pretend?
Or can it bestow, what I boast of in you,
    That blessing of blessings, a friend?

We may pay some regard to the rich and the great,
    But how seldom we love them you know;
Or if we do love them, it is not their state,
    The tinsel and plume of the show,

But some secret virtues we find in the heart,
  When the mask is laid kindly aside,
Which birth cannot give them, nor riches impart,
  And which never once heard of their pride.

A show of good spirits I've seen with a smile,
  To worth make a shallow pretence ;
And the chat of good breeding with ease, for a while,
  May pass for good nature and sense ;

But where is the bosom untainted by art,
  The judgment so modest and stay'd,
That union so rare of the head and the heart
  Which fixes the friends it has made ?

For those whom the great and the wealthy employ,
  Their pleasure or vanity's slaves,
Whate'er they can give I without them enjoy,
  And am rid of just so many knaves.

For the many whom titles alone can allure,
  And the blazon of ermine and gules,
I wrap myself round in my lowness secure,
  And am rid of just so many fools.

Then why should I covet what cannot increase
  My delights, and may lessen their store ;
My present condition is quiet and case,
  And what can my future be more ?

Should Fortune capriciously cease to be coy,
    And in torrents of plenty descend,
I, doubtless, like others, should clasp her with joy,
    And my wants and my wishes extend.

But since 'tis denied me, and heaven best knows,
    Whether kinder to grant it or not,
Say, why should I vainly disturb my repose,
    And peevishly carp at my lot?

No; still let me follow sage Horace's rule,
    Who tried all things and held fast the best;
Learn daily to put all my passions to school,
    And keep the due poise of my breast.

Thus, firm at the helm, I glide calmly away,
    Like the merchant long us'd to the deep,
Nor trust for my safety on life's stormy sea,
    To the gilding and paint of my ship.

Nor yet can the giants of honour and pelf
    My want of ambition deride,
He who rules his own bosom is lord of himself,
    And lord of all nature beside.

                                    W. WHITEHEAD.

CLXVII

CARELESS CONTENT

I AM content, I do not care,
    Wag as it will the world for me;
When Fuss and Fret was all my Fare,
    It got no ground, as I could see:
So when away my Caring went,
I counted Cost, and was Content.

With more of Thanks and less of Thought,
    I strive to make my Matters meet;
To seek what ancient sages sought,
    Physic and Food, in sour and sweet:
To take what passes in good Part,
And keep the Hiccups from the Heart.

With good and gentle humour'd Hearts,
    I choose to chat where'er I come,
Whate'er the Subject be that starts;
    But if I get among the Glum,
I hold my Tongue to tell the Troth,
And keep my Breath to cool my Broth.

For Chance or Change of Peace or Pain;
  For Fortune's Favour or her Frown ;
For Lack or Glut, for Loss or Gain,
  I never dodge, nor up nor down :
But swing what way the ship shall swim,
Or tack about, with equal Trim.

I suit not where I shall not speed,
  Nor trace the Turn of ev'ry Tide ;
If simple Sense will not succeed,
  I make no Bustling, but abide :
For shining Wealth, or scaring Woe,
I force no Friend, I fear no Foe.

I love my Neighbour as myself,
  Myself like him too, by his Leave ;
Nor to his Pleasure, Pow'r, or Pelf,
  Came I to crouch, as I conceive :
Dame Nature doubtless has design'd
A Man, the Monarch of his Mind.

Now taste and try this Temper, Sirs,
  Mood it, and brood it in your Breast ;
Or if ye ween, for worldly Stirs,
  That Man does right to mar his Rest,
Let me be deft, and debonair,
I am Content, I do not care.

                                    J. BYROM.

IN A HERMITAGE

THE man, whose days of youth and ease
   In Nature's calm enjoyments pass'd,
Will want no monitors, like these,
   To torture and alarm his last.

The gloomy grot, the cypress shade,
   The zealot's list of rigid rules,
To him are merely dull parade,
   The tragic pageantry of fools.

What life affords he freely tastes,
   When Nature calls, resigns his breath ;
Nor age in weak repining wastes,
   Nor acts alive the farce of death.

Not so the youths of Folly's train,
   Impatient of each kind restraint
Which parent Nature fix'd, in vain,
   To teach us man's true bliss, content.

For something still beyond enough,
   With eager impotence they strive,
'Till appetite has learn'd to loathe
   The very joys by which we live.

Then, fill'd with all which sour disdain
    To disappointed vice can add,
Tir'd of himself, man flies from man,
    And hates the world he made so bad.

W. WHITEHEAD.

CLXIX

TO THE CUCKOO

HAIL, beauteous stranger of the grove !
    Thou messenger of Spring !
Now Heaven repairs thy rural seat,
    And woods thy welcome sing.

What time the daisy decks the green,
    Thy certain voice we hear ;
Hast thou a star to guide thy path,
    Or mark the rolling year ?

Delightful visitant ! with thee
    I hail the time of flowers,
And hear the sound of music sweet
    From birds among the bowers.

The school-boy, wandering through the wood
    To pull the primrose gay,
Starts, the new voice of spring to hear,
    And imitates thy lay.

What time the pea puts on the bloom,
Thou fliest thy vocal vale,
An annual guest in other lands,
Another Spring to hail.

Sweet bird ! thy bower is ever green,
Thy sky is ever clear ;
Thou hast no sorrow in thy song,
No Winter in thy year !

Oh, could I fly, I'd fly with thee !
We'd make, with joyful wing,
Our annual visit o'er the globe,
Companions of the Spring.

J. LOGAN.

CLXX

NATURE'S CHARMS

OH, how canst thou renounce the boundless store
Of charms which Nature to her votary yields !
The warbling woodland, the resounding shore,
The pomp of groves, the garniture of fields ;
All that the genial ray of morning gilds,
And all that echoes to the song of even,
All that the mountain's sheltering bosom shields,
And all the dread magnificence of heaven,
Oh, how canst thou renounce, and hope to be forgiven ?

J. BEATTIE.

THE HAYMAKER'S ROUNDELAY

DRIFTED snow no more is seen,
Blust'ring Winter passes by ;
Merry Spring comes clad in green,
While woodlands pour their melody :
I hear him ! hark !
The merry lark
Calls us to the new-mown hay,
Piping to our roundelay.

When the golden sun appears,
On the mountain's surly brow,
When his jolly beams he rears,
Darting joy, behold them now :
Then, then, oh hark !
The merry lark
Calls us to the new-mown hay,
Piping to our roundelay.

What are honours ? What's a court ?
Calm Content is worth them all ;
Our honour is to drive the cart,
Our brightest court the harvest-hall :
But now—oh hark !
The merry lark
Calls us to the new-mown hay,
Piping to our roundelay.

ANON.

SNOWDROPS

WAN Heralds of the Sun and Summer gale,
   That seem just fall'n from infant Zephyr's wing ;
Not now, as once, with heart reviv'd I hail
   Your modest buds, that for the brow of Spring

Form the first simple garland—now no more,
   Escaping for a moment all my cares,
Shall I, with pensive, silent step explore
   The woods yet leafless ; where to chilling airs

Your green and pencill'd blossoms, trembling, wave.
   Ah ! ye soft, transient children of the ground,
More fair was she on whose untimely grave
   Flow my unceasing tears !   Their varied round

The seasons go ; while I through all repine,
For fix'd regret, and hopeless grief are mine.

                       CHARLOTTE SMITH.

THE HAMLET

THE hinds how blest, who ne'er beguil'd
To quit their hamlet's hawthorn wild,
Nor haunt the crowd, nor tempt the main,
For splendid care, and guilty gain !

When morning's twilight-tinctur'd beam
Strikes their low thatch with slanting gleam,
They rove abroad in ether blue,
To dip the scythe in fragrant dew:
The sheaf to bind, the beech to fell,
That nodding shades a craggy dell

'Midst gloomy glades, in warbles clear,
Wild nature's sweetest notes they hear:
On green untrodden banks they view
The hyacinth's neglected hue:
In their low haunts and woodland rounds,
They spy the squirrel's airy bounds:
And startle from her ashen spray,
Across the glen the screaming jay:
Each native charm their steps explore
Of Solitude's sequester'd store.

For them the moon with cloudless ray
Mounts, to illume their homeward way:
Their weary spirits to relieve,
The meadows incense breathe at eve.
No riot mars the simple fare,
That o'er a glimmering hearth they share:
But when the curfew's measur'd roar
Duly, the darkening valleys o'er,
Has echoed from the distant town,
They wish no beds of cygnet-down,
No trophied canopies, to close
Their drooping eyes in quick repose.

Their little sons, who spread the bloom
Of health around the clay-built room,
Or through the primros'd coppice stray,
Or gambol in the new-mown hay;
Or quaintly braid the cowslip-twine,
Or drive afield the tardy kine;
Or hasten from the sultry hill,
To loiter at the shady rill;
Or climb the tall pine's gloomy crest,
To rob the raven's ancient nest.

Their humble porch with honied flow'rs
The curling woodbine's shade imbow'rs:
From the small garden's thymy mound
Their bees in busy swarms resound:
Nor fell Disease, before his time,
Hastes to consume life's golden prime:
But when their temples long have wore
The silver crown of tresses hoar;
As studious still calm peace to keep,
Beneath a flowery turf they sleep.

T. WARTON.

CLXXIV

TO NIGHT

I LOVE thee, mournful, sober-suited Night!
    When the faint moon, yet lingering in her wane,
And veil'd in clouds, with pale uncertain light,
    Hangs o'er the waters of the restless main.

In deep depression sunk, the enfeebled mind
　Will to the deaf cold elements complain,
And tell the embosom'd grief, however vain,
　To sullen surges and the viewless wind.

Tho' no repose on thy dark breast I find,
　I still enjoy thee—cheerless as thou art ;
For in thy quiet gloom the exhausted heart
　Is calm, though wretched ; hopeless, yet resign'd.

While to the winds and waves its sorrows given,
　May reach—though lost on earth—the ear of Heaven !

CHARLOTTE SMITH.

CLXXV

LAST WORDS

　KIND companion of my youth,
　　Lov'd for genius, worth, and truth !
Take what friendship can impart,
Tribute of a feeling heart ;
Take the Muse's latest spark,
Ere we drop into the dark.
He, who parts and virtue gave,
Bade thee look beyond the grave ;

Genius soars, and virtue guides,
Where the love of God presides.
There's a gulf 'twixt us and God ;
Let the gloomy path be trod :
Why stand shivering on the shore?
Why not boldly venture o'er ?
Where unerring virtue guides
Let us brave the winds and tides ;
Safe, thro' seas of doubts and fears,
Rides the bark which virtue steers.
Love thy country, wish it well,
    Not with too intense a care,
'Tis enough, that, when it fell,
    Thou its ruin didst not share.
Envy's censure, Flattery's praise,
    With unmov'd indifference view ;
Learn to tread Life's dangerous maze
    With unerring Virtue's clue.
Void of strong desire and fear,
    Life's wide ocean trust no more ;
Strive thy little bark to steer
    With the tide, but near the shore.
Thus prepar'd, thy shorten'd sail
    Shall, whene'er the winds increase,
Seizing each propitious gale,
    Waft thee to the Port of Peace.
Keep thy conscience from offence
    And tempestuous passions free,
So, when thou art call'd from hence,
    Easy shall thy passage be ;

Easy shall thy passage be,
Cheerful thy allotted stay,
Short the account 'twixt God and thee,
Hope shall meet thee on the way.

BUBB DODINGTON, LORD MELCOMBE.

CLXXVI

AN EPISTLE TO A FRIEND IN TOWN

HAVE my friends in the Town, in the gay busy Town,
　　Forgot such a man as John Dyer?
Or heedless despise they, or pity the clown,
　　Whose bosom no pageantries fire?

No matter, no matter,—content in the shades,—
　　Contented? why everything charms me;
Fall in tunes all adown the green steep, ye cascades,
　　Till the trumpet of Virtue alarms me.

Till Outrage arises, or Misery needs
　　The swift, the intrepid avenger;
Till sacred Religion or Liberty bleeds—
　　Then mine be the deed and the danger.

Alas! what a folly, that wealth and domain
　　We heap up in sin and in sorrow!
Immense is the toil, yet the labour how vain!
　　Is not life to be over to-morrow?

Then glide on my moments, the few that I have,
  Sweet-shaded, and quiet, and even ;
While gently the body descends to the grave,
  And the spirit arises to heaven.

J. DYER.

CLXXVII

THE DILEMMA

THAT Jenny's my friend, my delight, and my pride,
I always have boasted, and seek not to hide ;
I dwell on her praises wherever I go,
They say I'm in love, but I answer "No, no."

At evening oft times with what pleasure I see
A note from her hand, " I'll be with you at tea ! "
My heart how it bounds, when I hear her below !
But say not 'tis love, for I answer "No, no."

She sings me a song, and I echo each strain.
" Again," I cry, " Jenny, sweet Jenny, again ! "
I kiss her soft lips, as if there I could grow,
And fear I'm in love, though I answer "No, no."

She tells me her faults, as she sits on my knee,
I chide her, and swear she's an angel to me :
My shoulder she taps, and still bids me think so ;
Who knows but she loves, though she tells me "No, no."

From beauty, and wit, and good humour, ah! why
Should prudence advise, and compel me to fly?
Thy bounties, O fortune! make haste to bestow,
And let me deserve her, or still I say "No!"

E. MOORE.

CLXXVIII

A USEFUL HINT

TENDER-HANDED stroke a nettle,
    And it stings you for your pains;
Grasp it like a man of mettle,
    And it soft as silk remains.

'Tis the same with common natures,
    Use them kindly they rebel;
But be rough as nutmeg graters,
    And the rogues obey you well.

A. HILL.

CLXXIX

LUCY'S FLITTIN'

'TWAS when the wan leaf frae the birk-tree was fa'in',
And Martinmas dowie had wound up the year,
That Lucy row'd up her wee kist wi' her a' in't,
And left her auld maister and neebours sae dear:

For Lucy had served in the Glen a' the simmer;
She cam there afore the flower blumed on the pea;
An orphan was she, and they had been kind till her,
Sure that was the thing brocht the tear to her ee.

She gaed by the stable where Jamie was stannin',
Richt sair was his kind heart, the flittin' to see:
"Fare ye weel, Lucy!" quo' Jamie, and ran in,
The gatherin' tears trickled fast frae his ee.
As down the burn-side she gaed slow wi' the flittin',
"Fare ye weel, Lucy!" was ilka bird's sang;
She heard the craw sayin't, high on the tree sittin',
And Robin was chirpin't the brown leaves amang.

"Oh, what is't that pits my puir heart in a flutter?
And what gars the tears come sae fast to my ee?
If I wasna ettled to be ony better,
Then what gars me wish ony better to be?
I'm just like a lammie that loses its mither;
Nae mither or friend the puir lammie can see;
I fear I hae tint my poor heart a'thegither,
Nae wonder the tear fa's sae fast frae my ee.

"Wi' the rest o' my claes I hae row'd up the ribbon,
The bonnie blue ribbon that Jamie gae me;
Yestreen when he gae me't, and saw I was sabbin',
I'll never forget the wae blink o' his ee.
Though now he said naething but Fare ye weel, Lucy,
It made me I neither could speak, hear, nor see;
He could nae say mair but just, Fare ye weel, Lucy!
Yet that I will mind till the day that I dee.

" The lamb likes the gowan wi' dew when it's droukit ;
The hare likes the brake and the braird on the lea :
But Lucy likes Jamie,"—she turn'd and she lookit,
She thocht the dear place she wad never mair see.
Ah, weel may young Jamie gang dowie and cheerless !
And weel may he greet on the bank o' the burn !
For bonnie sweet Lucy, sae gentle and peerless,
Lies cauld in her grave, and will never return !

W. LAIDLAW.

CLXXX

THE BRAES OF YARROW

" Thy braes were bonnie, Yarrow stream,
 When first on them I met my lover ;
Thy braes how dreary, Yarrow stream,
 When now thy waves his body cover !
For ever now, O Yarrow stream,
 Thou art to me a stream of sorrow !
For never on thy banks shall I
 Behold my love, the flower of Yarrow.

" He promised me a milk white steed,
 To bear me to his father's bowers ;
He promised me a little page,
 To squire me to his father's towers ;

He promised me a wedding ring—
The wedding-day was fix'd to-morrow ;—
Now he is wedded to his grave,
     Alas, his watery grave, in Yarrow !

"Sweet were his words when last we met ;
My passion I as freely told him ;
Clasp'd in his arms, I little thought
     That I should never more behold him !
Scarce was he gone, I saw his ghost ;
     It vanish'd with a shriek of sorrow ;
Thrice did the water-wraith ascend,
     And gave a doleful groan through Yarrow.

" His mother from the window look'd,
With all the longing of a mother ;
His little sister weeping walk'd
     The greenwood path to meet her brother.
They sought him east, they sought him west,
     They sought him all the forest thorough ;
They only saw the cloud of night,
     They only heard the roar of Yarrow !

" No longer from thy window look,—
Thou hast no son, thou tender mother !
No longer walk, thou lovely maid,
     Alas, thou hast no more a brother !
No longer seek him east or west,
     And search no more the forest thorough ;
For, wandering in the night so dark,
     He fell, a lifeless corpse, in Yarrow.

"The tear shall never leave my cheek,
  No other youth shall be my marrow;
I'll seek thy body in the stream,
  And then with thee I'll sleep in Yarrow."
The tear did never leave her cheek,
  No other youth became her marrow;
She found his body in the stream,
  And now with him she sleeps in Yarrow.

J. LOGAN.

CLXXXI

FRIENDSHIP

DISTILL'D amidst the gloom of night,
  Dark hangs the dew-drop on the thorn;
Till, notic'd by approaching light,
  It glitters in the smile of morn.

Morn soon retires, her feeble pow'r
  The sun out-beams with genial day,
And gently, in benignant hour,
  Exhales the liquid pearl away.

Thus on affliction's sable bed
  Deep sorrows rise of saddest hue;
Condensing round the mourner's head
  They bathe the cheek with chilly dew.

Though pity shows her dawn from heaven,
When kind she points assistance near,
To friendship's sun alone 'tis given
To soothe and dry the mourner's tear.

T. PENROSE.

CLXXXII

SONG TO DAVID

TELL them, I AM, Jehovah said
To Moses; while earth heard in dread,
   And, smitten to the heart,
At once above, beneath, around,
All Nature, without voice or sound,
   Replied, O Lord, Thou ART.

Thou art—to give and to confirm
For each his talent and his term;
   All flesh thy bounties share:
Thou shalt not call thy brother fool;
The porches of the Christian school
   Are meekness, peace, and pray'r.

.   .   .   .

Sweet is the dew that falls betimes,
And drops upon the leafy limes;
   Sweet Hermon's fragrant air:
Sweet is the lily's silver bell,
And sweet the wakeful tapers smell,
   That watch for early pray'r.

Sweet the young nurse with love intense,
Which smiles o'er sleeping innocence;
   Sweet when the lost arrive:
Sweet the musician's ardour beats,
While his vague mind's in quest of sweets,
   The choicest flow'rs to hive.

Sweeter in all the strains of love,
The language of thy turtle dove,
   Pair'd to thy swelling chord;
Sweeter with ev'ry grace endued,
The glory of thy gratitude,
   Respir'd unto the Lord.

Strong is the lion—like a coal
His eye-ball—like a bastion's mole
   His chest against the foes:
Strong the gier-eagle on his sail,
Strong against tide, th' enormous whale
   Emerges, as he goes.

But stronger still, in earth and air,
And in the sea, the man of pray'r;
   And far beneath the tide;
And in the seat to faith assign'd,
Where ask is have, where seek is find,
   Where knock is open wide.

Beauteous the fleet before the gale ;
Beauteous the multitudes in mail,
  Rank'd arms and crested heads :
Beauteous the garden's umbrage mild—
Walk, water, meditated wild,
  And all the bloomy beds.

Beauteous the moon full on the lawn ;
And beauteous, when the veil's withdrawn,
  The virgin to her spouse :
Beauteous the temple deck'd and fill'd,
When to the heav'n of heav'ns they build
  Their heart-directed vows.

Precious the penitential tear ;
And precious is the sigh sincere,
  Acceptable to God :
And precious are the winning flow'rs,
In gladsome Israel's feast of bow'rs
  Bound on the hallow'd sod.

More precious that diviner part
Of David, ev'n the Lord's own heart,
  Great, beautiful, and new :
In all things where it was intent,
In all extreams, in each event,
  Proof—answ'ring true to true.

Glorious the sun in mid career,
Glorious th' assembled fires appear,
    Glorious the comet's train :
Glorious the trumpet and alarm,
Glorious th' Almighty stretch'd-out arm,
    Glorious th' enraptur'd main :

Glorious the northern lights astream,
Glorious the song, when God's the theme,
    Glorious the thunder's roar :
Glorious hosanna from the den,
Glorious the Catholic amen,
    Glorious the martyr's gore :

Glorious, more glorious is the crown
Of Him, that brought salvation down
    By meekness, call'd Thy Son ;
Thou at stupendous truth believ'd,
And now the matchless deed's achiev'd,
    Determin'd, Dar'd, and Done.

                                C. SMART.

CLXXXIII

HOLY THURSDAY

'Twas on a Holy Thursday, their innocent faces clean,
Came children walking two and two, in red, and blue, and
    green :

Grey-headed beadles walked before, with wands as white
    as snow,
Till into the high dome of Paul's they like Thames
    waters flow.

Oh what a multitude they seemed, these flowers of
    London town !
Seated in companies they sit, with radiance all their own ;
The hum of multitudes was there, but multitudes of
    lambs,
Thousands of little boys and girls raising their innocent
    hands.

Now, like a mighty wind, they raise to heaven the voice
    of song,
Or like harmonious thunderings the seats of heaven
    among ;
Beneath them sit the aged men, wise guardians of the
    poor,
Then cherish pity, lest you drive an angel from your
    door.   W. BLAKE.

CLXXXIV

THE DAY OF JUDGEMENT

WHEN the fierce northwind with his airy forces
Rears up the Baltic to a foaming fury;
And the red lightning, with a storm of hail comes
                 Rushing amain down.

P

How the poor sailors stand amaz'd and tremble!
While the hoarse thunder, like a bloody trumpet,
Roars a loud onset to the gaping waters
          Quick to devour them.

Such shall the noise be, and the wild disorder,
(If things eternal may be like these earthly)
Such the dire terror when the great Archangel
          Shakes the creation;

Tears the strong pillars of the vault of Heaven,
Breaks up old marble, the repose of princes;
See the graves open, and the bones arising,
          Flames all around them.

Hark, the shrill outcries of the guilty wretches!
Lively bright horror, and amazing anguish,
Stare through their eyelids, while the living worm lies
          Gnawing within them.

Thoughts, like old vultures, prey upon their heart-strings,
And the smart twinges, when the eye beholds the
Lofty Judge frowning, and a flood of vengeance
          Rolling afore him.

Hopeless immortals! how they scream and shiver
While devils push them to the pit wide-yawning,
Hideous and gloomy, to receive them headlong
          Down to the centre.

Stop here, my fancy : (all away, ye horrid
Doleful ideas !) come, arise to Jesus,
How he sits God-like ! and the saints around him
        Thron'd, yet adoring !

O may I sit there when He comes triumphant,
Dooming the nations ! then ascend to glory,
While our hosannas all along the passage
        Shout the Redeemer.

                DR. I. WATTS.

CLXXXV

HOPE

SUN of the Soul ! whose cheerful ray
   Darts o'er this gloom of life a smile ;
Sweet Hope, yet further gild my way,
   Yet light my weary steps awhile,
Till thy fair lamp dissolve in endless day.

              DR. J. LANGHORNE.

CLXXXVI

THE WORM

TURN, turn thy hasty foot aside,
   Nor crush that helpless worm !
The frame thy scornful looks deride
   Requir'd a God to form.

The common Lord of all that move,
    From whom thy being flow'd,
A portion of His boundless love
    On that poor worm bestow'd.

The sun, the moon, the stars He made
    To all His creatures free:
And spreads o'er earth the grassy blade
    For worms as well as thee.

Let them enjoy their little day,
    Their lowly bliss receive;
O do not lightly take away
    The life thou canst not give!

                  T. GISBORNE.

CLXXXVII

FATI VALET HORA BENIGNI

In myriad swarms, each summer sun
    An insect nation shows;
Whose being, since he rose begun,
    And e'er he sets will close.

Brief is their date, confin'd their powers,
    The fluttering of a day;—
Yet life's worth living, e'en for hours,
    When all those hours—are play.

                  S. BISHOP.

CLXXXVIII

INSCRIPTION ON A FOUNTAIN

O you, who mark what flowrets gay,
 What gales, what odours breathing near,
What sheltering shades from summer's ray
 Allure my spring to linger here :

Yet see me quit this margin green,
 Yet see me deaf to pleasure's call,
Explore the thirsty haunts of men,
 Yet see my bounty flow for all.

O learn of me—no partial rill,
 No slumbering selfish pool be you ;
But social laws alike fulfil ;
 O flow for all creation too !

                                        E. LOVIBOND.

CLXXXIX

WRITTEN AT AN INN AT HENLEY

To thee, fair freedom ! I retire
 From flattery, cards, and dice, and din ;
Nor art thou found in mansions higher
 Than the low cot, or humble inn.

'Tis here with boundless power, I reign;
    And every health which I begin,
Converts dull port to bright champagne;
    Such freedom crowns it, at an inn.

I fly from pomp, I fly from plate!
    I fly from falsehood's specious grin!
Freedom I love, and form I hate,
    And choose my lodgings at an inn.

Here, waiter! take my sordid ore,
    Which lacqueys else might hope to win;
It buys, what courts have not in store,
    It buys me freedom at an inn.

Whoe'er has travell'd life's dull round,
    Where'er his stages may have been,
May sigh to think he still has found
    The warmest welcome at an inn.

                              W. SHENSTONE.

CXC

HYMN TO SCIENCE

SCIENCE! thou fair effusive ray
From the great source of mental day,
    Free, generous, and refin'd!
Descend with all thy treasures fraught,
Illumine each bewilder'd thought,
    And bless my labouring mind.

But first with thy resistless light,
Disperse those phantoms from my sight,
   Those mimic shades of thee;
The scholiast's learning, sophist's cant,
The visionary bigot's rant,
   The monk's philosophy.

O! let thy powerful charms impart
The patient head, the candid heart
   Devoted to thy sway;
Which no weak passions e'er mislead,
Which still with dauntless steps proceed
   Where Reason points the way.

Then launch through Being's wide extent;
Let the fair scale, with just ascent
   And cautious steps, be trod;
And from the dead, corporeal mass,
Through each progressive order pass
   To Instinct, Reason, God.

That last, best effort of thy skill,
To form the life, and rule the will,
   Propitious power! impart;
Teach me to cool my passion's fires,
Make me the judge of my desires,
   The master of my heart.

Sun of the soul ! thy beams unveil !
Let others spread the daring sail,
　　On Fortune's faithless sea ;
While, undeluded, happier I
From the vain tumult timely fly,
　　And sit in peace with thee.

　　　　　　　　　　　M. AKENSIDE.

CXCI

THE ENTHUSIAST

ONCE, I remember well the day,
'Twas ere the blooming sweets of May
　　Had lost their freshest hues,
When every flower on every hill,
In every vale, had drunk its fill
　　Of sun-shine and of dews.

'Twas that sweet season's loveliest prime
When Spring gives up the reins of time
　　To Summer's glowing hand,
And doubting mortals hardly know
By whose command the breezes blow
　　Which fan the smiling land.

'Twas then beside a green-wood shade
Which cloth'd a lawn's aspiring head
   I urg'd my devious way,
With loitering steps, regardless where,
So soft, so genial was the air,
   So wond'rous bright the day.

And now my eyes with transport rove
O'er all the blue expanse above,
   Unbroken by a cloud !
And now beneath delighted pass,
Where, winding through the deep-green grass,
   A full-brimm'd river flow'd.

I stop, I gaze ; in accents rude
To thee, serenest Solitude,
   Bursts forth th' unbidden lay ;
Begone, vile world ; the learn'd, the wise,
The great, the busy, I despise,
   And pity e'en the gay.

These, these are joys alone, I cry,
'Tis here, divine Philosophy,
   Thou deign'st to fix thy throne !
Here contemplation points the road
Thro' Nature's charms to Nature's God !
   These, these, are joys alone !

Adieu, ye vain, low-thoughted cares,
Ye human hopes, and human fears,
   Ye pleasures, and ye pains !—
While thus I spake, o'er all my soul
A philosophic calmness stole,
   A Stoic stillness reigns.

The tyrant passions all subside,
Fear, anger, pity, shame, and pride,
   No more my bosom move.
Yet still I felt, or seem'd to feel
A kind of visionary zeal
   Of universal love.

When lo ! a voice ! a voice I hear !
'Twas Reason whisper'd in my ear
   These monitory strains :
What mean'st thou, man ? would'st thou unbind
The ties which constitute thy kind,
   The pleasures and the pains ?

The same Almighty Power unseen,
Who spreads the gay or solemn scene
   To Contemplation's eye :
Fix'd every movement of the soul,
Taught every wish its destined goal,
   And quicken'd every joy.

He bids the tyrant passions rage,
He bids them war eternal wage,
  And combat each his foe :
Till from dissensions concords rise,
And beauties from deformities,
  And happiness from woe.

Art thou not man ? and dar'st thou find
A bliss which leans not to mankind ?
  Presumptuous thought, and vain !
Each bliss unshar'd is unenjoy'd,
Each power is weak, unless employ'd
  Some social good to gain.

Shall light, and shade, and warmth, and air,
With those exalted joys compare
  Which active virtue feels.
When on she drags, as lawful prize,
Contempt, and Indolence, and Vice,
  At her triumphant wheels.

As rest to labour still succeeds,
To man, while Virtue's glorious deeds
  Employ his toilsome day,
This fair variety of things
Are merely life's refreshing springs
  To soothe him on his way.

Enthusiast, go, unstring thy lyre ;
In vain thou sing'st if none admire,
   How sweet soe'er the strain ;
And is not thy o'erflowing mind,
Unless thou mixest with thy kind,
   Benevolent in vain ?

Enthusiast, go, try every sense ;
If not thy bliss, thy excellence
   Thou yet hast learn'd to scan ;
At least thy wants, thy weakness know,
And see them all uniting show,
   That man was made for man.

W. WHITEHEAD.

CXCII

NIGHT-FALL

OH, soothing hour, when glowing day
   Low on the western wave declines,
And village murmurs die away,
   And bright the vesper planet shines !

I love to hear the gale of even,
   Breathing along the dew-leaf'd copse,
And feel the fresh'ning dew of heaven
   Fall silently in limpid drops.

For like a friend's consoling sighs,
   That breeze of night to me appears ;
And as soft dew from pity's eyes,
   Descend those pure celestial tears.

Alas ! for those, who long have borne,
Like me, a heart by sorrow riven,
Who, but the plaintive winds will mourn ?
What tears will fall but those of heaven ?

CHARLOTTE SMITH.

CXCIII

TIME AND GRIEF

O TIME ! who know'st a lenient hand to lay
Softest on sorrow's wound, and slowly thence
(Lulling to sad repose the weary sense)
The faint pang stealest unperceived away ;

On thee I rest my only hope at last,
And think, when thou hast dried the bitter tear
That flows in vain o'er all my soul held dear,
I may look back on every sorrow past,

And meet life's peaceful evening with a smile :—
As some lone bird, at day's departing hour,
Sings in the sunbeam, of the transient shower,
Forgetful, though its wings are wet the while :—

Yet ah ! how much must the poor heart endure,
Which hopes from thee, and thee alone, a cure !

W. LISLE BOWLES.

REMEMBRANCE

THE season comes when first we met,
　But you return no more ;
Why cannot I the days forget,
　Which time can ne'er restore ?
O days too sweet, too bright to last,
Are you indeed for ever past ?

The fleeting shadows of delight,
　In memory I trace ;
In fancy stop their rapid flight
　And all the past replace :
But ah ! I wake to endless woes,
And tears the fading visions close !

　　　　　　　　MRS. ANNE HUNTER.

A POET'S EPITAPH

O STRANGER ! if thy wayward lot
Through Folly's heedless maze has led,
Here nurse the true, the tender thought,
And fling the wild flow'r on his head.

For he, by this cold hillock clad,
Where tall grass twines the pointed stone,
Each gentlest balm of feeling had,
To soothe all sorrow but his own.

For he, by tuneful Fancy rear'd,
(Though ever dumb he sleeps below),
The stillest sigh of anguish heard,
And gave a tear to ev'ry woe.

Then, stranger, be his foibles lost ;
At such small foibles virtue smil'd :
Few was their number, large their cost,
For he was Nature's orphan child.

When taught by life its pangs to know,
Ah ! as thou roam'st the checker'd gloom,
Bid the sweet night-bird's numbers flow,
And the last sunbeam light his tomb.

T. DERMODY.

CXCVI

THE FLOWERS OF THE FOREST

I've heard them lilting, at the ewe milking,
  Lasses a' lilting, before dawn of day ;
But now they are moaning, on ilka green loaning ;
  The flowers of the forest are a' wede awae.

At bughts in the morning, nae blithe lads are scorning;
    Lasses are lonely, and dowie and wae ;
Nae dagging, nae gabbing, but sighing and sabbing;
    Ilk ane lifts her leglin, and hies her awae.

In har'st at the shearing, nae youths now are jeering;
    Bandsters are runkled, and lyart or gray ;
At fair, or at preaching, nae wooing, nae fleeching;
    The flowers of the forest are a' wede awae.

At e'en, in the gloaming, nae swankies are roaming,
    'Bout stacks, wi' the lasses at bogle to play ;
But ilk maid sits drearie, lamenting her dearie—
    The flowers of the forest are a' wede awae.

Dule and wae for the order, sent our lads to the border !
    The English, for ance, by guile wan the day;
The flowers of the forest, that foucht aye the foremost,
    The prime o' our land, are cauld in the clay.

We hear nae mair lilting, at the ewe milking,
    Women and bairns are heartless and wae :
Sighing and moaning on ilka green loaning—
    The flowers of the forest are a' wede awae.

                                        JANE ELLIOT.

A RETROSPECT

Twenty lost years have stolen their hours away,
Since in this inn, e'en in this room I lay.
How chang'd! what then was rapture, fire, and air,
Seems now sad silence all and blank despair.

Is it that youth paints every view too bright,
And, life advancing, fancy fades her light!
Ah! no,—nor yet is day so far declin'd,
Nor can time's creeping coldness reach the mind.

'Tis that I miss th' inspirer of that youth;
Her, whose soft smile was love, whose soul was truth;
Death snatch'd my joys, by cutting off her share,
But left her griefs to multiply my care.

Pensive and cold this room in each chang'd part,
I view, and shock'd from ev'ry object start;
There hung the watch that, beating hours from day,
Told its sweet owner's lessening life away.

There her dear diamond taught the sash my name,
'Tis gone! frail image of love, life, and fame;
That glass she dress'd at, keeps her form no more,
Not one dear footstep tunes th' unconscious floor.

Oh life ! deceitful lure of lost desires !
How short thy period, yet how fierce thy fires !
Scarce can a passion start, we change so fast,
Ere new lights strike us, and the old are past.

Schemes following schemes, so long life's taste explore,
That ere we learn to live, we live no more.
Who then can think, yet sigh to part with breath,
Or shun the healing hand of friendly death ?

A. HILL.

CXCVIII

EVENING

EVENING ! as slow thy placid shades descend,
   Veiling with gentlest hush the landscape still,
   The lonely battlement, the farthest hill
And wood, I think of those who have no friend ;

Who now, perhaps, by melancholy led,
   From the broad blaze of day, where pleasure flaunts,
   Retiring, wander to the ring-dove's haunts
Unseen ; and watch the tints that o'er thy bed

Hang lovely ; oft to musing Fancy's eye
   Presenting fairy vales, where the tired mind
   Might rest beyond the murmurs of mankind,
Nor hear the hourly moans of misery !

Alas for man ! that Hope's fair views the while
Should smile like you, and perish as they smile !

W. LISLE BOWLES.

CXCIX

EPITAPH

TAKE, holy earth, all that my soul holds dear ;
 Take that best gift which heaven so lately gave ;
To Bristol's fount I bore with trembling care
 Her faded form ; she bow'd to taste the wave,

And died. Does Youth, does Beauty, read the line ?
 Does sympathetic fear their breast alarm ?
Speak, dead Maria ! breathe a strain divine,
 Ev'n from the grave thou shalt have power to charm.

Bid them be chaste, be innocent, like thee ;
 Bid them in duty's sphere as meekly move ;
And if so fair, from vanity as free,
 So firm in friendship, and as fond in love ;

Tell them, tho' 'tis an awful thing to die,
 ('Twas ev'n to thee) yet the dread path once trod,
Heaven lifts its everlasting portals high,
 And bids the pure in heart behold their God.

W. MASON.

CC

"SECURE OF FAME AND JUSTICE IN THE GRAVE"

AH! no—when once the mortal yields to Fate,
The blast of Fame's sweet trumpet sounds too late,
Too late to stay the spirit on its flight,
Or soothe the new inhabitant of light;
Who hears regardless, while fond man, distress'd,
Hangs on the absent, and laments the blest.

Farewell, then, Fame, ill sought thro' fields and blood,
Farewell unfaithful promiser of good:
Thou music, warbling to the deafen'd ear!
Thou incense wasted on the funeral bier!
Through life pursued in vain, by death obtain'd,
When ask'd, deny'd us, and when giv'n, disdain'd.

T. TICKELL.

CCI

TO-MORROW

IN the down-hill of life, when I find I'm declining,
  May my fate no less fortunate be,
Than a snug elbow-chair will afford for reclining,
  And a cot that o'erlooks the wide sea;

With an ambling pad-pony to pace o'er the lawn,
  While I carol away idle sorrow,
And blithe as the lark that each day hails the dawn,
  Look forward with hope for To-morrow.

With a porch at my door, both for shelter and shade too,
  As the sunshine or rain may prevail,
And a small spot of ground for the use of the spade too,
  With a barn for the use of the flail :
A cow for my dairy, a dog for my game,
  And a purse when a friend wants to borrow ;
I'll envy no Nabob his riches or fame,
  Or what honours may wait him To-morrow.

From the bleak northern blast may my cot be completely
  Secured by a neighbouring hill ;
And at night may repose steal upon me more sweetly
  By the sound of a murmuring rill.
And while peace and plenty I find at my board,
  With a heart free from sickness and sorrow,
With my friends may I share what To-day may afford,
  And let them spread the table To-morrow.

And when I at last must throw off this frail cov'ring,
  Which I've worn for three score years and ten,
On the brink of the grave I'll not seek to keep hov'ring
  Nor my thread wish to spin o'er again ;

But my face in the glass I'll serenely survey,
   And with smiles count each wrinkle and furrow ;
As this old worn-out stuff, which is threadbare To-day,
   May become everlasting To-morrow.

J. COLLINS.

CCII

DEATH IN LIFE

As those we love decay, we die in part,
Tie after tie is sever'd from the heart ;
Till loosen'd life, at last but breathing clay,
Without one pang is glad to fall away.

Unhappy he, who latest feels the blow,
Whose eyes have wept o'er every friend laid low,
Dragg'd ling'ring on from partial death to death,
Till, dying, all he can resign is—breath.

J. THOMSON.

CCIII

On Parent knees, a naked new-born child,
Weeping thou sat'st while all around thee smil'd ;
So live, that sinking on thy last long sleep,
Thou then mayst smile, while all around thee weep.

SIR W. JONES.

ON THE DEATH OF MR. ROBERT LEVET

CONDEMN'D to Hope's delusive mine,
  As on we toil from day to day,
By sudden blasts, or slow decline,
  Our social comforts drop away.

Well try'd through many a varying year,
  See Levet to the grave descend,
Officious, innocent, sincere,
  Of ev'ry friendless name the friend.

Yet still he fills affection's eye,
  Obscurely wise, and coarsely kind;
Nor, letter'd Arrogance, deny
  Thy praise to merit unrefin'd.

When fainting nature call'd for aid,
  And hov'ring death prepar'd the blow,
His vigorous remedy displayed
  The power of art without the show.

In misery's darkest cavern known,
  His useful care was ever nigh,
Where hopeless anguish pour'd his groan,
  And lonely want retir'd to die.

No summons mock'd by chill delay,
　　No petty gain disdain'd by pride ;
The modest wants of ev'ry day
　　The toil of ev'ry day supply'd.

His virtues walk'd their narrow round,
　　Nor made a pause, nor left a void ;
And sure th' Eternal Master found
　　The single talent well employ'd.

The busy day—the peaceful night,
　　Unfelt, uncounted, glided by ;
His frame was firm—his powers were bright,
　　Though now his eightieth year was nigh.

Then with no fiery throbbing pain,
　　No cold gradations of decay,
Death broke at once the vital chain,
　　And freed his soul the nearest way.

DR. JOHNSON.

CCV

LINES WRITTEN AT THE HOT-WELLS, BRISTOL

WHOE'ER, like me, with trembling anguish brings
His dearest earthly treasure to these springs ;
Whoe'er, like me, to soothe distress and pain,
Shall court these salutary springs in vain ;

Condemned, like me, to hear the faint reply,
To mark the fading cheek, the sinking eye,
From the chill brow to wipe the damps of death,
And watch in dumb despair the shortening breath ;

If chance should bring him to this humble line,
Let the sad mourner know his pangs were mine.
Ordained to love the partner of my breast,
Whose virtue warmed me, and whose beauty blessed ;

Framed every tie that binds the heart to prove,
Her duty friendship, and her friendship love ;
But yet remembering that the parting sigh
Appoints the just to slumber, not to die,

The starting tear I checked—I kissed the rod,
And not to earth resigned her—but to God.

LORD PALMERSTON.

CCVI

To him is reared no marble tomb,
     Within the dim cathedral fane ;
But some faint flowers of summer bloom,
     And silent falls the wintry rain.

No village monumental stone
     Records a verse, a date, a name—
What boots it ? when thy task is done,
     Christian, how vain the sound of fame !

W. LISLE BOWLES.

LIFE! we've been long together,
Through pleasant and through cloudy weather;
'Tis hard to part when friends are dear,
Perhaps 'twill cost a sigh, a tear;
Then steal away, give little warning,
    Choose thine own time,
Say not "Good-night," but in some brighter clime
    Bid me "Good-morning."

MRS. BARBAULD.

THE DIVINE IMAGE

To Mercy, Pity, Peace, and Love,
    All pray in their distress,
And to these virtues of delight
    Return their thankfulness.

For Mercy, Pity, Peace, and Love,
    Is God our Father dear;
And Mercy, Pity, Peace, and Love,
    Is man, his child and care.

For Mercy has a human heart,
Pity, a human face ;
And Love, the human form divine,
And Peace, the human dress.

Then every man, of every clime,
That prays in his distress,
Prays to the human form divine :
Love, Mercy, Pity, Peace.

And all must love the human form,
In Heathen, Turk, or Jew ;
Where Mercy, Love, and Pity dwell,
There God is dwelling too.

W. BLAKE.

BOOK IV

LOVE'S DIET

Tell me, fair maid, tell me truly,
    How should infant Love be fed;
If with dew-drops, shed so newly
    On the bright green clover blade;
Or, with roses plucked in July,
    And with honey liquored?
        O, no! O, no!
        Let roses blow,
And dew-stars to green blade cling:
        Other fare,   ·
        More light and rare,
Befits that gentlest Nursling.

Feed him with the sigh that rushes
    'Twixt sweet lips, whose muteness speaks
With the eloquence that flushes
    All a heart's wealth o'er soft cheeks;
Feed him with a world of blushes,
    And the glance that shuns, yet seeks:
        For 'tis with food,
        So light and good,

That the spirit child is fed ;
　　And with the tear
　　Of joyous fear,
That the small Elf's liquorèd.

W. MOTHERWELL.

CCX

TO HELENE—ON A GIFT-RING CARELESSLY LOST

I SENT a ring—a little band
　　Of emerald and ruby stone,
And bade it, sparkling on thy hand,
　　Tell thee sweet tales of one
　　　　Whose constant memory
　　　　Was full of loveliness and thee.

A shell was graven on its gold,—
　　'Twas Cupid fix'd without his wings—
To Helene once it would have told
　　More than was ever told by rings,
　　　　But now all's past and gone,
　　　　Her love is buried with that stone.

Thou shalt not see the tears that start
　　From eyes by thoughts like these beguil'd ;
Thou shalt not know the beating heart,
　　Ever a victim and a child :
　　　　Yet, Helene, love—believe
　　　　The heart that never could deceive.

I'll hear thy voice of melody
  In the sweet whispers of the air ;
I'll see the brightness of thine eye
  In the blue evening's dewy star ;
  In crystal streams thy purity,
  And look on Heaven to look on thee.

G. DARLEY.

CCXI

THE TRYSTING HOUR

THE gowan glitters on the sward,
  The lavrock's in the sky,
And Collie on my plaid keeps ward,
  And time is passing by.
    Oh, no ! sad an' slow,
    And lengthen'd on the ground,
  The shadow of our trystin' bush
  It wears sae slowly round !

My sheep-bell tinkles frae the west,
  My lambs are bleating near,
But still the sound I lo'e the best,
  Alack ! I canna' hear.
    Oh, no ! sad an' slow,
    The shadow lingers still,
  And like a lanely ghaist I stand
  And croon upon the hill.

R

I hear below the water roar,
   The mill wi' clackin' din,
And Lucky scoldin' frae her door,
   To ca' the bairnies in.
     Oh, no! sad an' slow,
   These are na' sounds for me,
The shadow of our trystin' bush
   It creeps sae drearily!

Oh, now I see her on the way,
   She's past the witch's knowe,
She's climbin' up the brownies' brae,
   My heart is in a lowe!
     Oh, no! 'tis no' so,
   'Tis glam'rie I hae seen,
The shadow of that hawthorn bush
   Will move na' more till e'en.

My book o' grace I'll try to read,
   Though conn'd wi' little skill;
When Collie barks I'll raise my head,
   And find her on the hill;
     Oh, no! sad an' slow,
   The time will ne'er be gane,
The shadow of the trystin' bush
   Is fix'd like ony stane.

                   JOANNA BAILLIE.

SONG

THEY who may tell love's wistful tale,
Of half its cares are lighten'd ;
Their bark is tacking to the gale,
The sever'd cloud is brighten'd.

Love, like the silent stream, is found
Beneath the willows lurking,
The deeper, that it hath no sound
To tell its ceaseless working.

Submit, my heart ; thy lot is cast,
I feel its inward token ;
I feel this mis'ry will not last,
Yet last till thou art broken.

JOANNA BAILLIE.

A PICTURE

MY Love o'er the water bends dreaming ;
It glideth and glideth away :
She sees there her own beauty, gleaming
Through shadow and ripple and spray.

Oh, tell her, thou murmuring river,
  As past her your light wavelets roll,
How steadfast that image for ever
  Shines pure in pure depths of my soul.

J. THOMSON.

CCXIV

MEET WE NO ANGELS, PANSIE?

CAME, on a Sabbath noon, my sweet,
  In white, to find her lover;
The grass grew proud beneath her feet,
  The green elm-leaves above her;—
    Meet we no angels, Pansie?

She said, "We meet no angels now";
  And soft lights stream'd upon her;
And with white hand she touch'd a bough;
  She did it that great honour;—
    What! meet no angels, Pansie?

O sweet brown hat, brown hair, brown eyes,
  Down-dropp'd brown eyes, so tender!
Then what said I? gallant replies
  Seem flattery, and offend her;—
    But,—meet no angels, Pansie?

T. ASHE.

JEANIE MORRISON

I'VE wandered east, I've wandered west,
 Through mony a weary way ;
But never, never can forget
 The luve o' life's young day !
The fire that's blawn on Beltane e'en,
 May weel be black gin Yule ;
But blacker fa' awaits the heart
 Where first fond luve grows cule.

O dear, dear Jeanie Morrison,
 The thochts o' bygane years
Still fling their shadows ower my path,
 And blind my een wi' tears :
They blind my een wi' saut, saut tears,
 And sair and sick I pine,
As memory idly summons up
 The blithe blinks o' langsyne.

My head rins round and round about,
 My heart flows like a sea,
As ane by ane the thochts rush back
 O' scule-time and o' thee.
Oh, mornin' life ! oh, mornin' luve !
 Oh lichtsome days and lang,
When hinnied hopes around our hearts
 Like simmer blossoms sprang !

Oh mind ye, luve, how aft we left
    The deavin' dinsome toun,
To wander by the green burnside,
    And hear its waters croon?
The simmer leaves hung ower our heads,
    The flowers burst round our feet,
And in the gloamin' o' the wood,
    The throssil whusslit sweet;

The throssil whusslit in the wood,
    The burn sang to the trees,
And we with Nature's heart in tune,
    Concerted harmonies;
And on the knowe abune the burn,
    For hours thegither sat
In the silentness o' joy, till baith
    Wi' very gladness grat.

Aye, aye, dear Jeanie Morrison,
    Tears trinkled doun your cheek,
Like dew-beads on a rose, yet nane
    Had ony power to speak!
That was a time, a blessed time,
    When hearts were fresh and young,
When freely gushed all feelings forth,
    Unsyllabled—unsung!

I marvel, Jeanie Morrison,
    Gin I hae been to thee

As closely twined wi' earliest thochts,
　　As ye hae been to me?
Oh! tell me gin their music fills
　　Thine ear as it does mine;
Oh! say gin e'er your heart grows grit
　　Wi' dreamings o' langsyne?

I've wandered east, I've wandered west,
　　I've borne a weary lot;
But in my wanderings, far or near,
　　Ye never were forgot.
The fount that first burst frae this heart,
　　Still travels on its way;
And channels deeper as it rins,
　　The luve o' life's young day.

O dear, dear Jeanie Morrison,
　　Since we were sindered young,
I've never seen your face, nor heard
　　The music o' your tongue;
But I could hug all wretchedness,
　　And happy could I dee,
Did I but ken your heart still dreamed
　　O' bygane days and me!

W. MOTHERWELL.

CCXVI

LOVE

Love has turned his face away,
    Weep, sad eyes!
Love is now of yesterday.
    Time that flies,
Bringing glad and grievous things,
Bears no more Love's shining wings.

Love was not all glad, you say;
    Tears and sighs
In the midst of kisses lay.
    Were it wise,
If we could, to bid him come,
Making with us once more home?

Little doubts that sting and prey,
    Hurt replies,
Words for which a life should pay,—
    None denies
These of Love were very part,—
Thorns that hurt the rose's heart.

Yet should we beseech Love stay,
    Sorrow dies;
And if Love will but delay,
    Joy may rise.

Since, with all its thorns, the rose
Is the sweetest flower that blows.

P. B. MARSTON.

CCXVII

SERENADE

Awake thee, my Lady-love!
   Wake thee, and rise!
The sun through the bower peeps
   Into thine eyes!

Behold how the early lark
   Springs from the corn!
Hark, hark how the flower-bird
   Winds her wee horn!

The swallow's glad shriek is heard
   All through the air!
The stock-dove is murmuring
   Loud as she dare!

Then wake thee, my Lady-love!
   Bird of my bower!
The sweetest and sleepiest
   Bird at this hour.

G. DARLEY.

SONG OF THE FORSAKEN

My cheek is faded sair, love,
 An' lichtless fa's my e'e ;
My breast a' lane and bare, love,
 Has aye a beild for thee.
My breast, though lane and bare, love,
The hame o' cauld despair, love,
Yet ye've a dwallin' there, love,
 A' darksome though it be.

Yon guarded roses glowin',
 It's wha daur min't to pu' ?
But aye the wee bit gowan
 Ilk reckless hand may strew.
An' aye the wee, wee gowan,
Unsheltered, lanely growin',
Unkent, uncared its ruin,
 Sae marklessly it grew.

An' am I left to rue, then,
 Wha ne'er kent Love but thee ;
An' gae a love as true, then,
 As woman's heart can gie ?
But can ye cauldly view, then,
A bosom burstin' fu', then ?
An' hae ye broken noo, then,
 The heart ye *sought* frae me ?

W. THOM.

LIGHT

THE night has a thousand eyes,
And the day but one ;
Yet the light of the bright world dies,
With the dying sun.

The mind has a thousand eyes,
And the heart but one ;
Yet the light of a whole life dies,
When love is gone.

F. W. BOURDILLON.

Too solemn for day, too sweet for night,
Come not in darkness, come not in light ;
But come in some twilight interim,
When the gloom is soft, and the light is dim.

W. S. WALKER.

.

CCXXI

WIFE, CHILDREN, AND FRIENDS

WHEN the black-letter'd list to the gods was presented,
(The list of what fate for each mortal intends),
At the long string of ills a kind goddess relented,
And slipp'd in three blessings—wife, children, and friends.

In vain surly Pluto maintain'd he was cheated,
For justice divine could not compass its ends;
The scheme of man's penance he swore was defeated,
For earth becomes heav'n with wife, children, and friends.

If the stock of our bliss is in stranger hands vested,
The fund ill-secur'd oft in bankruptcy ends;
But the heart issues bills which are never protested,
When drawn on the firm of wife, children, and friends.

Though valour still glows in his life's waning embers,
The death-wounded tar who his colours defends,
Drops a tear of regret as he dying remembers
How blest was his home with wife, children, and friends.

The soldier, whose deeds live immortal in story,
Whom duty to far distant latitudes sends,
With transport would barter whole ages of glory
For one happy day with wife, children, and friends.

Though spice-breathing gales o'er his caravan hover,
Though round him Arabia's whole fragrance ascends,
The merchant still thinks of the woodbines that cover
The bower where he sate with wife, children, and friends.

The day-spring of youth, still unclouded by sorrow,
Alone on itself for enjoyment depends ;
But drear is the twilight of age if it borrow
No warmth from the smiles of wife, children, and friends.

Let the breath of renown ever freshen and nourish
The laurel which o'er her dead favourite bends ;
O'er me wave the willow ! and long may it flourish,
Bedew'd with the tears of wife, children, and friends.

Let us drink—for my song, growing graver and graver,
To subjects too solemn insensibly tends ;
Let us drink—pledge me high—love and virtue shall
    flavour
The glass which I fill to wife, children, and friends.

W. R. SPENCER.

CCXXII

LITTLE AGLAE

TO HER FATHER, ON HER STATUE BEING CALLED LIKE HER

FATHER ! the little girl we see
Is not, I fancy, so like me ;
You never hold her on your knee.

When she came home the other day
You kiss'd her ; but I cannot say
She kiss'd you first and ran away.

W. S. LANDOR.

CCXXIII

A PETITION TO TIME

Touch us gently, Time !
 Let us glide adown thy stream
Gently,—as we sometimes glide
 Through a quiet dream !
Humble voyagers are We,
Husband, wife, and children three—
(One is lost, an angel, fled
To the azure overhead !)

Touch us gently, Time !
 We've not proud nor soaring wings :
Our ambition, our content
 Lies in simple things.
Humble voyagers are We
O'er Life's dim unsounded sea,
Seeking only some calm clime ;—
Touch us gently, gentle Time !

B. WALLER PROCTER.

LOVE AND DEATH

I THOUGHT once how Theocritus had sung
Of the sweet years, the dear and wished-for years,
Who each one in a gracious hand appears
To bear a gift for mortals, old or young :
And, as I mused it in his antique tongue,
I saw, in gradual vision through my tears,
The sweet, sad years, the melancholy years,
Those of my own life, who by turns had flung
A shadow across me.   Straightway I was 'ware,
So weeping, how a mystic shape did move
Behind me, and drew me backward by the hair ;
And a voice said in mastery, while I strove :
" Guess now who holds thee ? "—" Death ! " I said.   But,
    there,
The silver answer rang, " Not Death, but Love ! "

MRS. BROWNING.

THERE are who say we are but dust ;
    We may be soon, but are not yet :
Nor should be while in Love we trust,
    And never what he taught forget.

W. S. LANDOR.

SONG

Go, forget me—why should sorrow
   O'er that brow a shadow fling?
Go, forget me—and to-morrow
   Brightly smile and sweetly sing.
Smile—though I shall not be near thee;
Sing—though I shall never hear thee;
   May thy soul with pleasure shine,
   Lasting as the gloom of mine.

Like the sun, thy presence glowing,
   Clothes the meanest things in light;
And when thou, like him, art going,
   Loveliest objects fade in night.
All things look'd so bright about thee,
That they nothing seem without thee;
   By that pure and lucid mind
   Earthly things were too refined.

Go, thou vision wildly gleaming,
   Softly on my soul that fell;
Go, for me no longer beaming—
   Hope and Beauty! fare ye well!

Go, and all that once delighted
Take, and leave me all benighted ;
Glory's burning—generous swell,
Fancy and the Poet's shell.

REV. C. WOLFE.

CCXXVII

Jenny kiss'd me when we met,
    Jumping from the chair she sat in ;
Time, you thief ! who love to get
    Sweets into your list, put *that* in :
Say I'm weary, say I'm sad,
    Say that health and wealth have miss'd me,
Say I'm growing old, but add,
    Jenny kiss'd me.

LEIGH HUNT.

CCXXVIII

THE NUN

If you become a nun, dear,
    A friar I will be ;
In any cell you run, dear,
    Pray look behind for me.

S

The roses all turn pale, too;
The doves all take the veil, too;
    The blind will see the show.
What! you become a nun, my dear!
    I'll not believe it, no.

If you become a nun, dear,
    The bishop Love will be;
The Cupids every one, dear,
    Will chaunt "We trust in thee."
The incense will go sighing,
The candles fall a-dying,
    The water turn to wine;
What! you go take the vows, my dear!
    You may—but they'll be mine.

LEIGH HUNT.

CCXXIX

A BOY'S SONG

WHERE the pools are bright and deep,
Where the grey trout lies asleep,
Up the river and o'er the lea,
That's the way for Billy and me.

Where the blackbird sings the latest,
Where the hawthorn blooms the sweetest,
Where the nestlings chirp and flee,
That's the way for Billy and me.

Where the mowers mow the cleanest,
Where the hay lies thick and greenest ;
There to trace the homeward bee,
That's the way for Billy and me.

Where the hazel bank is steepest,
Where the shadow falls the deepest,
Where the clustering nuts fall free,
That's the way for Billy and me.

Why the boys should drive away
Little sweet maidens from the play,
Or love to banter and fight so well,
That's the thing I never could tell.

But this I know, I love to play,
Through the meadow, among the hay ;
Up the water and o'er the lea,
That's the way for Billy and me.

J. HOGG.

CCXXX

THE SKYLARK

BIRD of the wilderness,
Blithesome and cumberless,
Sweet be thy matin o'er moorland and lea !
Emblem of happiness,
Blest is thy dwelling-place,—
Oh to abide in the desert with thee !

Wild is thy lay and loud,
Far in the downy cloud,
Love gives it energy, love gave it birth.
Where, on thy dewy wing,
Where art thou journeying?
Thy lay is in heaven, thy love is on earth.

O'er fell and fountain sheen,
O'er moor and mountain green,
O'er the red streamer that heralds the day,
Over the cloudlet dim,
Over the rainbow's rim,
Musical cherub, soar, singing, away!

Then, when the gloaming comes,
Low in the heather blooms
Sweet will thy welcome and bed of love be!
Emblem of happiness,
Blest is thy dwelling-place—
Oh to abide in the desert with thee!

J. HOGG.

CCXXXI

ECHO AND SILENCE

In eddying course when leaves began to fly,
And autumn in her lap the stores to strew,
As 'mid wild scenes I chanced the muse to woo
Thro' glens untrod, and woods that frown'd on high,

Two sleeping nymphs, with wonder mute I spy :—
And lo ! she's gone—in robe of dark green hue
'Twas Echo from her sister Silence flew :
For quick the hunter's horn resounded to the sky.

In shade affrighted Silence melts away.
Not so her sister.   Hark ! for onward still
With far-heard step she takes her listening way,
Bounding from rock to rock, and hill to hill :

Ah ! mark the merry maid, in mockful play,
With thousand mimic tones the laughing forest fill !

SIR EGERTON BRYDGES.

CCXXXII

THE HERON

O MELANCHOLY Bird, a winter's day,
Thou standest by the margin of the pool,
And, taught by God, dost thy whole being school
To Patience, which all evil can allay.

God has appointed thee the Fish thy prey ;
And giv'n thyself a lesson to the Fool
Unthrifty, to submit to moral rule,
And his unthinking course by thee to weigh.

There need not schools, nor the Professor's chair,
Though these be good, true wisdom to impart ;
He, who has not enough for these to spare,
Of time, or gold, may yet amend his heart,

And teach his soul, by brooks and rivers fair :
Nature is always wise in every part.

EDWARD, LORD THURLOW.

CCXXXIII

SNOWDROPS

O DARLING spirits of the snow,
    Who hide within your heart the green,
Howe'er the wintry wind may blow,
    The secret of the summer sheen
        Ye smile to know !

By frozen rills, in woods and mead,
    A mild pure sisterhood ye grow,
Who bend the meek and quiet head,
    And are a token from below
        From our dear dead.

As in their turf ye softly shine
Of innocent white lives they lead,
With healing influence Divine
For souls who on their memory feed,
World-worn like mine.

RODEN NOEL.

CCXXXIV

SONG TO MAY

May, queen of blossoms,
And fulfilling flowers,
With what pretty music
Shall we charm the hours?
Wilt thou have pipe and reed,
Blown in the open mead?
Or to the lute give heed
In the green bowers?

Thou hast no need of us,
Or pipe or wire,
That hast the golden bee
Ripened with fire;
And many thousand more
Songsters, that thee adore
Filling earth's grassy floor
With new desire.

Thou hast thy mighty herds,
  Tame, and free-livers;
Doubt not, thy music too
  In the deep rivers;
And the whole plumy flight,
Warbling the day and night—
Up at the gates of light,
  See, the lark quivers!

EDWARD, LORD THURLOW.

CCXXXV

OSME'S SONG

HITHER! hither!
O come hither!
Lads and lasses come and see!
  Trip it neatly,
  Foot it featly,
O'er the grassy turf to me!

Here are bowers
Hung with flowers,
Richly curtain'd halls for you!
  Meads for rovers,
  Shades for lovers,
Violet beds, and pillows too!

Purple heather
You may gather,
Sandal-deep in seas of bloom !
Pale-faced lily,
Proud Sweet-Willy,
Gorgeous rose, and golden broom !

Odorous blossoms
For sweet bosoms,
Garlands green to bind the hair ;
Crowns and kirtles
Weft of myrtles,
You may choose, and Beauty wear !

Brightsome glasses
For bright faces
Shine in ev'ry rill that flows ;
Every minute
You look in it
Still more bright your beauty grows !

Banks for sleeping,
Nooks for peeping,
Glades for dancing, smooth and fine !
Fruits delicious
For who wishes,
Nectar, dew, and honey wine !

Hither ! hither !
O come hither !
Lads and lasses come and see !
Trip it neatly,
Foot it featly,
O'er the grassy turf to me !

G. DARLEY.

CCXXXVI

BUTTERFLY BEAU

I'M a volatile thing, with an exquisite wing,
  Sprinkled o'er with the tints of the rainbow ;
All the Butterflies swarm to behold my sweet form,
  Though the Grubs may all vote me a vain beau.
I my toilet go through, with my rose-water dew,
  And each blossom contributes its essence ;
Then all fragrance and grace, not a plume out of place,
  I adorn the gay world with my presence—
    In short, you must know,
    I'm the Butterfly Beau.

At first I enchant a fair Sensitive plant,
  Then I flirt with the Pink of perfection :
Then I seek a sweet Pea, and I whisper, " For thee
  I have long felt a fond predilection."

A Lily I kiss, and exult in my bliss,
 But I very soon search for a new lip ;
And I pause in my flight to exclaim with delight,
 " Oh ! how dearly I love you, my Tulip ! "
  In short, you must know,
  I'm the Butterfly Beau.

Thus for ever I rove, and the honey of love
 From each delicate blossom I pilfer ;
But though many I see pale and pining for me,
 I know none that are worth growing ill for :
And though I must own, there are some that I've
  known,
 Whose external attractions are splendid ;
On myself I most doat, for in my pretty coat
 All the tints of the garden are blended—
  In short, you must know,
  I'm the Butterfly Beau.

T. HAYNES BAYLY.

CCXXXVII

AFTER SUMMER

WE'LL not weep for summer over,
  No, not we ;
Strew above his head the clover,
  Let him be !

Other eyes may weep his dying,
    Shed their tears
There upon him where he's lying
    With his peers.

Unto some of them he proffered
    Gifts most sweet;
For our hearts a grace he offered,—
    Was this meet?

All our fond hopes, praying, perished
    In his wrath,—
All the lovely dreams we cherished
    Strewed his path.

Shall we in our tombs, I wonder,
    Far apart,
Sundered wide as seas can sunder
    Heart from heart,

Dream at all of all the sorrows
    That were ours,—
Bitter nights, more bitter morrows;
    Poison-flowers

Summer gathered, as in madness,
    Saying, "See,
These are yours, in place of gladness,—
    Gifts from me!"

Nay, the rest that will be ours
Is supreme,—
And below the poppy flowers
Steals no dream.

P. B. MARSTON.

CCXXXVIII

BUTTERFLY LIFE

WHAT, though you tell me each gay little rover
  Shrinks from the breath of the first autumn day !
Surely 'tis better, when summer is over,
  To die when all fair things are fading away.
Some in life's winter may toil to discover
  Means of procuring a weary delay—
I'd be a Butterfly ; living, a rover,
  Dying when fair things are fading away !

T. HAYNES BAYLY.

CCXXXIX

THE BLIND LASSIE

O HARK to the strain that sae sweetly is ringin',
  And echoing clearly o'er lake and o'er lea ;
Like some fairy bird in the wilderness singin',
  It thrills to my heart, yet nae minstrel I see ;
Round yonder rock knittin', a dear child is sittin',
  Sae toilin' her pitifu' pittance is won,
Hersell tho' we see nae, 'tis mitherless Jeanie,—
  The bonnie blind lassie that sits i' the sun.

Five years syne, come autumn, she cam' wi' her mither,
  A sodger's puir widow, sair wasted an' gane ;
As brown fell the leaves, sae wi' them did she wither,
  An' left the sweet child on the wide world alane.
She left Jeanie weepin', in His holy keepin',
  Wha shelters the lamb frae the cauld wintry win',
We had little siller, yet a' were gude till her,—
  The bonnie blind lassie that sits i' the sun.

An' blythe now an' cheerfu', frae mornin' to e'enin',
  She sits thro' the simmer, an' gladdens ilk ear ;
Baith auld and young daut her, sae gentle an' winnin',
  To a' the folks round, the wee lassie is dear.
Braw leddies caress her, wi' bounties would press her,
  The modest bit darlin' their notice would shun,
For though she has naething, proud hearted this wee
    thing—
  The bonnie blind lassie that sits i' the sun.

T. C. LATTO.

CCXL

IT'S HAME AND IT'S HAME

It's hame, and it's hame, hame fain wad I be,
An' it's hame, hame, hame, to my ain countree !
When the flower is i' the bud and the leaf is on the tree,
The lark shall sing me hame in my ain countree ;
It's hame, and it's hame, hame fain wad I be,
An' it's hame, hame, hame, to my ain countree !

The green leaf o' loyaltie's beginning for to fa',
The bonnie white rose it is withering an' a';
But I'll water't wi' the blude of usurping tyrannie,
An' green it will grow in my ain countree ;
It's hame, and it's hame, hame fain wad I be,
And it's hame, hame, hame, to my ain countree !

There's naught now frae ruin my country can save,
But the keys o' kind heaven to open the grave,
That a' the noble martyrs who died for loyaltie,
May rise again and fight for their ain countree ;
It's hame, and it's hame, hame fain wad I be,
An' it's hame, hame, hame, to my ain countree.

The great now are gane, a' who ventured to save,
The new grass is springing on the tap o' their grave ;
But the sun thro' the mirk blinks blythe in my ee :
"I'll shine on ye yet in your ain countree";
It's hame, and it's hame, hame fain wad I be,
An' it's hame, hame, hame, to my ain countree.

A. CUNNINGHAM.

CCXLI

THE STANDING TOAST

THE moon on the ocean was dimm'd by a ripple,
  Affording a chequer'd delight,
The gay jolly tars pass'd the word for the tipple,
  And the toast, for 'twas Saturday night :

Some sweetheart or wife that he loved as his life
    Each drank while he wish'd he could hail her;
But the standing toast that pleased the most
    Was—The wind that blows, the ship that goes,
And the lass that loves a sailor!

Some drank the king and his brave ships,
    And some the constitution,
Some, "May our foes and all such rips
    Own English resolution!"
That fate might bless some Poll or Bess,
    And that they soon might hail her,
But the standing toast that pleased the most
    Was—The wind that blows, the ship that goes,
And the lass that loves a sailor!

Some drank our queen, and some our land,
    Our glorious land of freedom!
Some that our tars might never stand
    For heroes brave to lead 'em!
That beauty in distress might find
    Such friends as ne'er would fail her;
But the standing toast that pleased the most
    Was—The wind that blows, the ship that goes,
And the lass that loves a sailor!

C. DIBDIN.

CCXLII

THE SEA PINK

I'VE a yacht in the Island, the Sea Pink, of Ryde,
  Not a craft in the club can be better;
I own, when she goes very much on one side,
  I'm afraid that the wind will upset her.
I belong to the Club, which is very genteel—
  We ne'er let a Scamp or a Shab in;
But though it's the fashion, I own that I feel
  More at ease in my Cab than my Cabin!

'Tis true, I know little of nautical ways,
  And less about charts of the ocean;
And what's rather odd, on the quietest days
  I always grow queer with the motion!
I've sunk a large sum on the toy, and 'tis well
  If the toy and I don't sink together;
Oh! talking of sinking—nobody can tell
  What I suffer in very bad weather!

When I sigh for the land, sailors talk of "sea-room,"
  All sense of propriety lacking;
And they gave me a knock-me-down blow with the boom,
  T'other day, in the hurry of tacking.
I sported one morning a water-proof cap,
  And a Mackintosh—all India-rubber;
And a sailor cried, "Jack, look at that 'ere queer chap,
  Did you ever see such a land-lubber?"

T

What a bother the wind is ! one day we were caught
 In a bit of a breeze in the offing ;
And we tack'd, and we tack'd, till I verily thought
 Every tack was a nail in my coffin !
Cried one, " Never fear, we shall soon reach the shore,"
 (To me that word reach is pathetic !)
I've heard of perpetual Blisters before,
 But I've an eternal emetic !

The Captain and Crew are of course in my pay,
 I expect them to pay me attention ;
But they push me about, and they now and then say
 Little words it would shock me to mention !
The smell of the tar I detest, and I think
 That the sea breeze quite spoils the complexion,
But the ladies all say, when they've seen the Sea Pink,
 That her Owner's the Pink of Perfection.

T. HAYNES BAYLY.

CCXLIII

SONG

 Blow high, blow low, let tempests tear
  The mainmast by the board ;
 My heart with thoughts of thee, my dear,
  And love, well-stored,

Shall brave all danger, scorn all fear,
 The roaring winds, the raging sea,
  In hopes on shore
  To be once more,
 Safe moor'd with thee !

Aloft, while mountains high we go,
 The whistling winds that scud along,
And the surge roaring from below,
  Shall my signal be,
  To think on thee,
 And this shall be my song :
  Blow high, blow low, let tempests tear
  The mainmast from the board.

And on that night when all the crew,
 The memory of their former lives
O'er flowing cups of flip renew,
 And drink their sweethearts and their wives,
I'll heave a sigh, and think on thee ;
And, as the ship rolls through the sea,
 The burden of my song shall be—
  Blow high, blow low, let tempests tear
  The mainmast by the board.

C. DIBDIN.

A PICTURE

Lo ! in storms, the triple-headed
  Hill, whose dreaded
Bases battle with the seas,
Looms across fierce widths of fleeting
  Waters beating
Evermore on roaring leas !

Arakoon, the black, the lonely !
  Housed with only
Cloud and rain-wind, mist and damp ;
Round whose foam-drenched feet and nether
  Depths, together
Sullen sprites of thunder tramp !

There the East hums loud and surly,
  Late and early,
Through the chasms and the caves,
And across the naked verges
  Leap the surges !
White and wailing waifs of waves.

Day by day the sea fogs gathered—
  Tempest-fathered—
Pitch their tents on yonder peak,
Yellow drifts and fragments lying
  Where the flying
Torrents chafe the cloven creek !

And at nightfall, when the driven
    Bolts of heaven
Smite the rock and break the bluff,
Thither troop the elves whose home is
    Where the foam is,
And the echo, and the clough.

Ever girt about with noises,
    Stormy voices,
And the salt breath of the Strait,
Stands the steadfast Mountain Giant,
    Grim, reliant,
Dark as Death, and firm as Fate.

                                    H. C. KENDALL.

CCXLV

THE TAMAR SPRING

Fount of a rushing river! wild flowers wreathe
    The home where thy first waters sunlight claim;
The lark sits hushed beside thee, while I breathe,
    Sweet Tamar Spring! the music of thy name.

On! through thy goodly channel, on! to the sea!
    Pass amid heathery vale, tall rock, fair bough;
But nevermore with footstep pure and free,
    Or face so meek with happiness as now.

Fair is the future scenery of thy days,
    Thy course domestic, and thy paths of pride;
Depths that give back the soft-eyed violet's gaze,
    Shores where tall navies march to meet the tide.

Yet false the vision, and untrue the dream,
    That lures thee from thy native wilds to stray;
A thousand griefs will mingle with that stream,
    Unnumbered hearts shall sigh those waves away.

Scenes fierce with men, thy seaward current laves,
    Harsh multitudes will throng thy gentle brink;
Back with the grieving concourse of thy waves,
    Home to the waters of thy childhood shrink!

Thou heedest not! thy dream is of the shore,—
    Thy heart is quick with life; on! to the sea!
How will the voice of thy far streams implore,
    Again amid these peaceful weeds to be!

My Soul! my Soul! a happier choice be thine,—
    Thine the hushed valley, and the lonely sod;
False dream, far vision, hollow hope resign,
    Fast by our Tamar Spring, alone with God!

                                        R. S. HAWKER.

CCXLVI

MIDNIGHT

O God ! this is a holy hour,
Thy breath is o'er the land ;
I feel it in each little flower
Around me where I stand,—
In all the moonshine scattered fair,
Above, below me, everywhere,—
In every dew-bead glistening sheen,
In every leaf and blade of green,—
And in this silence grand and deep
Wherein Thy blessed creatures sleep.

Men say, that in this midnight hour,
The disembodied have power
To wander as it liketh them,
By wizard oak and fairy stream,
Through still and solemn places,
And by old walls and tombs, to dream,
With pale, cold, mournful faces.
I fear them not ; for they must be
Spirits of kindest sympathy,
Who choose such haunts, and joy to feel
The beauties of this calm night steal
Like music o'er them, while they woo'd
The luxury of Solitude.

W. MOTHERWELL.

KIRKSTALL ABBEY REVISITED

LONG years have passed since last I strayed,
   In boyhood, through thy roofless aisle,
And watched the mists of eve o'ershade
   Day's latest, loveliest smile ;—
And saw the bright, broad, moving moon
Sail up the sapphire skies of June !

The air around was breathing balm ;
   The aspen scarcely seemed to sway ;
And, as a sleeping infant calm,
   The river flowed away,
Devious as error, deep as love,
   And blue and bright as heaven above !

How bright is every scene beheld
   In youth and hope's unclouded hours ;
How darkly, youth and hope dispelled,
   The loveliest prospect lowers :
Thou wert a splendid vision then ;—
When wilt thou seem so bright again !

Yet still thy turrets drink the light
   Of summer evening's softest ray,
And ivy garlands, green and bright,
   Still mantle thy decay ;

And calm and beauteous as of old,
Thy wandering river glides in gold.

But life's gay morn of ecstasy,
    That made thee seem so passing fair,—
The aspirations wild and high,
    The soul to nobly dare,—
Oh, where are they, stern ruin, say?—
Thou dost but echo—where are they!

Adieu!—Be still to other hearts
    What thou wert long ago to mine;
And when the blissful dream departs,
    Do thou a beacon shine,
To guide the mourner, through his tears,
    To the blest scenes of happier years.

A. A. WATTS.

CCXLVIII

THE soul of music slumbers in the shell,
Till waked and kindled by the master's spell;
And feeling hearts—touch them but rightly—pour
A thousand melodies unheard before.

S. ROGERS.

CCXLIX

RETIREMENT

RETIRE, and timely, from the world, if ever
    Thou hopest tranquil days;
Its gaudy jewels from thy bosom sever,
    Despise its pomp and praise.
The purest star that looks into the stream
    Its slightest ripple shakes,
And Peace, where'er its fiercer splendours gleam,
    Her brooding nest forsakes.
The quiet planets roll with even motion
    In the still skies alone;
O'er ocean they dance joyously, but ocean
    They find no rest upon.

W. S. LANDOR.

CCL

NIGHT AND DEATH

MYSTERIOUS Night! when our first Parent knew
Thee from report divine, and heard thy name,
Did he not tremble for this lovely Frame,
This glorious canopy of Light and Blue?

Yet 'neath a curtain of translucent dew,
Bathed in the rays of the great setting Flame,
Hesperus with the Host of Heaven came,
And lo! Creation widen'd on Man's view.

Who could have thought such Darkness lay concealed
Within thy beams, O Sun! or who could find,
Whilst flow'r, and leaf, and insect stood revealed,
That to such countless orbs thou mad'st us blind!

Why do we then shun Death with anxious strife?
If Light can thus deceive, wherefore not Life?

J. BLANCO WHITE.

CCLI

THERE IS A LIGHT

THERE is a light unseen of eye,
   A light unborn of sun or star,
Pervading earth, and sea, and sky,
   Beside us still, yet still afar:

A power, a charm, whose web is wrought
   Round all we see, or feel, or know,
Round all the world of sense and thought,
   Our love and hate, our joy and woe.

It goes, it comes; like wandering wind,
   Unsought it comes, unbidden goes:
Now flashing sun-like o'er the mind,
   Now quench'd in dark and cold repose.

It sweeps o'er the great frame of things,
   As o'er a lyre of varied tone,
Searching the sweets of all its strings,
   Which answer to that touch alone.

From midnight darkness it can wake
   A glory, bright as summer sea;
And can of utter silence make
   A vast and solemn harmony.

To the white dawn and moonlight heaven,
   The flower's soft breath, the breeze's moan,
The rain-cloud's hues, its spell hath given
   A life, a meaning not their own.

W. S. WALKER.

CCLII

THE GIFT

O happy glow, O sun-bathed tree,
   O golden-lighted river,
A love-gift has been given to me,
   And which of you is giver?

I came upon you something sad,
   Musing a mournful measure,
Now all my heart in me is glad
   With a quick sense of pleasure.

I came upon you with a heart
   Half sick of life's vexed story,
And now it grows of you a part,
   Steep'd in your golden glory.

A smile into my heart has crept
   And laughs through all my being ;
New joy into my life has leapt,
   A joy of only seeing !

O happy glow, O sun-bathed tree,
   O golden-lighted river,
A love gift has been given to me,
   And which of you is giver ?

                AUGUSTA WEBSTER.

CCLIII

MAIDEN MAY

MAIDEN May sat in her bower ;
Her own face was like a flower
   Of the prime,
Half in sunshine, half in shower,
   In the year's most tender time.

Her own thoughts in silent song
Musically flowed along,
    Wise, unwise,
Wistful, wondering, weak or strong,
   As brook shallows sink or rise.

Other thoughts another day,
Maiden May, will surge and sway
    Round your heart;
Wake, and plead, and turn at bay,
   Wisdom part, and folly part.

Time not far remote will borrow
Other joys, another sorrow,
    All for you;
Not to-day, and yet to-morrow
   Reasoning false and reasoning true.

Wherefore greatest? Wherefore least?
Hearts that starve and hearts that feast?
    You and I?
Stammering oracles have ceased,
   And the whole earth stands at " why? "

Underneath all things that be
Lies an unsolved mystery;
    Over all
Spreads a veil impenetrably,
   Spreads a dense unlifted pall.

Mystery of mysteries :
This creation hears and sees
 High and low—
Vanity of vanities :
 This we test and *this* we know.

Maiden May, the days of flowering
Nurse you now in sweet embowering,
 Sunny days ;
Bright with rainbows all the showering,
 Bright with blossoms all the ways.

Close the inlet of your bower,
Close it close with thorn and flower,
 Maiden May ;
Lengthen out the shortening hour,—
 Morrows are not as to-day.

Stay to-day which wanes too soon,
Stay the sun and stay the moon,
 Stay your youth ;
Bask you in the actual noon,
 Rest you in the present truth.

Let to-day suffice to-day :
For itself to-morrow may
 Fetch its loss,
Aim and stumble, say its say,
 Watch and pray and bear its cross.

CHRISTINA G. ROSSETTI.

BY AND BY

WAITING, waiting. 'Tis so far
  To the day that is to come :
One by one the days that are
  All to tell their countless sum ;
Each to dawn and each to die—
What so far as by and by ?

Waiting, waiting. 'Tis not ours,
  This to-day that flies so fast :
Let them go, the shadowy hours
  Floating, floated, into Past.
Our day wears to-morrow's sky,—
What so near as by and by ?

AUGUSTA WEBSTER.

MIMNERMUS IN CHURCH

You promise heavens free from strife,
  Pure truth, and perfect change of will ;
But sweet, sweet is this human life,
  So sweet, I fain would breathe it still :
Your chilly stars I can forego,
This warm, kind world is all I know.

You say there is no substance here,
  One great reality above :
Back from that void I shrink in fear,
  And child-like hide myself in love.
Show me what angels feel ; till then,
I cling, a mere weak man, to men.

You bid me lift my mean desires
  From faltering lips and fitful veins
To sexless souls, ideal quires,
  Unwearied voices, wordless strains ;
My mind with fonder welcome owns
One dear dead friend's remembered tones.

Forsooth the present we must give
  To that which cannot pass away ;
All beauteous things for which we live
  By laws of time and space decay.
But oh, the very reason why
I clasp them, is because they die.

W. CORY.

CCLVI

CARPE DIEM

YOUTH, that pursuest with such eager pace
    Thy even way,
Thou pantest on to win a mournful race :
    Then stay ! oh, stay !

U

Pause and luxuriate in thy sunny plain ;
                    Loiter,—enjoy :
Once past, thou never wilt come back again,
                    A second Boy.

The hills of Manhood wear a noble face,
                    When seen from far ;
The mist of light from which they take their grace
                    Hides what they are.

The dark and weary path those cliffs between
                    Thou canst not know,
And how it leads to regions never green,
                    Dead fields of snow.

Pause, while thou mayst, nor deem that fate thy gain,
                    Which, all too fast,
Will drive thee forth from this delicious plain,
                    A Man at last.

                              LORD HOUGHTON.

CCLVII

THE CHAUNT OF THE BRAZEN HEAD

I THINK, whatever mortals crave,
        With impotent endeavour,—
A wreath, a rank, a throne, a grave,—
        The world goes round for ever :

I think that life is not too long;
And therefore I determine,
That many people read a song
Who will not read a sermon.

I think you've looked through many hearts,
And mused on many actions,
And studied Man's component parts,
And Nature's compound fractions:
I think you've picked up truth by bits
From foreigner and neighbour;
I think the world has lost its wits,
And you have lost your labour.

I think the studies of the wise,
The Hero's noisy quarrel,
The majesty of Woman's eyes,
The poet's cherished laurel,
And all that makes us lean or fat,
And all that charms and troubles,—
This bubble is more bright than that,
But still they all are bubbles.

I think the thing you call Renown,
The unsubstantial vapour,
For which the soldier burns a town,
The sonneteer a taper,
Is like the mist which, as he flies,
The horseman leaves behind him;
He cannot mark its wreaths arise,
Or if he does they blind him.

I think one nod of Mistress Chance
    Makes creditors of debtors,
And shifts the funeral for the dance,
    The sceptre for the fetters :
I think that Fortune's favoured guest
    May live to gnaw the platters,
And he that wears the purple vest
    May wear the rags and tatters.

I think the Tories love to buy
    "Your Lordship"s and "your Grace"s,
By loathing common honesty,
    And lauding commonplaces :
I think that some are very wise,
    And some are very funny,
And some grow rich by telling lies,
    And some by telling money.

I think the Whigs are wicked knaves—
    (And very like the Tories)—
Who doubt that Britain rules the waves,
    And ask the price of glories :
I think that many fret and fume
    At what their friends are planning,
And Mr. Hume hates Mr. Brougham
    As much as Mr. Canning.

I think that friars and their hoods,
    Their doctrines and their maggots,

Have lighted up too many feuds,
    And far too many faggots.
I think, while zealots fast and frown,
    And fight for two or seven,
That there are fifty roads to Town,
    And rather more to Heaven.

I think that Love is like a play,
    Where tears and smiles are blended,
Or like a faithless April day,
    Whose shine with shower is ended :
Like Colnbrook pavement, rather rough,
    Like trade, exposed to losses,
And like a Highland plaid,—all stuff,
    And very full of crosses.

I think the world, though dark it be,
    Has aye one rapturous pleasure
Concealed in life's monotony,
    For those who seek the treasure :
One planet in a starless night,
    One blossom on a briar,
One friend not quite a hypocrite,
    One woman not a liar !

I think poor beggars court St. Giles,
    Rich beggars court St. Stephen ;
And Death looks down with nods and smiles,
    And makes the odds all even.

I think some die upon the field,
  And some upon the billow,
And some are laid beneath a shield,
  And some beneath a willow.

I think that very few have sighed
  When Fate at last has found them,
Though bitter foes were by their side,
  And barren moss around them :
I think that some have died of drought,
  And some have died of drinking ;
I think that nought is worth a thought,—
  And I'm a fool for thinking !

W. M. PRAED.

CCLVIII

HOPE AND WISDOM

YOUTH is the virgin nurse of tender Hope,
  And lifts her up and shows a far-off scene :
When Care with heavy tread would interlope,
  They call the boys to shout her from the green

Ere long another comes, before whose eyes
  Nurseling and nurse alike stand mute and quail :
Wisdom : to her Hope not one word replies,
  And Youth lets drop the dear romantic tale.

W. S. LANDOR.

HOPE

Gate that never wholly closes,
    Opening yet so oft in vain !
Garden full of thorny roses !
    Roses fall, and thorns remain.

Wayward lamp, with flickering lustre
    Shining far or shining near,
Seldom words of truth revealing,
    Ever showing words of cheer.

Promise-breaker, yet unfailing !
    Faithless flatterer ! comrade true !
Only friend, when traitor proven,
    Whom we always trust anew.

Courtier strange, whom triumph frighteth,
    Flying far from pleasure's eye,
Who by sorrow's side alighteth
    When all else are passing by.

Syren-singer ! ever chanting
    Ditties new to burdens old ;
Precious stone the sages sought for,
    Turning everything to gold !

True philosopher ! imparting
　　Comfort rich to spirits pained ;
Chider of proud triumph's madness,
　　Pointing to the unattained !

Timid warrior !　Doubt, arising,
　　Scares thee with the slightest breath ;
Matchless chief ! who, fear despising,
　　Tramples on the darts of death !

O'er the grave, past Time's pursuing,
　　Far thy flashing glory streams,
Too unswerving, too resplendent,
　　For a child of idle dreams.

Still, life's fitful vigil keeping,
　　Feed the flame and trim the light :
Hope's the lamp I'll take for sleeping
　　When I wish the world good-night.

E. C. JONES.

CCLX

EARTHLY AND HEAVENLY HOPE

REFLECTED on the lake I love
　　To see the stars of evening glow,
So tranquil in the heavens above,
　　So restless in the wave below.

Thus heavenly hope is all serene,
But earthly hope, how bright soe'er,
Still fluctuates o'er this changing scene
As false and fleeting as 'tis fair.

BISHOP HEBER.

CCLXI

DREAM PEDLARY

IF there were dreams to sell,
    What would you buy?
Some cost a passing bell,
    Some a light sigh;
That shakes from Life's fresh crown
Only a rose-leaf down.
If there were dreams to sell
Merry and sad to tell,
And the crier rang the bell,
    Which would you buy?

A cottage lone and still,
    With bowers nigh,
Shadowy, my woes to still
    Until I die.
Such pearl from Life's fresh crown
Fain would I shake me down;
Were dreams to have at will,
This would best heal my ill,
    This would I buy.

T. L. BEDDOES.

POPULAR THEOLOGY

"There is no God," the wicked saith,
  "And truly it's a blessing,
For what He might have done with us
  It's better only guessing."

"There is no God," a youngster thinks,
  "Or really, if there may be,
He surely didn't mean a man
  Always to be a baby."

"There is no God, or, if there is,"
  The tradesman thinks, "'twere funny
If He should take it ill in me
  To make a little money!"

"Whether there be," the rich man says,
  "It matters very little;
For I and mine, thank somebody,
  Are not in want of victual."

Some others, also, to themselves,
  Who scarce so much as doubt it,
Think there is none, when they are well,
  And do not think about it.

But country folks who live beneath
  The shadow of the steeple ;
The parson and the parson's wife,
  And mostly married people ;

Youths green and happy in first love,
  So thankful for illusion ;
And men caught out in what the world
  Calls guilt, in first confusion ;

And almost every one when age,
  Disease, or sorrows strike him,
Inclines to think there is a God,
  Or something very like Him.

                        A. H. CLOUGH.

CCLXIII

PRAYER TO DIANA

SINCE thou and the stars, my dear goddess, decree,
That, old maid as I am, an old maid I must be,
Oh ! hear the petition I offer to thee,
  For to bear it must be my endeavour ;
From the grief of my friendships, all dropping around,
Till not one whom I loved in my youth can be found,
From the legacy-hunters that near us abound,
  Diana, thy servant deliver !

From the scorn of the young, or the flouts of the gay,
From all the trite ridicule tattled away
By the pert ones who know nothing better to say,
　　(Or a spirit to laugh at them give her);
From repining at fancied neglected desert,
Or vain of a civil speech, bridling alert,
From finical niceness, or slatternly dirt,
　　　Diana, thy servant deliver !

From over-solicitous guarding of pelf,
From humour unchecked, that most pestilent elf,
From every unsocial attention to self,
　　Or ridiculous whim whatsoever :
From the vapourish freaks or methodical airs,
Apt to sprout in a brain that's exempted from cares,
From impertinent meddling in others' affairs,
　　　Diana, thy servant deliver !

From the erring attachments of desolate souls,
From the love of spadille and of matadore boles,
Or of lapdogs, and parrots, and monkeys, and owls,
　　Be they ne'er so uncommon and clever ;
But chief from the love of all loveliness flown
Which makes the dim eye condescend to look down,
On some ape of a fop, or some owl of a clown,
　　　Diana, thy servant deliver !

From spleen at beholding the young more caressed,
From pettish asperity, tartly expressed,
From scandal, detraction, and every such pest,
　　From all thy true servant deliver ;

Nor let satisfaction depart from her lot,
Let her sing, if at ease, and be patient if not,
Be pleased when regarded, content when forgot,
   Till fate her slight thread shall dissever !

                       ANON.

CCLXIV

PRUDENCE

   BEHAVE yoursel' before folk,
   Behave yoursel' before folk,
And dinna be sae rude to me,
   As kiss me sae before folk.
It wouldna' give me meikle pain,
Gin we were seen and heard by nane,
To tak' a kiss, or grant you ane ;
   But gudesake ! no before folk.
   Behave yoursel' before folk,
   Behave yoursel' before folk—
Whate'er you do when out o' view,
   Be cautious aye before folk !

Consider, lad, how folks will crack,
And what a great affair they'll mak'
O' naething but a simple smack,

That's gi'en or ta'en before folk.
Behave yoursel' before folk,
Behave yoursel' before folk—
Nor gi'e the tongue o' old and young
Occasion to come o'er folk.

I'm sure wi' you I've been as free
As ony modest lass should be;
But yet it doesna' do to see
    Sic freedom used before folk.
    Behave yoursel' before folk,
    Behave yoursel' before folk—
I'll ne'er submit again to it;
    So mind you that—before folk!

Ye tell me that my face is fair:
It may be sae—I dinna care—
But ne'er again gar't blush so sair
    As ye hae done before folk.
    Behave yoursel' before folk,
    Behave yoursel' before folk—
Nor heat my cheeks wi' your mad freaks,
    But aye be douce before folk!

Ye tell me that my lips are sweet;
Sic tales, I doubt, are a' deceit—
At ony rate, it's hardly meet

To prie their sweets before folk.
Behave yoursel' before folk,
Behave yoursel' before folk—
Gin that's the case, there's time and place,
But surely no before folk !

But gin you really do insist
That I should suffer to be kissed,
Gae get a license frae the priest,
  And mak' me yours before folk !
Behave yoursel' before folk,—
Behave yoursel' before folk—
And when we're ane, baith flesh and bane,
  Ye may tak' ten—before folk !

A. RODGER.

CCLXV

A HUMAN SKULL

A HUMAN skull ! I bought it passing cheap,—
Indeed 'twas dearer to its first employer !
I thought mortality did well to keep
  Some mute memento of the old destroyer.

It is a ghostly monitor, and most
  Experienced our wasting sand in summing ;
It is a grave domestic finger-post
  That warning points the way to kingdom—coming.

Time was, some may have prized its blooming skin;
  Here lips were woo'd, perhaps, in transport tender;
Some may have chuck'd what was a dimpled chin,
  And never had my doubt about its gender!

Did she live yesterday or ages back?
  What colour were the eyes when bright and waking?
And were your ringlets fair, or brown, or black,
  Poor little head! that long has done with aching?

It may have held (to shoot some random shots)
  Thy brains, Eliza Fry, or Baron Byron's;
The wits of Nelly Gwynn, or Dr. Watts,—
  Two quoted bards! two philanthropic syrens!

But this I surely knew before I closed
  The bargain on the morning that I bought it;
It was not half so bad as some supposed,
  Nor quite as good as many may have thought it.

Who love, can need no special type of death;
  Death steals his icy hand where Love reposes.
Alas for love, alas for fleeting breath,
  Immortelles bloom with Beauty's bridal roses.

O, true love mine, what lines of care are these?
  The heart still lingers with its golden hours,
But fading tints are on the chestnut trees,
  And where is all that lavish wealth of flowers?

The end is near.   Life lacks what once it gave,
   Yet death has promises that call for praises ;
A very worthless rogue may dig the grave,
   But hands unseen will dress the turf with daisies.

F. L. LAMPSON.

CCLXVI

THINK NOT OF THE FUTURE

THINK not of the future, the prospect is uncertain ;
   Laugh away the present, while laughing hours remain :
Those who gaze too boldly through Time's mystic
      curtain
   Soon will wish to close it, and dream of joy again.
I, like thee, was happy, and, on hope relying,
   Thought the present pleasure might revive again ;
But receive my counsel ! time is always flying,
   Then laugh away the present, while laughing hours
      remain.

I have felt unkindness, keen as that which hurts thee ;
   I have met with friendship fickle as the wind ;
Take what friendship offers ere its warmth deserts thee ;
   Well I know the kindest may not long be kind.

X

Would you waste the pleasure of the summer season,
  Thinking that the winter must return again?
If our summer's fleeting, surely that's a reason
  For laughing off the present, while laughing hours
    remain.

T. HAYNES BAYLY.

CCLXVII

A LIFE IN THE COUNTRY

"Oh! a life in the country how joyous,
  How ineffably charming it is;
With no ill-mannered crowds to annoy us
  Nor odious neighbours to quiz!"
So murmured the beautiful Harriet
  To the fondly affectionate Brown,
As they rolled in the flame-coloured chariot
  From the nasty detestable town:
Singing, "Oh, a life in the country how joyous,
  How ineffably charming it is!"

"I shall take a portfolio quite full
  Of the sweetest conceivable glees;
And at times manufacture delightful
  Little Odes to the doves on the trees.
There'll be dear little stockingless wretches
  In those hats that are so picturesque,
Who will make the deliciousest sketches,
  Which I'll place in my Theodore's desk.

" Then how pleasant to study the habits
    Of the creatures we meet as we roam:
And perhaps keep a couple of rabbits,
    Or some fish and a bullfinch at home !
The larks, when the summer has brought 'em,
    Will sing overtures quite like Mozart's,
And the black-berries, dear, in the autumn
    Will make the most exquisite tarts.

" The bells of the sheep will be ringing
    All day amid sweet-scented showers,
As we sit by some rivulet singing
    About May and her beautiful bowers.
We'll take intellectual rambles
    In those balm-laden evenings of June,
And say it reminds one of Campbell's
    (Or somebody's) lines to the moon."

But these charms began shortly to pall on
    The taste of the gay Mrs. Brown ;
She hadn't a body to call on,
    Nor a soul that could make up a gown.
She was yearning to see her relations,
    And besides had a troublesome cough ;
And in fact she was losing all patience,
    And exclaimed, " We must really be off,
Though a life in the country so joyous,
    So ineffably charming it is.

"But this morning I noticed a beetle
   Crawl along on the dining-room floor,
If we stay till the summer, the heat 'll
   Infallibly bring out some more.
Now few have a greater objection
   To beetles than Harriet Brown :
And, my dear, I think, on reflection—
   I should like to go back to the town."

C. S. CALVERLEY.

CCLXVIII

MY CREAM-COLOURED PONIES

Go order my ponies ; so brilliant a Sunday
   Is certain to summon forth all the élite ;
And cits who work six days, and revel but one day,
   Will trudge to the West End from Bishopsgate Street :
See ! two lines of carriages almost extending
   The whole way from Grosvenor to Cumberland Gate ;
The Duchess has bow'd to me ! how condescending !
   I came opportunely—I thought I was late.

I'm certain my ponies, my cream-colour'd ponies,
   Will cause a sensation wherever I go ;
My page, in his little green jacket, alone is
   The wonder of all !   Oh, I hope he won't grow !

How young Sir Charles looks, with his hat so well fitted
To show on the left side the curls of his wig!
I wonder that yellow post-chaise was admitted;
And there's an enormity—three in a gig!

Dear me! Lady Emily bow'd to me coolly;
Oh! look at that crazy old family-coach!
That cab is a mercantile person's—'tis truly
Amazing how those sort of people encroach!
Good gracious! the pole of that carriage behind us
Is going to enter my phaeton's back!
Do call to them, Robert! Oh! why won't they mind us?
I hear it! I feel it! bless me what a crack!

Don't glance at the crowd of pedestrians yonder,
There's vulgar Miss Middleton looking this way.
Let's drive down to Kensington Gardens; I wonder
We haven't met Stanmore this beautiful day.
They've upset the Countess's carriage, how frightful!
Do look at Sir David—he'll drive here till dark;
Let's go where the crowd is the thickest; delightful!
My cream-colour'd ponies, the pride of the Park!

T. HAYNES BAYLY.

IN THE GLOAMING

In the gloaming to be roaming, where the crested waves
    are foaming,
And the shy mermaidens combing locks that ripple to
    their feet;
Where the gloaming is, I never made the ghost of an
    endeavour
To discover—but whatever were the hour, it would be
    sweet.

"To their feet," I say, for Leech's sketch indisputably
    teaches
That the mermaids of our beaches do not end in ugly
    tails,
Nor have homes among the corals; but are shod with
    neat balmorals,
An arrangement no one quarrels with, as many might
    with scales.

Sweet to roam beneath a shady cliff, of course with some
    young lady,
Lalage, Neæra, Haidee, or Elaine, or Mary Ann:
Love, you dear delusive dream you! Very sweet your
    victims deem you,
When heard only by the seamew, they talk all the stuff
    one can.

Sweet to haste, a licensed lover, to Miss Pinkerton the
    glover,
Having managed to discover what is dear Neæra's
    " size,"
P'raps to touch that wrist so slender, as your tiny gift
    you tender,
And to read you're no offender in those laughing hazel
    eyes.

Then to hear her call you " Harry," when she makes
    you fetch and carry—
O young men about to marry, what a blessed thing it is !
To be photographed—together—cased in pretty Russia
    leather—
Hear her gravely doubting whether they have spoilt your
    honest phiz !

Then to bring your plighted fair one first a ring—a rich
    and rare one—
Next a bracelet, if she'll wear one, and a heap of things
    beside ;
And serenely bending o'er her, to inquire if it would
    bore her
To say when her own adorer may aspire to call her
    bride !

Then, the days of courtship over, with your WIFE to
    start for Dover
Or Dieppe—and live in clover evermore, whate'er
    befalls :

For I've read in many a novel that, unless they've souls
    that grovel,
Folks *prefer* in fact a hovel to your dreary marble halls :

To sit, happy married lovers ; Phillis trifling with a
    plover's
Egg, while Corydon uncovers with a grace the Sally
    Lunn,
Or dissects the lucky pheasant—that, I think, were
    passing pleasant ;
As I sit alone at present, dreaming darkly of a Dun.

C. S. CALVERLEY.

CCLXX

THE EPICUREAN

Upon an everlasting tide
    Into the silent seas we go ;
But verdure laughs along the side,
    And on the margin roses blow.

Nor life, nor death, nor aught they hold,
    Rate thou above their natural height ;
Yet learn that all our eyes behold,
    Has value, if we mete it right.

Pluck then the flowers that line the stream,
Instead of fighting with its power;
But pluck as flowers, not gems, nor deem
That they will bloom beyond their hour.

Whate'er betides, from day to day,
An even pulse and spirit keep;
And like a child, worn out with play,
When wearied with existence, sleep.

SIR F. DOYLE.

CCLXXI

QUA CURSUM VENTUS

As ships, becalmed at eve, that lay
With canvas drooping, side by side,
Two towers of sail at dawn of day
Are scarce long leagues apart descried;

When fell the night, up sprung the breeze,
And all the darkling hours they plied,
Nor dreamt but each the self-same seas
By each was cleaving, side by side:

E'en so—but why the tale reveal
Of those, whom year by year unchanged,
Brief absence joined anew to feel,
Astounded, soul from soul estranged?

At dead of night their sails were filled,
  And onward each rejoicing steered—
Ah, neither blame, for neither willed,
  Or wist, what first with dawn appeared.

To veer, how vain! On, onward strain,
  Brave barks ! In light, in darkness too,
Through winds and tides one compass guides—
  To that, and your own selves, be true.

But O blithe breeze ; and O great seas,
  Though ne'er, that earliest parting past,
On your wide plain they join again,
  Together lead them home at last.

One port, methought, alike they sought,
  One purpose hold where'er they fare,—
O bounding breeze, O rushing seas !
  At last, at last, unite them there !

A. H. CLOUGH.

CCLXXII

HYMN TO FREEDOM

O Freedom ! who can tell thy worth,
Thou sent of Heaven to suffering earth !
Save him that hath thee in his lot ;
And him who seeks, but finds thee not ?

Thou art the chain, from Heaven suspended,
By which great Truth to earth descended ;
Thou art the one selected shrine
Whereon the fires of Virtue shine.

At thy approach, the startled mind
Quakes, as before some stirring wind,
And with glad pain, sets wide her door
To the celestial visitor.

And chased before thy presence pure
Fly sinful creeds, and fears obscure ;
And flowers of hope before thee bloom,
And new-born wisdom spreads its plume.

Blithe fancies, morning birds that sing
Around the soul's awakening ;
Firm faith is thine, and darings high,
And frank and fearless purity.

Before thy throne, a various band,
Of many an age, and class, and land,
Now waiting in the world's great hour,
We kneel for comfort and for power.

Our wills, O Freedom, are thy own,
Our trust is in thy might alone ;
But we are scatter'd far apart,
Feeble, and few, and faint of heart.

Look on us, Goddess! smile away
Low-minded hopes, and weak dismay;
That our exorcised souls may be
A living mansion, worthy thee.

Against thee league the powers of wrong,
The bigot's sword, the slanderer's tongue;
And thy worse foe, the seeming wise,
Veiling his hate in friendship's guise.

But weak to thee the might of earth,
For thou art of ethereal birth;
And they that love shall find thee still,
Despite blind wrath, and evil will.

In vain before thine altars crowd
The light, the sensual, and the proud:
The meek of mind, the pure of heart,
Alone shall see thee as thou art.

Sustain'd by thee, untired we go
Through doubt and fear, through care and woe;
O'er rough and smooth we toil along,
Led by thy far and lovely song.

We will not shrink, we will not flee,
Though bitter tears have flow'd for thee,
And bitter tears are yet to flow;
Be thou but ours, come bliss, come woe!

Awake, O Queen!—we call thee not
From favour'd land, or hallow'd spot;
Where'er man lifts to heaven his brow,
Where love and right are, there art thou.

Awake, O Queen! put forth that might
Wherewith thou warrest for the right;
Speed on, speed on the conquering hour,
Spirit of light, and love, and power!

By baffled hopes, by wrong, by scorn,
By all that man hath done or borne,
Oh come! let fear and falsehood flee,
And earth, at length, find rest in thee!

W. S. WALKER.

CCLXXIII

FLOWERS WITHOUT FRUIT

PRUNE thou thy words, the thoughts control
    That o'er thee swell and throng;
They will condense within thy soul,
    And change to purpose strong.

But he who lets his feelings run
    In soft luxurious flow,
Shrinks when hard service must be done,
    And faints at every woe.

Faith's meanest deed more favour bears,
　　Where hearts and wills are weigh'd,
Than brightest transports, choicest prayers,
　　Which bloom their hour and fade.

CARDINAL NEWMAN.

CCLXXIV

THE ISLES OF THE SIRENS

CEASE, Stranger, cease those piercing notes,
　　The craft of Siren choirs ;
Hush the seductive voice, that floats
　　Upon the languid wires.

Music's ethereal fire was given,
　　Not to dissolve our clay,
But draw Promethean beams from Heaven,
　　And purge the dross away.

Weak self! with thee the mischief lies,
　　Those throbs a tale disclose ;
Nor age nor trial has made wise
　　The Man of many woes.

CARDINAL NEWMAN.

THE WORLD'S AGE

Who will say the world is dying?
  Who will say our prime is past?
Sparks from Heaven, within us lying,
  Flash, and will flash till the last.
Fools! who fancy Christ mistaken;
  Man a tool to buy and sell;
Earth a failure, God-forsaken,
  Ante-room of Hell.

Still the race of Hero-spirits
  Pass the lamp from hand to hand;
Age from age the Words inherits—
  " Wife, and Child, and Fatherland."
Still the youthful hunter gathers
  Fiery joy from wold and wood;
He will dare as dared his fathers
  Give him cause as good.

While a slave bewails his fetters;
  While an orphan pleads in vain;
While an infant lisps his letters,
  Heir of all the age's gain;

While a lip grows ripe for kissing;
   While a moan from man is wrung;
Know, by every want and blessing,
   That the world is young.

C. KINGSLEY.

CCLXXVI

THE PRIVATE OF THE BUFFS

LAST night, among his fellow-roughs
   He jested, quaffed, and swore ;
A drunken private of the Buffs,
   Who never looked before.
To-day, beneath the foeman's frown,
   He stands in Elgin's place,
Ambassador from Britain's crown,
   And type of all her race.

Poor, reckless, rude, low-born, untaught,
   Bewildered and alone,
A heart, with English instinct fraught,
   He yet can call his own.
Ay, tear his body limb from limb,
   Bring cord, or axe, or flame,
He only knows, that not through him
   Shall England come to shame.

For Kentish hop-fields round him seem'd,
  Like dreams, to come and go ;
Bright leagues of cherry-blossom gleam'd,
  One sheet of living snow ;
The smoke, above his father's door,
  In gray soft eddyings hung ;
Must he then watch it rise no more,
  Doom'd by himself, so young ?

Yes, honour calls ! with strength like steel
  He puts the vision by.
Let dusky Indians whine and kneel,
  An English lad must die.
And thus, with eyes that would not shrink,
  With knee to man unbent,
Unfaltering on its dreadful brink,
  To his red grave he went.

Vain, mightiest fleets of iron framed ;
  Vain, those all-shattering guns ;
Unless proud England keep, untamed,
  The strong heart of her sons.
So let his name through Europe ring—
  A man of mean estate,
Who died, as firm as Sparta's king,
  Because his soul was great.

SIR F. DOYLE.

SIR BEVILLE

ARISE ! and away ! for the King and the land ;
　　Farewell to the couch and the pillow :
With spear in the rest, and with rein in the hand,
　　Let us rush on the foe like a billow.

Call the hind from the plough, and the herd from the
　　　　fold,
　　Bid the wassailer cease from his revel :
And ride for old Stowe, where the banner's unrolled,
　　For the cause of King Charles and Sir Beville.

Trevanion is up, and Godolphin is nigh,
　　And Harris of Hayne's o'er the river,
From Lundy to Looe, " One and all " is the cry,
　　And the King and Sir Beville for ever.

Aye ! by Tre, Pol, and Pen, ye may know Cornish men,
　　'Mid the names and the nobles of Devon ;—
But if truth to the King be a signal, why then
　　Ye can find out the Grenville in heaven.

Ride ! ride ! with red spur, there is death in delay,
　　'Tis a race for dear life with the devil ;
If dark Cromwell prevail, and the King must give way,
　　This earth is no place for Sir Beville.

So with Stamford he fought, and at Lansdown he fell,
  But vain were the visions he cherished ;
For the great Cornish heart, that the King loved so well,
  In the grave of the Grenville it perished.

R. S. HAWKER.

CCLXXVIII

HALBERT THE GRIM

THERE is blood on that brow,
  There is blood on that hand ;
There is blood on that hauberk,
  And blood on that brand.

Oh ! bloody all o'er is
  His war-cloak, I weet ;
He is wrapped in the cover
  Of murder's red sheet.

There is pity in man—
  Is there any in him ?
No ! ruth were a strange guest
  To Halbert the Grim.

The hardest may soften,
  The fiercest repent ;
But the heart of Grim Halbert
  May never relent.

Death doing on earth is
        For ever his cry;
And pillage and plunder
        His hope in the sky!

'Tis midnight, deep midnight,
        And dark is the heaven;
Sir Halbert, in mockery,
        Wends to be shriven.

He kneels not to stone,
        And he bends not to wood;
But he swung round his brown blade,
        And hewed down the Rood!

He stuck his long sword, with
        Its point in the earth;
And he prayed to its cross hilt,
        In mockery and mirth.

Thus lowly he louteth,
        And mumbles his beads;
Then lightly he riseth,
        And homeward he speeds.

His steed hurries homewards,
        Darkling and dim;
Right fearful it prances,
        With Halbert the Grim.

Still fiercer it tramples,
  The spur gores its side;
Now downward and downward
  Grim Halbert doth ride.

The brown wood is threaded,
  The gray flood is past;
Yet hoarser and wilder
  Moans ever the blast.

No star lends its taper,
  No moon sheds her glow;
For dark is the dull path
  That Baron must go.

Though starless the sky, and
  No moon shines abroad,
Yet, flashing with fire, all
  At once gleams the road.

And his black steed, I trow,
  As it galloped on,
With a hot sulphur halo,
  And flame-flash all shone.

From eye and from nostril,
  Out gushed the pale flame,
And from its chafed mouth, the
  Churn'd fire-froth came.

They are two ! they are two !—
  They are coal-black as night,
That now staunchly follow
  That grim Baron's flight.

In each lull of the wild blast,
  Out breaks their deep yell ;
'Tis the slot of the Doomed One,
  These hounds track so well.

Ho ! downward, still downward,
  Sheer slopeth his way ;
No let hath his progress,
  No gate bids him stay.

No noise had his horse-hoof
  As onward it sped ;
But silent it fell, as
  The foot of the dead !

Now redder and redder
  Flares far its bright eye,
And harsher these dark hounds
  Yell out their fierce cry.

Sheer downward ! right downward !
  Then dashed life and limb,
As careering to hell,
  Sank Halbert the Grim !

  Orate pro anima ejus.

W. MOTHERWELL.

PLAINT

DARK, deep, and cold the current flows
Unto the sea where no wind blows,
Seeking the land which no one knows.

O'er its sad gloom still comes and goes
The mingled wail of friends and foes,
Borne to the land which no one knows.

Why shrieks for help yon wretch, who goes
With millions, from a world of woes,
Unto the land which no one knows?

Though myriads go with him who goes,
Alone he goes where no wind blows,
Unto the land which no one knows.

For all must go where no wind blows,
And none can go for him who goes;
None, none return whence no one knows.

Yet why should he who shrieking goes
With millions, from a world of woes,
Reunion seek with it or those?

Alone with God, where no wind blows,
And Death, his shadow—doom'd, he goes :
That God is there the shadow shows.

Oh, shoreless Deep, where no wind blows !
And, thou, oh Land which no one knows !
That God is all, His shadow shows.

E. ELLIOTT.

CCLXXX

DESPAIR is not for good or wise,
    And should not be for love ;
We all must bear our destinies,
    And bend to those above.
Birds flying o'er the stormy seas
Alight upon their proper trees,
Yet wisest men not always know
Where they should stop or whither go.

W. S. LANDOR.

CCLXXXI

THE COMMON LOT

ONCE, in the flight of ages past,
    There lived a man :—and who was he ?
Mortal ! howe'er thy lot be cast,
    That man resembled thee.

Unknown the region of his birth,
    The land in which he died unknown :
His name has perished from the earth,
    This truth survives alone :—

That joy and grief, and hope, and fear,
    Alternate triumphed in his breast ;
His bliss and woe,—a smile, a tear !
    Oblivion hides the rest.

The bounding pulse, the languid limb,
    The changing spirits' rise and fall,
We know that these were felt by him,
    For these are felt by all.

He suffered,—but his pangs are o'er ;
    Enjoyed,—but his delights are fled ;
Had friends,—his friends are now no more ;
    And foes,—his foes are dead.

He saw whatever thou hast seen ;
    Encountered all that troubles thee :
He was—whatever thou hast been ;
    He is what thou shalt be.

The rolling seasons, day and night,
    Sun, moon, and stars, the earth and main,
Erewhile his portion, life, and light,
    For him exist in vain.

The clouds and sunbeams, o'er his eye
   That once their shades and glory threw,
Have left in yonder silent sky
   No vestige where they flew.

The annals of the human race,
   Their ruins, since the world began,
Of him afford no other trace
   Than this,—there lived a man !

                     J. MONTGOMERY.

CCLXXXII

A VOICE FROM THE GRAVE

ALL needful works accomplished and endured,
   Nearer, and yet more near, my God to Thee ;
Touch we the things that are, with hand assured,
   With hand relaxed, the things that seem to be.

Lest, like the expiration of a breath,
   Which a child breathes and watches on a glass,
Our breath of being all absorbed, in Death,
   With all those things that pass away, we pass.

For where the treasure is the heart, we know,
   Is ; and where the heart is there the life has root ;
And in what soil soever ye may sow,—
   There,—and there only, may ye seek your fruit.

And many seeds men sow in many soils,
  Watering the ground about with many tears
And sweat of brow, who yet from all their toils
  And sorrows pluck no other fruit than fears.

For so is man, as one who in a dream
  Of pleasantness would fain see all as sooth ;
Yet knows the things he sees are things that seem,
  And dreads the hour of waking into Truth.

For what is Truth ?   The Altar, or the Fire ;
  Blood, or the Life ; the Sabbath, or the Rest ;
Words, or the Thought ; the Deed, or the Desire ;
  The expressive symbol, or the thing expressed ?

Is it the furtive hour on drowsy wing ;—
  Is it the dial whereon the sunbeams play ;—
That is the Truth?   Is Time the real thing ?
  Time,—or the shifting sand that marks its way ?

Aspiring to the home from whence it came,
  The spark of life, lent only and not given,
Plays o'er the altar-stone of Time in flame,
  Consumes   the   form, — but   clothes   the   soul   for
    Heaven.

Wherefore, dear Child, live in the Soul of things.
  There is thy home ; thence is thy place of birth ;
So to the parent Sun all flame upsprings ;
  While earthy things but gravitate to earth.

A. A. WATTS.

PRAYER

BE not afraid to pray—to pray is right.
Pray, if thou canst, with hope; but ever pray,
Though hope be weak, or sick with long delay;
Pray in the darkness, if there be no light.

Far is the time, remote from human sight,
When war and discord on the earth shall cease;
Yet every prayer for universal peace
Avails the blessed time to expedite.

Whate'er is good to wish, ask that of Heaven,
Though it be what thou canst not hope to see:
Pray to be perfect, though material leaven
Forbid the Spirit so on earth to be;

But if for any wish thou dar'st not pray,
Then pray to God to cast that wish away.

H. COLERIDGE.

DESIDERIUM

WEARY is the life I lead,
    Beating air with vain endeavour;
Love is left to weep, to bleed;
    Those dear eyes are closed for ever!

Closed for ever and for ever !
Not again shall I behold thee,
Not again these arms enfold thee !
    Thou art gone for ever !

Nothing now is left for mirth ;
    All my dreams were false and hollow ;
Thou, alas ! hast left the earth,
    May it soon be mine to follow !
    Mine to pass the veil and follow !
Eyes of olden hours shall meet me,
Lips of olden love shall greet me,
    In the day I follow.

P. S. WORSLEY.

CCLXXXV

CHILD of a day, thou knowest not
    The tears that overflow thine urn,
The gushing eyes that read thy lot,
    Nor, if thou knewest, couldst return !

And why the wish ! the pure and blest
    Watch, like thy mother, o'er thy sleep ;
O peaceful night !   O envied rest !
    Thou wilt not ever see her weep.

W. S. LANDOR.

CCLXXXVI

SAY NOT THE STRUGGLE NOUGHT AVAILETH

Say not the struggle nought availeth,
   The labour and the wounds are vain,
The enemy faints not, nor faileth,
   And as things have been they remain.

If hopes were dupes, fears may be liars;
   It may be, in yon smoke concealed,
Your comrades chase e'en now the flyers,
   And, but for you, possess the field.

For while the tired waves, vainly breaking,
   Seem here no painful inch to gain,
Far back, through creeks and inlets making,
   Comes silent, flooding in, the main.

And not by eastern windows only,
   When daylight comes, comes in the light,
In front, the sun climbs slow, how slowly,
   But westward, look, the land is bright.

A. H. CLOUGH.

A THANKSGIVING

WE thank Thee, O God of earth and heaven,
    Source and essence of all we know,
Thou, who the power to man has given
    Thy life to witness,—Thy life to show.
To us it is nothing to call Thee Father,
    Mother, or Brother, or Bride, or Friend;
Manifold motions of Thee; or rather
    The manifold rays in Thy love that blend.

Whether we see Thee as sole and single;—
    Whether as Three on Thy name we call,—
Many natures in all things mingle,
    Why not Three, in the source of all?
Whether in form as of Son and Father,
    A dual Being Thou seem'st to bear;
Or whether in nature we see Thee rather,
    Worshipping Godhood everywhere.

Whether in shape as of outer being
    Fitted for flesh Thy face to see;
Or whether unto us Thy spirit seeing,
    Thy flesh and Thy bones have ceased to be;

We bless Thy goodness, that workest to free us,
　　In all these forms Thy spirit to know ;
What, alas ! were we, should'st Thou only see us
　　In the shapes of our life which to men we show.

For the motions of life that make up being ;
　　For being that blends them all in one ;
For thought and emotion—for feeling and seeing
　　In the warmth and the light of an inner sun ;
For life, with its joys of gaining and giving,
　　For death, which is life in another dress ;—
Life,—that is more than merely living,—
　　Death, that is more than life,—and less !

For joys whereby the warmth is given
　　That eases the strain of the Spirit's strife ;
For sorrows, that are as the winds of heaven,
　　Bracing the nerves of the inner life ;
For strife springing forth from the just reaction
　　Of forces moving the life within ;
For peace, whereto by some subtle paction
　　Strife moveth ever, its way to win.

For Fate, which setteth a bound to being,
　　A limit to knowledge, a law to ill ;
For faith,—which is as the spirit of seeing,
　　For love,—which is as the soul of will ;

For these, and how many a boon and blessing,
From these outpouring in gladsomeness ;
Thy love, as the spirit of all confessing,
Thy Spirit, O Infinite Love ! we bless !

A. A. WATTS.

CCLXXXVIII

EARLY DEATH

SHE pass'd away, like morning dew,
    Before the sun was high ;
So brief her time, she scarcely knew
    The meaning of a sigh.

As round the rose its soft perfume,
    Sweet love around her floated ;
Admired she grew—while mortal doom
    Crept on, unfear'd, unnoted.

Love was her guardian Angel here,
    But Love to Death resign'd her ;
Tho' Love was kind, why should we fear,
    But holy Death is kinder ?

H. COLERIDGE.

Z

THE BIRD'S RELEASE

Go forth, for she is gone!
With the golden light of her wavy hair,
She is gone to the fields of the viewless air;
    She hath left her dwelling lone!

Go forth, and like her be free!
With thy radiant wing, and thy glancing eye,
Thou hast all the range of the sunny sky,
    And what is our grief to thee?

Is it aught e'en to her we mourn?
Doth she look on the tears by her kindred shed?
Doth she rest with the flowers o'er her gentle head,
    Or float, on the light wind borne?

We know not—but she is gone!
Her step from the dance, her voice from the song,
And the smile of her eye from the festal throng;
    She hath left her dwelling lone!

MRS. HEMANS.

ON A CHILD'S TOMB

THINE was a blessed flight,
Ere sorrow faded and ere sin could slay !
No weary way was thine, no arduous fight,
And but an hour on Earth, of labour light,
    With hire for all the day.

ANON.

AN EPITAPH

FORTH now through all the sad cold earth
Our love goes weeping : Time, nor space, nor breath
Can chain again life's past glad mysteries of birth,
    Abashed before the deeper mystery of death.
We cling to Hope with tender child-like fear,
And hide within her breast and clasp the truth she saith,
That love and lives like thine bring God to man more
        near.
Oh, thou wert gentle, true, ethereal, and how dear,
A song-fulfilling lark that soared with what pure might
To Heaven,—yet built so low her nest earth wets it with
        her tear,

Ah, who shall shield it now when falls the Night !
Strong lover of the true—for ever may the light
Of thy fair words shine o'er life's troubled shore,
And he "who cannot speak man well, be silent evermore."

ANON.

CCXCII

A DEATH SCENE

ONE long look that sore reproved me
    For the woe I could not bear—
One mute look of suffering moved me
    To repent my useless prayer.

And, with sudden check, the heaving
    Of distraction passed away ;
Not a sign of further grieving
    Stirred my soul that awful day.

Paled, at length, the sweet sun setting ;
    Sunk to peace the twilight breeze ;
Summer dews fell softly, wetting
    Glen, and glade, and silent trees.

Then his eyes began to weary,
    Weighed beneath a mortal sleep ;
And their orbs grew strangely dreary,
    Clouded, e'en as they would weep.

But they wept not, but they changed not,
　　Never moved, and never closed ;
Troubled still, and still they ranged not—
　　Wandered not, nor yet reposed.

So I knew that he was dying—
　　Stooped, and raised his languid head ;
Felt no breath, and heard no sighing,
　　So I knew that he was dead.

　　　　　　　　　　　　EMILY BRONTË.

CCXCIII

A DIRGE

CALM on the bosom of thy God,
　　Young spirit ! rest thee now !
E'en while with us thy footstep trod,
　　His seal was on thy brow.

Dust, to its narrow house beneath !
　　Soul, to its place on high !—
They that have seen thy look in death,
　　No more may fear to die.

　　　　　　　　　　　　MRS. HEMANS.

THE LONG-AGO

ON that deep-retiring shore
Frequent pearls of beauty lie,
Where the passion-waves of yore
Fiercely beat and mounted high :
Sorrows that are sorrows still
Lose the bitter taste of woe ;
Nothing's altogether ill
In the griefs of Long-ago.

Tombs where lonely love repines,
Ghastly tenements of tears,
Wear the look of happy shrines
Through the golden mist of years :
Death, to those who trust in good,
Vindicates his hardest blow ;
Oh ! we would not, if we could
Wake the sleep of Long-ago !

Though the doom of swift decay
Shocks the soul where life is strong,
Though for frailer hearts the day
Lingers sad and overlong,—

Still the weight will find a leaven,
Still the spoiler's hand is slow,
While the Future has its Heaven,
And the Past its Long-ago.

LORD HOUGHTON.

CCXCV

THE VISIONARY

WHEN midnight o'er the moonless skies
    Her pall of transient death has spread,
When mortals sleep, when spectres rise,
    And nought is wakeful but the dead !

No bloodless shape my way pursues,
    No sheeted ghost my couch annoys,
Visions more sad my fancy views,
    Visions of long departed joys!

The shade of youthful Hope is there,
    That linger'd long, and latest died ;
Ambition all dissolved to air,
    With phantom honours at her side.

What empty shadows glimmer nigh !
    They once were Friendship, Truth, and Love !
Oh, die to thought, to memory die,
    Since lifeless to my heart ye prove !

W. R. SPENCER.

STANZAS

GENTLE mourner, fondly dreaming
    O'er the grave of buried years,
Where the cold pale stars are gleaming
    Far along this vale of tears ;—

Fond enthusiast, wildly gazing
    From the towers of childhood's home,
On the visioned beacon's blazing
    Bright o'er ocean's sun-flushed foam ;—

Hope's false mirage hides the morrow,
    Memory gilds the days gone by ;
Give not thy young life to sorrow,
    Trust not joys that bloom to die.

Fiercest throbs the pulse of gladness,
    Heralding a darker day ;
Sweetest spring from thoughts of sadness
    Eden flowers that ne'er decay.

Here, of mirth and anguish blended,
    Joys are born that cannot cloy,
Ending—not till life is ended—
    In the painless endless joy.

H. N. OXENHAM.

DEPARTED JOYS

AMONGST the thunder-splintered caves,
  On ocean's long and windy shore,
I catch the voice of dying waves
  Below the ridges old and hoar;

The spray descends in silver showers,
  And lovely whispers come and go,
Like echoes from the happy hours
  I never more may hope to know!

The moonlight dreams upon the sail
  That drives the restless ship to sea;
The clouds troop past the mountain vale,
  And sink like spirits down the lee;

Why comes thy voice, thou lonely One,
  Along the wild harp's wailing strings?
Have not our hours of meeting gone,
  Like fading dreams on phantom wings?

Are not the grasses round thy grave
  Yet springing green and fresh to view?
And does the gleam on Ocean's wave
  Tide gladness now to me and you?

H. C. KENDALL.

AN EPITAPH

THE pledge we wore I wear it still,
But where is thine? Oh! where art thou?
Oft have I borne the weight of ill,
But never bent beneath till now.

Well has thou left, in silent gloom,
The cup of woe for me to drain;
If rest alone be in the tomb,
I would not wish thee here again.

ANON.

CCXCIX

THE MARRIAGE RING

THE ring so worn, as you behold,
　　So thin, so pale, is yet of gold;
The passion such it was to prove,—
　　Worn with life's care, love yet was love.

G. CRABDE.

ccc

THE FUNERAL FEAST

OH think not that with garlands crown'd
Inhuman near thy grave we tread,
Or blushing roses scatter round,
To mock the paleness of the dead.

What though we drain the fragrant bowl
In flowers adorn'd, and silken vest ;
Oh think not, brave departed soul,
We revel to disturb thy rest.

Feign'd is the pleasure that appears,
And false the triumph of our eyes ;
Our draughts of joy are dash'd with tears,
Our songs imperfect end in sighs.

We only mourn ; o'er flowery plains
To roam in joyous trance is thine ;
And pleasures unallied to pains,
Unfading sweets, immortal wine.

E. BLAND.

CCCI

A DIRGE

Naiad, hid beneath the bank,
　By the willowy river-side,
Where Narcissus gently sank,
　Where unmarried Echo died,
Unto thy serene repose
Waft the stricken Anterôs.

Where the tranquil swan is borne,
　Imaged in a watery glass,
Where the sprays of fresh pink thorn
　Stoop to catch the boats that pass,
Where the earliest orchid grows,
Bury thou fair Anterôs.

Glide we by, with prow and oar :
　Ripple shadows off the wave,
And, reflected on the shore,
　Haply play about the grave.
Folds of summer-light enclose
All that once was Anterôs.

On a flickering wave we gaze,
　Not upon his answering eyes :

Flower and bird we scarce can praise,
  Having lost his sweet replies :
Cold and mute the river flows
With our tears for Anterôs.

W. CORY.

CCCII

SONG

Oh ! never, no, never,
  Thou 'lt meet me again !
Thy spirit for ever
  Has burst from its chain ;
The links thou has broken
  Are all that remain,
For never, oh ! never,
  Thou 'lt meet me again.

Like the sound of the viol,
  That dies on the blast ;
Like the shade on the dial,
  Thy spirit has pass'd.
The breezes blow round me,
  But give back no strain ;
The shade on the dial
  Returns not again.

Where roses enshrined thee,
  In light trellis'd shade,

Still hoping to find thee,
    How oft have I strayed !
Thy desolate dwelling
    I traverse in vain ;—
The stillness has whisper'd
    Thou 'lt ne'er come again.

CAROLINE OLIPHANT.

CCCIII

IN MEMORIAM

THOU wert the first of all I knew
    To pass unto the dead,
And Paradise hath seemed more true,
And come down closer to my view,
    Since there thy presence fled.

The whispers of thy gentle soul
    At silent lonely hours,
Like some sweet saint-bell's distant toll,
Come o'er the waters as they roll,
    Betwixt thy world and ours.

Oh ! still my spirit clings to thee,
    And feels thee at my side ;
Like a green ivy, when the tree,
Its shoots had clasped so lovingly,
    Within its arms hath died :

And ever round that lifeless thing
   Where first their clusters grew,
Close as while yet it lived they cling,
And shrine it in a second spring
   Of lustre dark and new.

T. WHYTEHEAD.

CCCIV

ON THE DEATH OF A LITTLE GIRL

Oh ! cold and drear my heart has grown
Since that sweet soul of thine is flown :
Like the warm ivy to the tree,
Wast thou, my darling child, to me.

And close as those green tendrils twine,
Thy gentle spirit clung to mine ;
Dismantled now and lone it grows,
And bare to every wind that blows.

To the cold world I turned, to rest
On its false lap my bleeding breast,
But eyes that weep, and hearts that care
For others' woes, I found not there.

I turned to home, but every spot
Tells me, sweet child, that thou art not ;
And she, my soother once, and thine,
Her tear-wet cheek is pale as mine.

I turned to Heaven my anguished look,
Remembered last, though first forsook ;
And angels whisper in my ear,
" Thy child, thy Saviour, all are here."

T. WHYTEHEAD.

CCCV

REMEMBRANCE

COLD in the earth—and the deep snow piled above thee,
Far, far removed, cold in the dreary grave !
Have I forgot, my only Love, to love thee,
Severed at last by Time's all-severing wave ?

Now, when alone, do my thoughts no longer hover
Over the mountains, on that northern shore,
Resting their wings where heath and fern-leaves cover
Thy noble heart for ever, ever more ?

Cold in the earth—and fifteen wild Decembers,
From those brown hills, have melted into Spring ;
Faithful, indeed, is the spirit that remembers
After such years of change and suffering !

Sweet Love of youth, forgive, if I forget thee,
While the world's tide is bearing me along,
Other desires and other hopes beset me,
Hopes which obscure, but cannot do thee wrong!

No later light has lightened up my heaven,
No second morn has ever shone for me;
All my life's bliss from thy dear life was given,
All my life's bliss is in the grave with thee.

But when the days of golden dreams had perished,
And even despair was powerless to destroy;
Then did I learn how existence could be cherished,
Strengthened, and fed without the aid of joy.

Then did I check the tears of useless passion—
Weaned my young soul from yearning after thine;
Sternly denied its burning wish to hasten
Down to that tomb, already more than mine.

And, even yet, I dare not let it languish,
Dare not indulge in memory's rapturous pain;
Once drinking deep of that divinest anguish,
How could I seek the empty world again?

EMILY BRONTË.

THE REQUIEM OF YOUTH

OH, whither does the spirit flee
  That makes existence seem
A day-dream of reality,
  Reality a dream?

We enter on the race of life,
  Like prodigals we live,
To learn how much the world exacts
  For all it hath to give.

The fine gold soon becometh dim,
  We prove its base alloy;
And hearts, enamoured once of bliss,
  Ask peace instead of joy.

Spectres dilate on every hand,
  That seemed but tiny elves;
We learn mistrust of all, when most
  We should suspect ourselves.

But why lament the common lot
  That all must share so soon;
Since shadows lengthen with the day,
  That scarce exist at noon.

MRS. ALARIC A. WATTS.

CCCVII

MELIORA LATENT

NAUGHT can cheer the dark existence
  Which we may not fly from yet;
But with Fate's severe assistance,
  Though we live, we may forget.

For while woe is broad and patent,
  Filling, clouding all the sight,
Ever *meliora latent*,
  And a dawn will end the night.

Meliora latent ever;
  Better than the seen lies hid;
Time the curtain's dusk will sever,
  And will raise the casket's lid.

This our hope for all that's mortal,
  And we too shall burst our bond;
Death keeps watch beside the portal,
  But 'tis Life that dwells beyond.

Still the final hour befriends us,
  Nature's direst though it be;
And the fiercest pang that rends us,
  Does its worst—and sets us free.

Then from earth's immediate sorrow
　Toward the skyey future turn ;
And from its unseen to-morrow,
　Fill to-day's exhausted urn.

J. STERLING.

CCCVIII

Ah what avails the sceptred race,
　Ah what the form divine !
What every virtue, every grace !
　Rose Aylmer, all were thine.

Rose Aylmer, whom these watchful eyes
　May weep, but never see,
A night of memories and of sighs
　I consecrate to thee.

W. S. LANDOR.

CCCIX

A RETROSPECT

Yes, I behold again the place,
　The seat of joy, the source of pain ;
It brings in view the form and face
　That I must never see again.

The night-bird's song that sweetly floats
  On this soft gloom—this balmy air,
Brings to the mind her sweeter notes
  That I again must never hear.

Lo ! yonder shines that window's light,
  My guide, my token, heretofore ;
And now again it shines as bright,
  When those dear eyes can shine no more.

Then hurry from this place away !
  It gives not now the bliss it gave ;
For Death has made its charm his prey,
  And joy is buried in her grave.

G. CRABBE.

CCCX

DESPAIR

THERE is a winter in my soul,
  A winter of despair :
Oh when will spring its rage control ?
  When shall the snowdrop blossom there ?
Cold gleams of comfort sometimes dart
  A dawn of glory on my heart,
    But quickly pass away.
Thus Northern Lights the gloom adorn,
  And give the promise of a dawn
    That never turns to day.

ANON.

DIRCE

Stand close around, ye Stygian set,
  With Dirce in one boat convey'd,
Or Charon, seeing, may forget
  That he is old, and she a shade.

Love ran with me, then walk'd, then sate,
Then said, *Come! come! it grows too late:*
And then he would have gone, but—no—
You caught his eye; he could not go.

W. S. LANDOR.

DIRGE AT SEA

Sleep!—we give thee to the wave,
Red with life-blood from the brave,
Thou shalt find a noble grave:
    Fare thee well!

Sleep! thy billowy field is won,
Proudly may the funeral gun,
Midst the hush at set of sun,
    Boom thy knell!

Lonely, lonely is thy bed,
Never there may flower be shed,
Marble reared, or brother's head
Bow'd to weep.

Yet thy record on the sea,
Borne through battle high and free,
Long the red-cross flag shall be :
Sleep ! oh, sleep !

MRS. HEMANS.

CCCXIII

YOUTH AND AGE

Now, between us all and Him,
There are rising mountains dim,
Forests of uncounted trees,
Spaces of unmeasured seas :
Think with Him how gay of yore
We made sunshine out of shade,—
Think with Him how light we bore
All the burden sorrow laid ;
All went happily about Him,—
How shall we toil on without Him ?

How without his cheering eye
Constant strength enbreathing ever?
How without Him standing by
Aiding every hard endeavour?
For when faintness or disease
Had usurped upon our knees,
If He deigned our lips to kiss
With those living lips of his,
We were lightened of our pain,
We were up and hale again :—
Now, without one blessing glance
From his rose-lit countenance,
We shall die deserted men,—
And not see Him, even then!

We are cold, very cold,—
All our blood is drying old,
And a terrible heart-dearth
Reigns for us in heaven and earth ;
Forth we stretch our chilly fingers
In poor effort to attain
Tepid embers, where still lingers
Some preserving warmth, in vain.
Oh ! if Love, the Sister dear
Of Youth that we have lost,
Come not in swift pity here,
Come not, with a host
Of affections, strong and kind,
To hold up our sinking mind,

If She will not, of her grace,
Take her Brother's holy place,
And be to us, at least, a part
Of what He was, in Life and Heart,
The faintness that is on our breath
Can have no other end but Death.

LORD HOUGHTON.

CCCXIV

LAST LINES

No coward soul is mine,
No trembler in the world's storm-troubled sphere:
I see Heaven's glories shine,
And faith shines equal, arming me from fear.

O God, within my breast,
Almighty, ever present Deity!
Life—that in me has rest,
As I—undying Life—have power in thee!

Vain are the thousand creeds
That move men's hearts: unutterably vain;
Worthless as withered weeds,
Or idlest froth amid the boundless main,

To waken doubt in one
Holding so fast by thine infinity;
So surely anchored on
The steadfast rock of immortality.

With wide-embracing love
Thy spirit animates eternal years,
Pervades and broods above,
Changes, sustains, dissolves, creates, and rears.

Though earth and man were gone,
And suns and universes ceased to be,
And Thou were left alone,
Every existence would exist in Thee.

There is not room for Death,
Nor atom that his might could render void:
Thou—Thou art Being and Breath,
And what Thou art may never be destroyed.

EMILY BRONTË.

CCCXV

AN EPITAPH

Too dearly loved, thy God hath called thee—go,
Go, thou best portion of this widow'd heart;
And thou, poor remnant lingering here in woe,
So learn to follow as no more to part.

EDWARD, LORD DERBY.

CCCXVI

HEAVENWARD

WOULD you be young again?
   So would not I—
One tear to memory giv'n,
   Onward I'd hie.
Life's dark flood forded o'er,
All but at rest on shore,
Say, would you plunge once more,
   With home so nigh?

If you might, would you now
   Retrace your way?
Wander through thorny wilds,
   Faint and astray?
Night's gloomy watches fled,
Morning all beaming red,
Hope's smiles around us shed,
   Heavenward—away.

Where are they gone, of yore
   My best delight?
Dear and more dear, tho' now
   Hidden from sight.
Where they rejoice to be,
There is the land for me;
Fly time—fly speedily,
   Come life and light.

LADY NAIRNE.

CCCXVII

LEBEWOHL

I

WITH these words, Good-bye, Adieu,
Take I leave to part from you,
Leave to go beyond your view,
Through the haze of that which is to be ;
Fare thou forth, and wing thy way,
So our language makes me say.
Though it yield, the forward spirit needs must pray
In the word that is hope's old token.

II

Though the fountain cease to play,
Dew must glitter near the brink ;
Though the weary mind decay,
As of old it thought so must it think.
Leave alone the darkling eyes
Fixed upon the moving skies,
Cross the hands upon the bosom, there to rise,
To the throb of the faith not spoken.

W. CORY.

NOTES

BOOK I

(1250–1625)

I

TRADITION assigns to this lively little lyric the honour of being the most ancient song, with or without the musical notes, in the English language. In all probability it was composed as early as 1250. It is preserved in the Harleian MS. No. 978, and was first published in Sir John Hawkins' *History of Music.*

II

This charming little song is from Harleian MS. No. 2253, and is printed by Ritson in his *Ancient Songs and Ballads*, vol. i. p. 58 ; it is also printed in Dr. Böddeker's *Altenglische Dichtungen des MS. Harl.* 2253, pp. 168-171 ; and his text I adopt.

III

Printed in Wright's *Songs and Carols* from Sloane MS. No. 2593 in the British Museum.

IV

From Harleian MS. 2253 ; printed by Wright and Ritson, and by Dr. K. Böddeker in his *Altenglische Dichtungen des MS. Harl.* 2253, p. 195. I give his text.

V

From the Egerton MS. No. 613, fol. 2, 20, of the thirteenth century. Printed in Wright's *Reliqiuæ Antiquæ*, vol. i. p. 89.

VI

It will be seen that the point of this graceful little poem turns on a pun between the herb "rew" and "rue" or pity. For William Dunbar see next note.

VII

William Dunbar, whom Sir Walter Scott pronounced to be "a poet unrivalled by any that Scotland has ever produced," was born some time about 1450 and died probably about 1530. Dunbar's fame has suffered from the obsolete language in which he wrote. There is a strange solemnity and power in many of his pieces. I only give a portion of the poem from which these stanzas are taken.

VIII

I have slightly modernised the spelling in this piece, which is to be found among Dunbar's miscellaneous poems.

IX

From the *Garlande of Laurell*. Skelton (1460?-1529) is chiefly known as the author of poems of a very different kind from this, but he had a versatile genius, and if he could revel in graceless ribaldry he could break out, as he does here, into charming song.

X

Sephestia's Song to her child in *Menaphon*. The middle stanza is omitted.

XI

From *Patient Grissell*, a comedy written in conjunction by Haughton, Chattle, and Dekker, 1600.

XII

From the *Phœnix Nest*, 1593.

From *Astrophel and Stella*, the Eleventh Song.

From *The Captain.* As *The Captain* was written in conjunction by Beaumont and Fletcher it is impossible to assign this lyric certainly either to the one or to the other. It is the most pathetic in their plays. In the last line the folio reads "day."

Printed in *Observations on the Art of English Poetry*, attributed to George Puttenham.

This has been attributed to Donne, but certainly belongs to Campion. For Campion see note on xliv.

From Britannia's *Pastorals*, the Third Song.

From *Blurt, Master Constable: or the Spaniard's Night Walke*, 1602. Owe = possess "Phœbe here" etc.; this is somewhat awkwardly expressed, and Dyce proposes to read "Did Phœbe here one night lie," thus ruining the rhythm, but making the sense clear.

Lady Mary Wroth, to whom Ben Jonson dedicated the *Alchemist*, was the daughter of Robert, second Earl of Leicester, a younger brother of Sir Philip Sidney, and the wife of Sir Robert Wroth of Durant. The extract given is from her romance *Urania*, an imitation of her uncle's *Arcadia*, published in 1621.

From Rossiter's *Consort Lessons*, 1609. Chappell's *Old English Popular Music*, vol. i. p. 148.

XXII

From Wilbye's *Second Set of Madrigales.'*

XXIII

From Robert Jones's *The Muses' Garden of Delights*—re printed in Beloes' *Literary Anecdotes*, vol. vi. p. 168, and by Mr. Bullen in his Lyrics from the Elizabethan Song-Books.

XXIV

From *Menaphon*.

XXV

From *England's Helicon*, where it is signed, like several other pieces in the same collection, "Shepheard Tonie." Sir Egerton Brydges, in his Introduction to his reprint of *England's Helicon*, conjectures that it might be a signature assumed by Anthony Munday. Munday's voluminous and varied writings show that he was certainly a very versatile genius, but nothing equal to this lyric, or to some of the others under this signature, is to be found in his acknowledged writings.

XXVI

In an old MS. formerly belonging to Sir John Cotton of Stratton in Huntingdonshire. This poem is attributed to Dr. Donne, among whose poems it is commonly printed. See Dr. Grosart's note in his edition of *Donne's Poems*, vol. ii. pp. 238, 239.

XXVII

This poem is generally attributed to Raleigh. In the *Phœnix Nest* it appears without any signature, and in *England's Helicon*, where it is printed as a dialogue between Melibœus and Faustus, it is signed Ignoto. In a MS. list of Francis Davison's it is assigned to Raleigh. The "sauncing," or "saunce" bell, is said to be the small bell which is rung when the clergyman enters the church, and also at funerals.

XXVIII

First printed under the title of the *Ploughman's Song* in *The Honourable Entertainment given to the Queen's Majesty in Progress at Elvetham in Hampshire by the Right Honourable the Earl of Hertford*, 1591, and afterwards in *England's Helicon*.

XXIX

From *The Rape of Lucrece*.

XXX

From *The Fair Maid of the Exchange*. I have excised one stanza.

XXXI

From *The Faithful Shepherdess*.

XXXII

From *Valentinian*. A mazer is a bowl or goblet.

XXXIII

From *England's Helicon*.

XXXIV

This charming lyric is from Captain Tobias Hume's *First Part* of Airs—French, Polish and others—together published in 1605. We owe its recovery to Mr. A. H. Bullen, who has printed it in his Lyrics from the Song-Books of the Elizabethan Age.

XXXV

From Davison's *Poetical Rhapsody*.

XXXVI

From *England's Helicon*, where it appears as one of three poems taken from John Dowland's *Book of Tablature for the Lute*.

XXXVII

From *A Handefull fo Pleasant Delites*, etc., 1584. The

initials appended to this quaint poem are T. P. ; who he was, I know not. I have shortened it by omitting three stanzas.

XXXVIII

From the *Arcadia.*

XXXIX

From the *Two Noble Kinsmen.* As this play was written after Beaumont's death, this lyric may be assigned to Fletcher; it is hardly likely that it belongs to Shakespeare, who is supposed to have assisted in the composition of the play.

XL

From Lodge's novel, *Rosalynde: or Euphues' Golden Legacy.*

XLI

From *England's Helicon.* Constable is one of the most charming and musical of the Elizabethan Lyrists. Born about 1555, he passed much of his life in exile, as he was a Roman Catholic. Beside contributing four beautiful lyrics to *England's Helicon,* he was the author of a collection of sonnets entitled *Diana,* and also of some religious sonnets. The date of his death is uncertain.

XLIII

From *The Captain.*

XLIV

From Philip Rosseter's *Booke of Ayres,* 1601. Little more is known of Thomas Campion, one of the most charming of Elizabethan lyric poets, than that he studied at Cambridge, belonged at one time to the society of Gray's Inn but subsequently became a physician and practised in London, dying in the spring of 1619-20. His poems have been collected and edited by Mr. A. H. Bullen, who may be said to have been the first to introduce him to modern readers. To the first couplet of the last stanza there is a curious parallel in Shakespeare's *2 Henry IV*. II. 2, "Well thus we play the fools with the time, and the spirits of the wise sit in the clouds and mock us."

XLV

The Petrarch of the North is far inferior to his master and model in sweetness, in grace, and in exquisite felicity of expression, but he is his rival in other respects.

XLVI

From *Astrophel and Stella*, sonnet cx, one of the noblest sonnets in our language. More than one passage in this sonnet shows that it found response in Shakespeare.

XLVII

Though this beautiful lyric is somewhat hackneyed I could not omit it. It is from the Comedy of *Patient Grissell*, written in conjunction by Dekker, Chettle, and Haughton.

XLVIII

This poem was no doubt suggested by Martial, Epigram xc. book ii. Mean = moderate, and sleeps probably = somnia, dreams.

XLIX

From the *Reliquiae Wottonianae*. I give Dr. Hannah's text. Ben Jonson was so fond of these verses that he transcribed them with his own hands and had them by heart. See his *Conversations with Drummond* and Gifford's note. Jonson seems to have transcribed them from memory.

L

From *Old Damon's Pastoral* in *England's Helicon*.

LI

From the *Reliquiae Wottonianae*. Dr. Hannah gives as the title of this poem " Upon the Sudden Restraint of the Earl of Somerset then falling from favour." It probably has reference to the fall of Somerset in 1615, but Park supposes, though on no good grounds, that it has reference to Bacon.

LII

The ordinary reading in the second line is "will serve Thee." I restore the rhyme.

LIII

From his Elegy on Sir Philip Sidney, printed in Todd's *Spenser*, vol. vi. pp. 82-96.

LV

From the *Paradise of Dainty Devices*. Appended to it are the initials M. T., which Percy who reprints it in his *Reliques* thinks may be the reversed initials of Thomas Marshall, whose initials are attached to another poem in the collection.

LVI

The author of this powerful poem, which was first printed in 1608 in the second edition of Davison's *Poetical Rhapsody*, cannot be ascertained with certainty. It has been commonly attributed to Sir Walter Raleigh, and is included by Birch in his edition of Raleigh's Works, and by Sir Egerton Brydges in his edition of Raleigh's Poems. It is attributed to Raleigh in a MS. poem in the Chetham Library at Manchester (8012, p. 107) undoubtedly written while Raleigh was still alive, and among the Ashmolean MSS. at Oxford are two poems, one purporting to be an answer to it, and the other a defence of it by Raleigh himself. The defence was probably not by Raleigh, but it is plain that the writer had no doubt that Raleigh was the author of the original poem. The presumptive evidence therefore in favour of Raleigh is strong. It has been assigned to Lord Essex, to Francis Davison, to Sir Edward Dyer, to Joshua Sylvester and to others, but on utterly unsatisfactory grounds. For a full discussion of the question see Dr. Hannah's admirable edition of *Poems by Sir Henry Wotton, Sir Walter Raleigh, and others*, pp. 188-199.

LVIII

From *Divine Meditations and Elegies*, 1622. The pathos and beauty of this lyric far outweigh its imperfect rhymes and the singular grammatical solecism in the first stanza. Of its author nothing more is known than that he belonged to a good family, was baptized in February 1585, and that he is probably to be identified with Captain John Hagthorpe, who was serving in the navy between April and September 1626.

LIX

From *Spectacles*, 25, 27. Joshua Sylvester (1563-1618) is one of the few Elizabethan poets who deserves more attention than he has received from modern students.

LX

From *Nosce Te-ipsum*, a poem on the Immortality of the Soul, first published in 1599; one of the most eloquent and powerful philosophic poems in our language.

LXI

From *Flowers of Zion*.

LXII

From the *History of Women*, book iv. It is an epitaph on Ethelburga, Queen of the West Saxons.

LXIII

From the *Maid's Tragedy*.

LXIV

From *Spectacles*, 10, 11.

LXV

William Alexander (1580-1640) created in June 1633 Earl of Stirling, was the author of a long and dreary poem on the *Day of Judgment*, some miscellaneous poems, and of four *Monarchicke Tragedies: Cræsus, Darius*, the *Alexandrian*

Tragedy and *Julius Cæsar.* The extract given is from *Darius*, which appeared in 1603. It has been supposed that Shakespeare had this passage in his mind when he wrote the superb verses in the *Tempest*, IV. i., "And like the baseless fabric," etc. Porson was fond of quoting Stirling's lines which he pronounced to be superior to Shakespeare's ; but, stately and majestic though they are, few would agree with Porson. It may be added that Stirling afterwards greatly altered and spoilt the second stanza : see the version in his Collected Works, 1637. I give the passage as it appears in the quarto, 1603.

LXIX

This eloquent religious poet, a member of the Society of Jesus, was born about 1562, and was executed, a martyr to his faith, in February 1594-95. Well might Ben Jonson say (*Conversations with Drummond*) that had he written this piece he would have been content to destroy many of his own pieces.

LXX

Written by Donne in the severe illness which brought him to the point of death three years after he became Dean of St. Paul's. See Walton's *Life.*

LXXI

These verses were written by Sir Walter Raleigh on the night before his execution, and were found in his Bible.

LXXII

From the 42nd section of Stephen Hawes' *Pastime of Pleasure*, first printed in 1509. Of Hawes nothing more is known than that he was a native of Suffolk, and was Groom of the Privy Chamber to Henry VII. His poem on the whole is tedious, but it has much more merit than is commonly allowed, and historically it is of great importance. Both Sir Walter Scott and Longfellow have appropriated the last beautiful couplet of the extract given in the text, without however acknowledging their indebtedness to Hawes.

BOOK II

(1625–1700)

LXXIII

To his son Vincent on his birthday, November 1630, being then three years old. Corbet (1582-1635) was successively Bishop of Oxford and Norwich, and no more jovial Bishop ever adorned or astonished the Episcopal bench. The poems by which he is best known are his *Faeries' Farewell* and his *Iter Boreale*, but Corbet had as little of the touch of the poet as Swift.

LXXIV

From *Silex Scintillans*, part i. In this beautiful poem is undoubtedly to be found the germ of Wordsworth's great Ode.

LXXV

From *The Mistress of Philarete*. Instead of selecting from Wither poems which are now somewhat hackneyed, viz. the lyrics " Shall I wasting in despair," and " Hence away thou siren leave me," and the fine passage about the power of poetry in the Fourth Eclogue of the *Shepherd's Hunting*, I have chosen this which Charles Lamb marked as " of pre-eminent merit," a judgment in which every one must concur.

LXXVI

From the Miscellaneous Thoughts in his *Remains*, vol. i, pp. 244, 245. I have connected the two fragments by omitting some verses which intervene. It is difficult to associate with the author of *Hudibras* sentiment so noble and refined as these verses express. No critic, so far as I know, has noticed that underlying the wit, worldliness, and cynicism of Butler was a fine, if thin, vein of poetic sensibility which peeps out timidly even in *Hudibras*.

LXXVII

From *Hesperides*. Herrick's best lyrics are among the commonplaces of every anthology, and are therefore excluded from this. If I cannot give his diamonds I have endeavoured to give two or three of his pearls.

LXXVIII

From *Castara*.

LXXIX

From *Castara*. Love has rarely found so pure and lofty a laureate as Habington. His Laura was Lucy Herbert. I have ventured to curtail this poem by the omission of the four stanzas which intervene in the original between the second and the last.

LXXX

From *Hesperides*. This pretty poem is in rhythm an echo of the second song in Ben Jonson's Masque *The Gipsies Metamorphosed*.

LXXXI

William Cartwright, born, according to one account, in 1615, to another in 1611, passed most of his life at Oxford, as a lecturer and preacher, dying prematurely in 1643. His Comedies, Tragi-Comedies, and poems were published posthumously in 1651. Ben Jonson is reported to have said of him, " My son Cartwright writes all like a man," a compliment which Cartwright rewarded by an eloquent poem to Jonson's memory. As a lyrical poet he belongs to the Metaphysical School.

LXXXII

I have been told that this poem was a great favourite with Tennyson, who was fond of quoting the lines beginning " But at my back." He has himself borrowed from it.

From the *Masque of Semele.* Act ii. Scene i.

Cotton's masterpiece is *Winter*, but it is much too long for introduction here, and it is impossible to shorten it without injury. In originality, vigour, and verve Cotton has no superior in that brilliant school of poets to which he belongs ; and yet it is remarkable that his miserable travesty of the first and second books of the *Æneid* should have gone through upwards of fifteen editions, while the poems printed in 1689, in which his genius displays itself, should never have been reprinted till 1810.

LXXXVII

From *Abdelazar: or The Moor's Revenge.* Mrs. Behn's lyrics are at their best among the best of their kind.

Dr. Walter Pope was a well-known figure among wits and men of science between about 1658, when he was proctor at Oxford, and 1714 when he died. In 1660 he succeeded Sir Christopher Wren as Gresham Professor of Astronomy. This poem was first published in 1693. It was reprinted in Nichols's Select Collection, vol. i. p. 173 ; and in *Songs and Ballads*, chiefly collected by Robert, Earl of Oxford, vol. ii. There are two versions, the shorter one, which I give, being the best. A charming Latin paraphrase of the longer version will be found in Vincent Bourne's *Poemata.* It is gratifying to know that fortune allowed Dr. Pope to realise his ideal. In his quaint and delightful *Life of Seth Ward* he says, " I thank God that I am arrived at a good old age without gout or stone, with my intellectual senses but little decayed and my intellectuals, though none of the best, yet as good as ever they were." In the last stanza but one the allusion is to a tradition of the Turks to the effect that, when any one is born into the world, a certain quantity of meat and drink is apportioned to him for consumption during his mortal existence, and that when it is consumed he dies ; the moral being that a man who desires to live long must be thrifty in his meat and drink.

XCI

From *Hesperides*.

XCII

Katherine Fowler, born in 1631, married about 1647 James Philips of Cardigan, died 22nd June 1664, in the thirty-third year of her age. "The matchless Orinda" is the author of many poems of a grave and serious cast, which by no means discredit the eulogies of Cowley and Dryden. Her poems were published in quarto in 1664, under the title of "*Poems*, by the incomparable Mrs. K." There were many subsequent editions. I give the text, not as it appears in the quarto, but as it appears in the *Poems*, by Eminent Ladies, for that is the best text.

XCIII

From *Epigrams of All Sorts*, 1670. This is not the only really beautiful poem written by Flecknoe. See note on cix.

XCIV

Burd, maiden. This pathetic poem is from Herd's Collection. It is printed in Chambers's *Scottish Songs*, and in Sir Walter Scott's *Minstrelsy*, and from thence has often been transcribed. The date and authorship are alike unknown. The story on which it was founded is briefly this. Helen Irving, the daughter of the Laird of Kirconnel in Dumfriesshire, had two suitors, Adam Fleming of Kirkpatrick and the Laird of Blacket House. Fleming was the favourite, and one afternoon, when the lovers were together, the Laird, mad with jealousy, levelled his cross-bow at his successful rival, and Helen, perceiving him doing so, threw herself before her lover to shield him from the arrow, and received it in her breast, dying instantly.

From *The Broken Heart*.

From *Clarastella*, 1650. Nothing is certainly known about Heath, but he is a very accomplished poet, who deserves to be rescued from the oblivion into which he has fallen.

Henry King (1591-1669) was a student of Christ Church in 1608 and afterwards Chaplain to Charles I. and Dean of Rochester. He died, Bishop of Chichester, in 1669. He versified the Psalms, and published in 1657 a small volume of " Poems, Elegies, Paradoxes, and Sonnets." Terse and serious reflection, clothed in fluent and often graceful verse, is the predominating characteristic of his poetry.

From the *Emblems*, Book ii. Epig. xv.

From the *Emblems*, Book ii. Embl. v.

In the original this Hymn comprises twenty-six stanzas. As the choice lay between omission and curtailment, I have adopted the latter, and not I think to the detriment of the poem, for many of the excised stanzas are flat and harsh and much below the level of what is best in it ; and what is best is truly noble. The only tolerable poem of Yalden—his *Hymn to Darkness*—is a parody of this.

From the poem entitled *Reason* in the Miscellanies. Never perhaps has the distinction between Reason and Faith

been so happily defined.   The poem may be compared with
the magnificent lines at the opening of Dryden's *Religio
Laici*.

CIV

From *Emblem* xiv. Book i.

CV

Robert Gomersal(1600-1646) was a student of Christ Church
and a distinguished preacher at Oxford.   He became subsequently Vicar of Thorncombe in Devonshire.   He was the
author of a volume of sermons, of some meditations in verse
on the nineteenth and twentieth chapters of Judges, of a
tragedy entitled *Lodowick Sforza*, and of some occasional
poems printed in 1633—from which the extract given is
taken.   I have freely excised without marking the excisions.
Readers will be reminded of Dryden's famous lines in
Aurengzebe, Act iv. Scene 1, " When I consider life," etc.

CVI

From the *Silex Scintillans*, Part i.   Vaughan has never
been so popular as Herbert, and yet, as a poet, he is greatly
superior to him.   How noble is his lyric commencing " Thou
that know'st for whom I mourn "; how really sublime his
poem *The World;* how pregnant the eloquence of his *Con-
stellation*, which anticipates, though with an infusion of lofty
piety, Matthew Arnold's *Self-dependence*.

CVII

From *Wit's Recreations*, ed. 1650.   It is not unlikely,
but it is by no means certain, that those verses were written
by Herrick.   They appear with poems which are unquestion-
ably his, and are very much in his style.   They were first
included among Herrick's poems by Mr. Carew Hazlitt.

CVIII

Poor Flecknoe's chief claim to immortality is his association with Dryden's satire on Shadwell—*Mac Flecknoe*. He was for upwards of half a century an industrious scribbler. His first poem is dated 1626, and he is supposed to have died about 1678. There are, however, one or two real gems to be found among his rubbish, and this is one of them.

CIX

To the harsh and uncouth style of this noble Platonist is probably to be attributed the fact that his works are so completely forgotten. Never perhaps has rapt mysticism found more intense expression than in his poems and prose discourses.

CX

From *Gondibert*, Canto vi. One of the distinguishing characteristics of Davenant is the gravity and stateliness of his paradoxes and conceits, but this poem is really fine.

CXI

From the *Sacred Poems*. This is Crashaw's note at perfection. In the expression of rapt enthusiasm he has no rival among English religious poets.

CXII

From the *Ode to the Memory of Charles Morwent*. John Oldham (1653-1683) whose premature death was lamented by Dryden, is chiefly known by his *Satires on the Jesuits*, but it is in Pindarics or irregular Odes, in the one from which this extract is taken, and particularly in those on Ben Jonson and Homer, and in his *Dithyramb*, that his genius, which had a touch of nobility in it, is discernible.

CXIII

From the *Fourth Emblem* of Book v.

CXIV

From the Sacred Poems.

CXV

From the Elegy *On the Death of Mr. William Hervey.*
I have considerably shortened this poem ; the original
consists of nineteen stanzas ; it has not, I venture to think,
suffered from curtailment.

CXVI

The date of this Epitaph is 1666, but I cannot remember
where I found it. The second couplet is to be found slightly
altered in Sir H. Wotton's poems.

CXVIII

This passage is the one good thing in Garth's once
famous mock-heroic poem, *The Dispensary* (1696) ; it is in
the third canto. Cowper has borrowed and inserted the
second line in his Lines on the Receipt of his Mother's Picture.

CXIX

These beautiful verses were written by Waller after he
had completed his eightieth year, if not even later. They
conclude his Divine Poems. I omit the six introductory
verses.

CXX

It is impossible to settle with certainty the authorship of
this poem. It is printed in Bishop King's Poems, and is
attributed to King by Headley, Hazlitt, Campbell, Johnstone,
and Cattermole. But it has also been attributed to Francis
Beaumont, though not on equally satisfactory evidence.

CXXI

This is the one poem in Herbert which is not marred by

his characteristic defects, affected quaintness, extravagance, prosaic baldness, and discordant rhythm.

CXXII

From the *Religio Medici*, Part ii. Sect. 12. "This," says Browne, "is the dormitive I take to bedward. I need no other *laudanum* than this to make me sleep ; after which I close mine eyes in security, content to take my leave of the sun, and sleep unto the resurrection."

CXXIII

From her *Poems and Fancies*, 1653, p. 135. There are beautiful little fragments to be found in the wilderness of the Duchess's poetry and prose.

CXXIV

These are the last three stanzas of the concluding poem of *Castara*.

CXXV

From Carew's *Cælum Britannicum*.

CXXVI

From *Microcosmus*, a moral masque, 1637. Of Thomas Nabbes nothing is certainly known beyond the facts that he was born in 1605, was matriculated at Exeter College, Oxford, in 1621, and contributed somewhat extensively to the drama during the reign of Charles I.

CXXVII

Epitaph on Eleanor Freeman, who died in 1650, aged 21, and was buried in Tewkesbury Church, Gloucestershire. It is printed in Headley's *Specimens*, vol. ii. p. 74.

BOOK III

CXXVIII

From Miscellany Poems by a Lady, 1713. Anne Kings-mill, born about 1660, married Heneage Finch, fourth Earl of Winchilsea, and died in August 1720. This poetess is chiefly known from Wordsworth's remark, that her *Nocturnal Reverie* is one of the few poems, in the interval intervening between the publication of *Paradise Lost* and the *Seasons*, which contain a new image of external nature. In a letter to Dyce, Wordsworth says, "There is one poetess to whose writings I am especially partial, the Countess of Winchilsea. I have perused her poems frequently, and should be happy to name such passages as I think most characteristic of her genius," and in a subsequent letter (see Wordsworth's *Memoirs*, vol. ii. pp. 228, 229) he names them. I have, how-ever, ventured to select a poem not noted by Wordsworth, as the object of these selections is not so much to illustrate the genius of particular poets, as to give poems interesting in themselves.

CXXIX

Poor Pattison's story is a very sad one. Born at Peas-marsh, near Rye, in 1706, he was educated at Sidney Sussex College, Cambridge. But quitting Cambridge, before taking his degree, he became involved in many troubles and difficulties, being at one time on the point of starvation. He died in London, July 1727, in his twenty-first year. His poems have much merit, and his *Morning Contemplation*, from which the extract is taken, is a very pleasing descriptive piece.

CXXX

This fine stanza is from Fenton's *Ode to Lord Gower*, which Pope, according to Johnson, pronounced to be the next Ode in the English language to Dryden's *Cecilia*. Modern criticism would not corroborate Pope's verdict. Fenton's *Pindaric Odes* have, at times, great dignity and eloquence, and some of his Tales, if they rival Prior's in indecency, rival them also in grace, terseness, and wit.

CXXXI

Of the author of this spirited Anacreontic, George Alexander Stevens, an account will be found in Baker's *Biographia Dramatica*. He wrote several plays, but made himself chiefly conspicuous by travelling about England and America, and delivering an extraordinary "medley of sense and nonsense, wit and ribaldry," which he called "a Lecture upon Heads." In 1761 he published a volume of Miscellanies entitled *The Choice Spirits' Chaplet*, to which he contributed several rollicking and most spirited ballads, among them *The Marine Medley*, and a song, "Once the Gods of the Greeks," which I have been almost tempted to add. He died in 1784. An edition of his poems, with a memoir of the author by W. H. Badham, appeared after his death.

CXXXII

Paraphrased from Fontenelle.

CXXXIII

Written by the famous Lord Peterborough to Mrs. Howard, afterwards Countess of Suffolk. The verses are printed in Swift's Works, and in the *Suffolk Papers*, Introduction, vol. i. p. 46.

CXXXIV

From Dodsley's Collection, vol. vi. p. 326.

CXXXV

From Dodsley's Collection, vol. viii. p. 243. Robert Craggs, Earl Nugent, was a conspicuous, but not eminent figure among politicians between 1741 and 1788. Some of his poems are printed in Dodsley's Collection, and in the *New Foundling Hospital for Wit*. The Ode which he wrote on his temporary conversion to Protestantism, though too highly praised by Walpole, is vigorous and eloquent.

CXXXVII

Aaron Hill (1685-1750) was an accomplished poet and dramatist, who had the distinction of being one of the very few gentlemen to be found among the Men of Letters of his time. This impressed Pope, who laid the scourge so lightly on him in the *Dunciad*, that the satire is scarcely to be distinguished from eulogy.

CXXXVIII

From a poem entitled *An Hymn to the Morning*. For an account of the authoress of this poem see note on cxlvi.

CXLI

The point of this trifle needs perhaps a little explanation. It is supposed to be Lord William Hamilton's retort to Lady Hertford, who had written to tell him that she had done all she could to show him that she was in love with him, imploring him to—

> Prevent my warm blushes
> Since how can I speak without pain ;

My eyes oft have told you my wishes,
Why don't you their meaning explain?

In Dodsley's Collection, vol. vi. p. 247, it is attributed to Sir William Yonge.

CXLII

From Chambers's *Scottish Songs.*

CXLIII

For an account of Bishop see note on clxxxvii.

CXLV

Ambrose Philips (1671-1749) is now chiefly known as the butt of Pope's ironical satire in prose and direct satire in verse. What distinction he has as a poet lies in his sprightly and graceful verses to the Misses Carteret and Pulteney, and in the fact that he was one of the few poets of his time who had an eye and a taste for the beauties of Nature.

CXLVI

Mary Leapor (1722-1746) appears now to be entirely forgotten, but she is a poetess of some merit. She was the daughter of a gardener, was self-educated, and is said to have served as a cookmaid in a gentleman's family. She died prematurely at Brackley, Northamptonshire, 12th November 1746. Her poems were collected after her death and published by subscription for the benefit of her father, the first volume appearing in 1748 and the second in 1751. As her poems are so little known, I have given three specimens.

CXLVII

First published in Johnson's *Musical Museum*, part iv., and reprinted in Chambers's *Scottish Songs.* I have ventured to omit the last stanza, though Burns wrote the closing quatrain.

CXLVIII

From Chambers's *Scottish Songs*. The poem is attributed to Dr. Alexander Webster, a well-known minister and preacher in Edinburgh, who died in 1784. There is a tradition that he wrote it early in life, and that it was inspired "by a lady of rank, whom he was engaged to woo for another, condescending to betray a passion for him."

CXLIX

From Sir Walter Scott's *Minstrelsy of the Scottish Border*. Scott was at first misled by them and printed them as a genuine poem of the age of Charles I., observing that they have "much of the romantic expression of passion common to the poets of that period, whose lays still reflected the setting beams of chivalry."

CLI

From *Fables for the Female Sex*. Edward Moore (1712-1757) was the editor of the once famous periodical, *The World*, and the author of a powerful tragedy, *The Gamester*. Goldsmith said that Moore was a poet who never had justice done to him while living; but his *Fables* were long very popular. I have not found anything in his smooth but commonplace poems equal in merit to the extract given.

CLII

From Elegy xi. Impressive and eloquent, but how inferior to the lyric which it recalls—Schiller's *Die Ideale*.

CLIII

To few poets could Pindar's words be applied with more truth than to Blake—

πολλά μοι ὑπ' ἀγκῶνος ὠκέα βέλη
ἔνδον ἐντι φαρέτρας,
φωνᾶντα συνετοῖσιν.   *Ol.* ii. 150-3.

CLIV

First printed in a collection of poems published by David Lewis in 1726. It is generally attributed to J. Gilbert Cooper, to whom it certainly cannot belong, as he was little more than a baby when it appeared. Cooper printed it in his *Letters on Taste* (1755), and Dr. Aikin, supposing Cooper was the author, assigned it to him, and has been followed by others. It has also been assigned to G. A. Stevens, who was a boy when Lewis published his Miscellany.

CLVI

From a volume of Miscellanies by Collins, published in 1804, by M. Swinney, at Birmingham, under the quaint title of *Scripscrapologia.* See Notes and Queries, Series vii., vol. i. pp. 310, 311. For Collins see note on ccii.

CLIX

Dr. Thomas Lisle was educated at Magdalen College, Oxford, where he took his M.A. degree in 1732, and his D.D. in 1743. He was for many years Rector of Burclere in Hants, where he died, in March 1767. This witty poem is, with other of Lisle's poems, printed in Dodsley's Collection, vol. vi. p. 178. His poems, and especially his humorous poems, have great merit.

CLX

From the *Night Piece on Death.* In his Essay on Simplicity and Refinement Hume says : " Parnell, after the fiftieth reading, is as fresh as at the first," and if Parnell be judged by what is best in his work, few readers would think Hume's praise preposterous. He here caught the note of *Il Penseroso*, and anticipated that of Gray's masterpiece.

John Byrom (1691-1763) is generally known as the author of the pretty pastoral poem, *My time, O ye Muses*, inspired by Joanna Bentley, and as a humorous poet ; his serious poetry, of which this is a specimen, is now almost forgotten, but is certainly remarkable.

From Green's poem, *On Barclay's Apology for the Quakers*. Of this delightful poet, whose *Spleen* is one of the jewels of our eighteenth-century humorous and ethical poetry, nothing more is certainly known than that he was a Quaker, who, born in 1696, held some office in the Custom House, and died in 1737.

These verses were left with the minister of Riponden—a "romantic village" in Yorkshire—to the scenery of which they refer. Dr. John Langhorne (1735-1779) is one of the most attractive minor poets of the period to which he belongs. Historically he is important ; he is one of the fathers of the sentimental school. As the author of the *Country Justice*, he anticipated Crabbe, and as the author of the *Fables of Flora*, in some respect, Wordsworth. His style is singularly pure and sweet ; his pathos, as in the verses on the death of his wife—*Verses in Memory of a Lady*—often exquisite, and his *Precepts of Conjugal Happiness* is a poem which deserves to be known to all whom such precepts may concern.

On no other poet perhaps does cynicism sit with so much grace as on Prior. It is the dominant note in all his poetry, —and *mille habet ornatus mille decenter habet*,—eloquent in his *Solomon*, deliciously humorous in his *Alma* and in his *Tales*, wit itself in his Epigrams, and touched with pathos

in his Odes. If in Tennyson, England just missed her
Virgil, in Prior she just missed her Horace.

CLXV

The author of this striking poem was Mrs. Fanny Greville,
wife of Fulke Greville, Envoy Extraordinary in 1776 to the
Elector of Bavaria, and Minister to the Diet of Ratisbon.
Her daughter married John, first Lord Crewe. Her poems,
of which some remain in manuscript at Crewe Hall and
elsewhere, have never been collected. If they are at all
equal to the present it is a pity they are not published. The
present poem was printed in Dodsley's Collection, vol. i.
pp. 314-317. I have omitted the first four stanzas.

CLXVI

For the author of this poem see note on cxci.

CLXVIII

"Monitors like these," a skull and hour-glass.

CLXIX

Well known as this poem is, I could not omit it. Simplicity, pathos, delicacy of taste, and a pure and musical
style distinguish the poetry of Logan, and give him a high
place among minor lyrical poets. His *Ode on the death of a
young lady*, his *Odes* written in spring and in autumn, his
song, *The day is departed*, his *Lovers*, and one or two of his
Hymns, have much of the charm of the two poems selected
from him. He was born at Soutra in East Lothian, and
died, worn out with disappointments and troubles, in his
fortieth year, 28th December 1788. This is not the place
to discuss Logan's treatment of Bruce's MSS., but this is
certain, that David Laing and Mr. Tidd Mason have proved
Logan's claim to the authorship of the *Cuckoo;* and this
also is certain, that Logan is incomparably superior to Bruce
as a poet.

CLXX

From *The Minstrel*, canto i. st. ix.

CLXXI

From *A Collection of songs with the music*, adapted and composed by Dr. Hague.

CLXXIV

Pensiveness and grace touched with deep melancholy, but brightened with an exquisite sensibility to the power and charm of Nature, are the characteristics of this pleasing, but nearly forgotten poetess. Her poems should be dear to all who love flowers, for seldom have they been described with so much accuracy and delicacy. Born in May 1749, she had a life full of sorrow and misfortune, of which her poetry is the reflection. Latterly, she herself and others were dependent on her pen, and she was the authoress of several novels and miscellaneous works. She died in October 1806. Wordsworth greatly admired the Sonnet here given.

CLXXV

From Dodsley's Collection, vol. i. p. 327. They were addressed by Bubb Dodington, Lord Melcombe, to the poet Young, not long before their author's death. It is difficult to associate such a poem with a man so profligate and un-principled as Dodington.

CLXXVI

Wordsworth has remarked that "the character of Dyer as a patriot, a citizen, and a tender-hearted friend of humanity, was, in some respects, injurious to him as a poet," but that "in point of imagination and purity of style, I am not sure that he is not superior to any writer in verse since the time of Milton." The scope of this work precludes extracts from *Grongar Hill*, *The Ruins of Rome*, and *The Fleece*—the poems on which Dyer's fame rests—so I have contented myself with giving a poem which very pleasingly illustrates his character.

CLXXIX

This touching dramatic lyric is taken from Chambers's *Scottish Songs*, vol. ii. p. 357. The last four lines were added by Hogg to make the story complete. The name of the author will be familiar to readers of Lockhart's *Life of Scott.* Meeting with misfortunes, he became Scott's bailiff. Beyond this poem he wrote nothing of any note.

CLXXX

This poem was suggested by, and is really a sequel to the old ballad—printed in Chambers's *Collection of Scottish Ballads,—Willie's drown'd in Yarrow*, but beautiful as the parent poem is, Logan's is still more beautiful. Wordsworth's reference to it in his *Yarrow Visited* will occur to most readers. The author, John Logan, was born about 1747, was educated at the University of Edinburgh, entered the Church, and died in December 1788; this poem, however, and the *Ode to the Cuckoo*, will always keep his memory alive.

CLXXXI

Thomas Penrose (1743-1779), after an adventurous life in the navy, subsequently entered the Church. He was the author of *Flights of Fancy*, and of a volume of miscellaneous poems, published after his death in 1781. He holds a respectable place among the minor representatives of the sentimental school. The grace and ingenuity of the idea in this little poem will, I trust, outweigh its somewhat cumbrous elaboration.

CLXXXII

This poem stands alone, the most extraordinary phenomenon, perhaps, in our literature, the one rapt strain in the poetry of the eighteenth century, the work of a poet who, though he produced much, has not produced elsewhere a single line which indicates the power here displayed ; it was composed, during the intervals of a fit of insanity, in an asylum. Published in 1763, it was in 1765 appended to a metrical version of the Psalms, a version, it may be added, which has nothing of the inspiration manifest in this poem. I have been obliged to curtail it, not perhaps to its disadvantage, the original consisting of eighty-six stanzas. My extract begins at the fortieth stanza, the stanzas I have given being as follows : xl., xli., lxxii.-lxxxvi., omitting lxxv., and lxxx., lxxxi. There is, as in parts of *Lucretius*, a peculiar exaltation and intensity in the poem, which it is not difficult to associate with the ecstasy of insanity. Poor Smart terminated a life of poverty and misfortune in 1770.

CLXXXIV

Many poets, from Sir Philip Sidney to Mr. Swinburne, have written English Sapphics, but there are none equal to these in our language. Readers may be reminded that the metrical scheme is as follows :—

$$
\begin{array}{cc}
\acute{-} \smile - \triangledown & \acute{-} \mid \smile \smile - \smile - \triangledown \\
\acute{-} \smile - \triangledown & \acute{-} \mid \smile \smile - \smile - \triangledown \\
\acute{-} \smile - \triangledown & \acute{-} \mid \smile \smile - \smile - \smile \\
& \acute{-} \smile \smile - \triangledown
\end{array}
$$

CLXXXV

From the Hymn to Hope.

CLXXXVI

Thomas Gisborne (1758-1846) was associated with the "Clapham Sect." As the author of *Poems Sacred and Moral*, from which this poem is selected, he was a disciple of Cowper.

CLXXXVII

Samuel Bishop (1731-1794) was long an assistant master at Merchant Taylors' School, becoming headmaster in 1783, which office he held till his death. His poems were collected and published with a memoir by the Rev. Thomas Clare in two volumes, quarto, in 1796. Mild and genial humour, tersely and gracefully expressed, is the characteristic of his trifles, which are generally pleasing and sometimes happy ; but they have not, like those of his models Prior and Swift, the note of distinction.

CLXXXVIII

Edward Lovibond (1724-1775) was one of the contributors to the *World.* As a poet he is an ingenious and graceful trifler, *magis extra vitia quam cum virtutibus.* His *Tears of Old May Day* was greatly admired by his contemporaries.

CXC

The author of *The Pleasures of Imagination* is not, it must be owned, very successful as a lyric poet, and I have had to suppress much in this Hymn to Science, not, I think, to its detriment.

CXCI

William Whitehead (1715-1785) succeeded Cibber as Poet Laureate in 1758. He is a poet, often it must be owned a tame and commonplace poet, who has never had justice done to his real merits, and I hope that the three poems here selected from his collected works will serve to show that the oblivion into which his writings have fallen is not altogether deserved.

CXCIV

Mrs. Anne Hunter (1742-1821) was the sister of Sir Everard Home and the wife of the famous surgeon John Hunter. She published a collection of her songs and lyrics in 1802, from which the extract given is taken. Her lyrics, some of which were set by Haydn, are marked by tenderness and grace.

CXCV

There are few sadder stories in literary history than the life of that hapless child of genius, Thomas Dermody, born 17th January 1775, died in July 1802. His touching and tragical story is told at length by his biographer, James Grant Raymond. His work is very unequal, but his pathos and humour are sometimes exquisite. He came very near to being the Burns of Ireland. In the present poem I have ventured to excise six stanzas.

CXCVI

Jane Elliot of Minto (1727-1805) was the daughter of Sir Gilbert Elliot. This beautiful poem was printed in Scott's *Minstrelsy of the Scottish Border*. *Lilting*, singing cheerfully. *Loaning*, a broad lane. *Wede awae*, weeded out. *Scorning*, rallying. *Dowie*, dreary. *Daffing* and *gabbing*, joking and chatting. *Leglin*, milk-pail. *Har'st*, harvest. *Shearing*, reaping. *Bandsters*, sheaf-binders. *Runkled*, wrinkled. *Lyart*, inclining to gray. *Fleeching*, coaxing. *Gloaming*, twilight. The reference is to the battle of Flodden Field.

CXCVII

These verses, which in simple, unaffected pathos anticipate Cowper, are entitled *Alone in an Inn at Southampton*, 25th April 1737. The reference is to the death of the author's wife. I have shortened the original.

CXCIX

The Rev. William Mason (1725-1797) is more generally known as the friend and biographer of Gray than as a poet. His poetry, which is somewhat voluminous, is for the most part frigid and commonplace, but his two tragedies *Elfrida* and *Caractacus* and some of his occasional poems are not without much merit. The lady on whom this epitaph was written was his wife, who died of consumption at Bristol in

1767. The last three lines were written by Gray. See Mitford's *Correspondence of Gray and Mason*, p. 380.

CC

From the Elegy on the Earl of Cadogan. Few poets so nearly forgotten have so narrowly missed eminence as Tickell. His Elegy on Addison, too well known for inclusion in this volume, is one of the most eloquent and pathetic poems in our language. His *Colin and Lucy* is among the best of our ballads, and his *Thersites*, in condensed energy of invective, is equal to anything of the same kind in Swift, to whom it might seem to belong.

CCI

John Collins was the author of this truly charming poem. He was born at Bath, but the date of his birth is not known. He went on the stage, became famous as a reciter and composer of humorous songs, some of which appeared in a Miscellany entitled *The Brush*, others in a volume called *Scripscrapologia: or Collins' Doggerel Dish of All Sorts*, and some in *The Birmingham Chronicle*, of which he became one of the proprietors. He died in May 1808. The play on the word "everlasting" in the last line should not be missed; "everlasting" was a stout strong cloth generally worn by sergeants. See Hallwell's *Dictionary of Archaic and Provincial Words*.

CCII

From Thomson's *Poems on Several Occasions*, where they are entitled *Verses occasioned by the Death of Mrs. Aikman, a particular friend of the author's*. A poet so well known as Thomson scarcely comes within the scope of this volume, but as these verses seem never quoted or noticed I have ventured to give them. They are a pathetic commentary on the curse in the old Roman epitaph *ultimus suorum moriatur*. The common reading in the second line is "string after string."

CCIII

This famous and beautiful epigram is from the Arabic of Ali-ibn-Ahmed-ibn Mansour, a famous satirist, who died at Bagdad in A.D. 914. The original is given in specimens of Arabian Poetry by A. D. Carlyle 1796. For the following literal version of the original I am indebted to my friend Mr. C. E. Wilson : "You are he whom your mother bore weeping whilst the people around you were smiling with joy. Strive for yourself that you may be, when they are weeping in the day of your death, smiling joyously." Carlyle's version is very inferior to that of Sir William Jones.

CCV

From Watt's *Poetical Album*, second series, p. 94. These touching verses were written by Henry, second Viscount Palmerston, father of the famous statesman, on the death of his first wife, Frances, who died in June 1769.

CCVI

I have ventured to detach these two stanzas from their context. They form part of a poem on Bishop Ken's Grave.

CCVII

How Anna Letitia Aikin, Mrs. Barbauld (1743-1825), could have deviated into lines so exquisite as these must be inexplicable to all who are acquainted with her poetry. They form the concluding verses of a poem entitled *Life*. Wordsworth said of this poem that though he was not in the habit of envying authors their good things, he would like to have written these lines.

BOOK IV

(1798-1880)

CCX

From poems published in a memorial volume printed, without date, for private circulation by Messrs. R. and M. J. Livingstone after Darley's death. I have taken the liberty to modernise the spelling of this poem.

CCXI

From *Fugitive Verses.*

CCXII

From *The Phantom :* a Drama ; Act I. sc. 4. Miss Baillie's purely lyrical genius was ill employed in dramatic composition. Her plays, which make up nearly two-thirds of her works, though they found a great admirer in J. S. Mill, are now deservedly all but forgotten ; but some of the songs, such as "The bride she is winsome and bonny," "My Nanny, O," "The gowan glitters on the sward," "The Weary Pund o' Tow," and one or two of her humorous poems, will keep her memory alive.

CCXIII

From *The City of Dreadful Night.* How nearly this hapless poet sometimes approached Heine !

CCXIV

Thomas Ashe (1836-1889). From the series of poems entitled *At Altenahr* in the later poems. When will some

2 D

competent critic do justice to poor Ashe ? His lyrics are full of beauty and charm.

CCXV

William Motherwell (1797-1835) is one of those poets to whom full justice has never been done ; he stands in the first rank of Scotch lyric poets. Essentially original, he was a man of rare and fine genius. I have omitted three stanzas from the middle of the poem.

CCXVI

P. B. Marston (1850-1887) was a son of the well-known dramatic poet Dr. Westland Marston. His poetry is the reflection of his life, and his life was one of the saddest recorded in the history of poets. His lyrics have occasionally great merit. His poems were collected in 1892 with a biographical sketch of the author by Miss Louise Chandler Moulton.

CCXVII

Romanzo's song in *Sylvia.* George Darley is one of those poets who have received hard measure from fame. The late Lord Houghton, who, like Tennyson, Sir Henry Taylor, and others, had a very high opinion of Darley's merits, intended to reprint his poems with a biographical introduction. Surely his poems should be collected and made popularly accessible.

CCXVIII

William Thom (1798-1848) was one of the many minor poets whom Burns and the school of Burns inspired, but he was no servile imitator. He was self-taught, and the greater part of his life was spent in drudging in the cotton mills, "a serf," as he once described himself, who had "to weave fourteen hours out of the four and twenty." Nature and genius speak in this and in others of his lyrics.

From *Among the Flowers and other Poems*, a volume of poems published at Belfast in 1878. Of the author I know nothing, but I know these stanzas are worthy of a place beside Plato's two exquisite epigrams. In the original the last verse runs "when love is *done*." I have taken the liberty to substitute "gone" for "done," feeling sure that "done" must be a misprint.

The Hon. W. R. Spencer, born in 1770, was long a familiar figure in fashionable circles at the beginning of this century and during the Regency. He was a friend of Sir Walter Scott. He realised his own vision (see ccxcv.), and died in distress at Paris in 1834. He is perhaps best known by his ballad *Beth-Gêlert;* he is certainly one of the most graceful of modern lyrical poets.

From *Pericles and Aspasia.*

From *Sonnets from the Portuguese.* The reference is to *Theocritus*, Idyll xv. 103-105.

Grace, fluency, and a fine sensibility mark every poem which has been preserved from Wolfe's papers. *The Burial of Sir John Moore* and the exquisite threnody, "If I had thought thou could'st have died," both of which, as stock pieces in every collection, are not included in the present volume, are the poems on which his fame rests; but I venture to think that the lyric here given is not unworthy to stand, at whatever interval, beside them. His poems were collected and his life written by his friend the Rev. John A. Russell.

CCXXVII

From *Men, Women, and Books*.

CCXXVIII

This witty poem was suggested by part of the famous Italian song, beginning "Se monaca ti fai."

CCXXXI

From *Sonnets and Poems*. Wordsworth placed this sonnet first among sonnets produced by "modern writers." Letter to Dyce, see Wordsworth's Memoirs, vol. ii. p. 279. Its originality is unquestionable and certainly startling. Brydges himself says of it, "It is my masterpiece. I have never written anything equal to it in originality, force, or finish." Sir Egerton Brydges (1762-1837) deserves an honourable place among those who revived and furthered the study of our old authors, as the editor of the *Censura Literaria*, and the principal editor of the *Retrospective Review*.

CCXXXII

Of this sonnet Charles Lamb, in the *London Magazine* for September 1823, remarks that "for quiet sweetness and un-affected morality it has scarcely its parallel in our language."

CCXXIII

From *Songs of the Heights and Depths*.

CCXXXIV

Edward, Lord Thurlow (1781-1839) was the son of the celebrated Lord Chancellor. He published two or three volumes of poems. In the *London Magazine* for September 1823, in a note to his paper on Sir Philip Sidney's sonnets, Lamb, speaking of Lord Thurlow's poetry, says that "on the score of exquisite diction alone it is entitled to something better than neglect," though he censures its "profusion of verbal dainties" and "disproportionate lack of matter and circumstance."

Osme's song in *Sylvia: or the May Queen.*

From *Loves of the Butterflies.* For Haynes Bayly see note on cclxvi.

From the *Loves of the Butterflies* I omit the two stanzas which precede.

From the *Minister's Kailyard and other Poems,* published at Edinburgh in 1845.

Allan Cunningham (1784-1842) is the author of lyrics which need fear no comparison with those of Burns. Such would be "She's gane to dwell in Heaven," "Thou hast sworne by thy God, my Jeannie," and the English ballad "A wet sheet and a flowing sea." Inferior to these, but very pretty, is his *Morning Song,* "O come! for the lily," etc.

Charles Dibdin (1745-1814) composed upwards of thirteen hundred songs, and the one selected is the last he wrote. It is thoroughly characteristic, and I give it in preference to the songs usually cited, such as "Poor Jack" and "Tom Bowling." Poetry has seldom been applied to a more practical purpose than by Dibdin, as Pitt recognised, who granted Dibdin a pension of £200 a year for his services in educating our sailors by his inspiring and manly lyrics. His songs were collected after his death by one of his sons and printed under the auspices of the Lords of the Admiralty.

From *Weeds of Witchery.*

CCXLIV

From Kendall's Collected Poems, 1886. The poem is a description of Arakoon, a mountainous promontory on the coast of New South Wales. I preserve the description but, excising the last two stanzas, omit the somewhat commonplace moral.

CCXLV

Robert Stephen Hawker (1803-1875) was for many years vicar of Morwenstow in the north-east corner of Cornwall; he was Newdigate prizeman at Oxford in 1827. His poems, which are marked by great vigour and originality, were collected by J. G. Godwin in 1879. The poem which is especially associated with Hawker is his fine ballad on *Trelawny*, but I have preferred to select two which are not so familiar.

CCXLVI

Extracted from a poem entitled *Midnight and Moonshine*.

CCXLVII

From *Lyrics of the Heart*.

CCXLVIII

From *Human Life*.

CCL

It is remarkable that what Coleridge has called the finest sonnet in our literature should have been written by a native of Spain who had no English blood in his veins, and to whom English was an acquired language. Blanco White, whose mother was Spanish and whose father was of Irish descent, was born at Seville 11th July 1775, settled in England in 1810, and died at Liverpool in May 1841. His character and career are of singular interest, and have been depicted by himself in an Autobiography. Coleridge's praise is exaggerated, but harsh and cumbersome as the versification is, it is a magnificent sonnet. I do not think it has been noticed that the germ and idea of the sonnet are to be found in Sir Thomas Browne's *Garden of Cyrus*, chap. iv., " Light that makes things seen, makes some things invisible ; were it not for darkness and the shadow of the earth the noblest part of the creation had remained unseen and the stars in heaven as invisible as on the fourth day when they were created above the horizon with the sun and there was not an eye to behold them." But the noble application and deduction are White's own. I should like to read " on " for " in " in the eighth line.

CCLI

I have omitted the two concluding stanzas of this poem. For Walker see note on cclxxii.

CCLIII

From *A Pageant and other Poems*. Surely in these stanzas we have the perfection of lyrical poetry. Had the muse who occasionally inspired Miss Rossetti been true to her she would have been perhaps the first of British poetesses.

CCLIV

From *Yu-pe-Ya's Lute*.

CCLV

From *Ionica*, a collection of poems which appeared anonymously in 1858. The author was an assistant master at Eton, named Johnson, but on resigning his mastership he took the name of Cory. He died at his residence in Pilgrim Lane, Hampstead, 11th June 1892, in the seventieth year of his age. It is gratifying to know that one of the most modest of poets found himself famous before he died. Surely these exquisite verses need fear no comparison with the immortal epigram in which Callimachus mourned Heraclitus ; they recall it in what they suggest, they rival it in perfection of expression. Cory's poetry is so exquisite and delicate that it will probably secure him lasting fame.

CCLVII

To this poem Praed prefixes the following prose introduction : " Brazen companion of my solitary hours ! do you, while I recline, pronounce a prologue to those sentiments of wisdom and virtue, which are hereafter to be the oracles of statesmen, and the guides of philosophers. Give me to-night a proem of our essay, an opening of our case, a division of our subject. Speak ! Slow music. The Friar falls asleep. The head chaunts as follows." The " Brazen Head." The reference of course is to the famous brazen head fabled to have been made by Roger Bacon, which, after uttering successively, "Time is"—" Time was "— and " Time is past," tumbled itself from the stand and was shattered to pieces, because the opportunity of catechising it was neglected.

CCLVIII

A melancholy philosophy, the truth of which is still, happily, questionable.

CCLIX

The heart of a hero beat in Ernest Charles Jones, and his noble and dauntless spirit burns in his poetry. His life (1819-1868) belongs to the history of the liberal cause : his chief contributions to poetry were *The Battle Day and other Poems*, 1855, and *Corayda and other Poems*, 1860. The poem in the text was, with others, written while Jones was undergoing two years' solitary confinement, the penalty imposed on him for sedition.

CCLXI

Morbid and sickly affectation, straying sometimes into grace and prettiness, as in the present poem, are the chief characteristics of Beddoes' lyrics, which are in one continued strain of falsetto.

CCLXII

From *Dipsychus*.

From Watt's *Poetical Album*, second series, p. 82.

From Alexander Rodger's *Poems and Songs*. Rodger (1784-1846) was a true poet with a rich vein of humour. His political views got him into trouble in 1819, when he was imprisoned. He published a collection of his poems, dedicated to Lord Brougham, in 1838.

From *London Lyrics*.

From *The Melodies of Various Nations*. Some seventy years ago Thomas Haynes Bayly, who belonged to the school of Moore, was one of the most popular song-writers in England. He was born at Bath, 13th October 1797, and died at Cheltenham, 22nd April 1839. His works were edited by his widow, with a Memoir. As a writer of sentimental and humorous *vers de société* he is at his best hardly inferior to his master Moore. I wish I had space for more selections from his poetry.

From the Literary Remains of Charles Stuart Calverley (1831-1884). The author of *Fly Leaves* and *Verses and Translations* stands with Praed at the head of modern writers of *vers de société*. In subtle felicity of expression he is superior to Praed.

From *Songs and Ballads*.

From verses entitled *The Epicurean*.

CCLXXII

The author of this noble poem was born in December 1795, was educated at Eton and at Trinity College, Cambridge, and died in London in 1846. His poems were collected and his life written by his friend the Rev. J. Moultrie. A man of genius, a finished classical scholar, and an accomplished critic, Walker might have won lasting fame, but eccentricities which bordered on insanity, an infirm will, and some mysterious nervous disease made his life an utter wreck. In his poetry fine genius reveals itself in fitful flashes. His only sustained effort is the above poem, which I have slightly curtailed by the omission of three somewhat weak and certainly not necessary stanzas.

CCLXXV

This poem is characteristic of Kingsley, but his strength is seen in his ballads, *The Sands of Dee*, *The Three Fishers*, and in such poems as *The Last Buccanier*, and above all *The Outlaw* and that masterpiece of pathos *The Mango-Tree*.

CCLXXVI

To this fine ballad Sir Francis Doyle prefixes the following extract from the *Times*. "Some Sheiks and a private of the Buffs, having remained behind with the grog-carts, fell into the hands of the Chinese. On the next morning they were brought before the authorities and commanded to perform the *kotow*. The Sheiks obeyed; but Moyse, the English soldier, declaring that he would not prostrate himself before any Chinaman alive, was immediately knocked upon the head, and his body thrown on a dunghill." If Doyle's poem is noble, the act it commemorates is nobler still, and I have taken some pains to ascertain the facts. The soldier's name was John Moyes (not Moyse), who enlisted at Edinburgh in July 1845, stating that he was then seventeen years of age, and a native of Burntisland, Co. Fife. There is no record of his service at the War Office ; but he was reported as "missing en route from Pehtang to Sien Ho, China, on 12th August 1860. Found dead, same date." From information courteously given by the War Office, in the *Times* for 25th August 1860 there is a graphic account of his arrest by some Tartars, and his being carried with his fellow-prisoners before a Mandarin in a neighbouring village, where he acquitted himself as the note to the poem describes. There can be no doubt of his identity, and assuredly the Buffs have cause to be proud of John Moyes.

CCLXXVII

For an account of Sir Bevil or Beville Grenville, "the most generally loved man" in Cornwall, and Hawker's allusions in this poem, see Clarendon's *History of the Rebellion*, books vi. and vii. I have corrected the spelling of "Granville," and have ventured also to correct an error in the last stanza. It cannot be *at* Stamford he fought, it must be with Stamford, *i.e.* with the Earl of Stamford, the reference plainly being to the engagement with Stamford's troops at Stratton, 16th May 1643. Sir Beville was killed in an engagement with Sir W. Waller at Landsdowne, July 1643.

CCLXXVIII

This fine ballad is taken from Motherwell's *Minstrelsy, Ancient and Modern*, p. 30. The name of the author is not given, but it is stated that it was suggested by the following passage in Matthew Paris : "Miles quidam, qui vitam suam in cædibus innocentium, et torneamentis peregerat, et rapinis. Hic omnibus armis militibus armatus, equo nigerrimo insidebat, qui piceam flammam cum fœtore spumeo, per os et nares, quum urgeretur calcaribus, efflabat" (*Matthew Paris*, p. 219. Motherwell's note). It is hardly necessary to say that Motherwell himself was the author. I print Motherwell's later text.

CCLXXIX

Not a poem characteristic of the Corn Law Rhymer, though occasionally its note may be caught in his lyrics.

CCLXXX

From *Pericles and Aspasia.*

CCLXXXI

James Montgomery is no contemptible poet, but he has written nothing else equal to this poem. With its stern pathos may be compared the epigram of Ausonius, *Epith.* xxxviii.—

Non nomen, non quo genitus, non unde, quid egi,
    Mutus in æternum sum, cinis, ossa, nihil.
Non sum, nec fueram : genitus tamen e nihilo sum ;
    Mitte, nec exprobres singula, talis eris.

CCLXXXII

From *Aurora : a Volume of Verse*, published anonymously in 1875. Mr. Watts' poems are perhaps too esoteric for popular appreciation, but they deserve to be known—and some day will be known—more widely than they are now.

CCLXXXIV

From *Poems and Translations* by Philip Stanhope Worsley. Worsley is chiefly known by his translations of the *Iliad*, and of part of the *Odyssey* into English Spenserian stanzas.

CCLXXXVI

This noble poem was the last which Clough wrote.

CCLXXXVII

From *Aurora;* see note on cclxxxii.

CCLXXXVIII

I detach the gem from the setting, and omit the four preceding stanzas.

CCXC

I read these verses on a tombstone some twenty-five years ago, but I have quite forgotten where I saw them, nor do I know whether they are original ; I can only say I have never met with them elsewhere.

CCXCI

I transcribed this epitaph from a tombstone in the Balls Pond Cemetery. The impressive beauty of its imagery and the intensity of its pathos disarm what would be impertinent criticism. It may not be the work of a poetic artist, it is for that very reason, I think, the more affecting. I know nothing of its history or of its authorship.

CCXCII

Seldom has pathos found more piercing expression than here : it is as though the note of him who told the story of Ugolino and of the supreme lyrist of love's agony had blended. The notes of Dante and Sappho seem to meet, not here only but elsewhere and often, in Emily Brontë's lyrics.

CCXCIV

Sir Walter Scott in his diary, 13th May 1827, quotes the last two stanzas of this poem as expressive of his own feelings, adding, "Ay and can I forget the author, the frightful moral of his own vision. What is this world? a dream within a dream, and as we grow older each step is an awakening."

CCXCV

From a collection of poems entitled *The Sentence of Kaires and other Poems* printed at Oxford in 1854, by Henry Nutcombe Oxenham (1829-1888). He was a scholar of Balliol who subsequently entered the Church. In 1857 he seceded to the Church of Rome, and became a distinguished theological writer.

CCXCVII

From *Poems and Songs*. The verses I have given form the greater part of a poem entitled *Bellambi's Maid*, but I think they gain by being detached from the context. Henry Clarence Kendall (1841-1882) was a poet of really fine genius ; his poems, partly descriptive and partly lyrical, deserve to be better known. He was an Australian, and was engaged in journalism at Melbourne. An English Review, the *Athenœum*, first welcomed his poetry into the world, and I am glad to have the opportunity of giving him a place in a collection of British poetry. I wish I had space to give more from Kendall.

CCXCVIII

I copied this from a tombstone, not now to be found there, in Old Saint Pancras Churchyard. I presume it is original, I know it is touching, and therefore it is here.

CCXCIX

These verses were found after Crabbe's death on a paper enclosing his wife's wedding ring " nearly worn through before she died." See *Life of Crabbe*, by his son.

CCC

From *Collections from the Greek Anthology and from the Pastoral, Elegiac, and Dramatic Poets*, by Rev. Robert Bland. The lines are paraphrased from or rather suggested by the following verses preserved in Stobaeus :—

> οὐ μὲν γὰρ οὕτως ἄν ποτ' ἐστεφανωμένοι
> προύκειμεθ' ἄνθεσ' οὐδὲ κατακεχρισμένοι,
> εἰ μὴ καταβάντας εὐθέως πίνειν ἔδει.
> διὰ ταῦτα γάρ τοι καὶ καλοῦνται μακάριοι,
> πᾶς γὰρ λέγει τις " ὁ μακαρίτης οἴχεται."

CCCI

From *Ionica.*

CCCII

Caroline Oliphant (1807-1831) was the niece and namesake of Lady Nairne, the author of *The Land o' the Leal.* Some selections from her papers were published by the Rev. Charles Rogers, in 1869, in a volume containing the poems of Lady Nairne. From the selection given by Rogers I have taken the extract given; I have omitted the last stanza in the original.

CCCIII

From Whytehead's *Poetical Remains and Letters.* Thomas Whytehead (born 30th November 1815 at Thormanby in the North Riding of Yorkshire, died in New Zealand 19th March 1843) was a Fellow of St. John's College, Cambridge, who, subsequently entering the Church, went out with Bishop Selwyn to New Zealand. His poems have the note of distinction, and deserve to be known better than they are. I wish I had had space for a poem by him entitled *The Second Day*, which is a truly magnificent piece.

CCCVII

From *Poems* published in 1839. Sterling is now chiefly remembered, not from any achievements of his own, but from Carlyle's singularly interesting biography of him.

CCCVIII

The lady to whose memory these lines are dedicated was one of Landor's early loves; she died suddenly and prematurely in India. Her very name is a poem, and it is amazing to learn that instead of its repetition Landor originally wrote in the second stanza "Sweet Aylmer."

CCCIX

" Before finally quitting Leicestershire my father paid a short visit to his sister at Alborough ; and one day was given

to a solitary ramble among the scenery of bygone years—
Parkham and the woods of Glenham then in the first blossom
of May.   He did not return until night, and in his note-book
I find the following brief record of this mournful visit."
—*Crabbe's Life*, by his son, chap. viii.

CCCX

These exquisitely pathetic verses were found in the pocket-
book of a patient suffering from monomania, who was under
the care of Sir Alexander Morrison.   They are to be found
in Sir Alexander's *Lectures on Insanity*, p. 137, note.

CCCXIV

These noble lines were written by Emily Brontë very
shortly before her death.

CCCXV

This is Lord Derby's exquisite paraphrase of Bishop
Wordsworth's beautiful epitaph on his wife :

I, nimium dilecta, vocat Deus ; I. bona nostræ
Pars animæ ; mœrens altera, disce sequi.

The translation in the text appeared in the *Guardian* for
1st May 1867.   The Latin original will be found in Bishop
Charles Wordsworth's *Annals of My Early Life*.

CCCXVI

Composed in 1842 when Lady Nairne had reached her
seventy-sixth year.   Lady Nairne's three well-known Scotch
lyrics and her incomparable *Land o' the Leal* have not been
included in this collection for the reasons explained in the
preface.

CCCVII

From *Ionica*.

INDEX OF FIRST LINES

2 E

INDEX OF WRITERS

GIVING DATES OF BIRTH AND DEATH

INDEX OF POEMS

2 F

Printed by R. & R. CLARK, LIMITED, *Edinburgh*